Tilly and the Crazy Eights

Tilly and the Crazy Eights

Monique Gray Smith

Second Story Press

Library and Archives Canada Cataloguing in Publication

Copyright
TK

ISBN: 978-1-77260-075-9 (softcover)
ISBN 978-1-77260-078-0 (e-book)

Printed and bound in Canada

Text © Monique Gray Smith
Cover image © Niki Watts
Edited by Rhonda Kronyk
Designed by Ellie Sipila

Every effort has been made to secure permission and provide appropriate
credit for photographic material. The publisher deeply regrets any omission
and pledges to correct errors called to its attention in subsequent editions.

*Second Story Press gratefully acknowledges the support of the
Ontario Arts Council and the Canada Council for the Arts for our
publishing program. We acknowledge the financial support of the
Government of Canada through the Canada Book Fund.*

ONTARIO ARTS COUNCIL
CONSEIL DES ARTS DE L'ONTARIO
an Ontario government agency
un organisme du gouvernement de l'Ontario

Canada Council   Conseil des Arts
for the Arts   du Canada

Funded by the Government of Canada
Financé par le gouvernement du Canada

 Canadä

Published by
SECOND STORY PRESS
20 Maud Street, Suite 401
Toronto, ON M5V 2M5
www.secondstorypress.ca

Dedication

Contents

1

Stitch 'n Bitch

I'm told this is how it all began...

THEY'D BEEN MEETING like this every Thursday. No one could actually remember when they'd started, or maybe they didn't want to as it might remind them of how old they were becoming. Somewhere along the way, they'd come to fondly know their Thursday night gathering as their Stitch 'n Bitch meeting.

The new moon barely lit a path for the elders into their meeting in the basement of the community hall. The wind howled through the valley and would've caused the sagebrush to blow about had it not been covered with snow. Not only was the landscape feeling the brunt of a long, harsh winter, but so were the women. Each of them was in need of a spark or something to give them hope to get through the rest of the season that was wearing on them in ways they couldn't describe. Or didn't dare describe.

Sarah could feel the tension weaving its way into their meeting, like a snake waiting to strike. She was all too familiar with this scene. Over the years, the unresolved pain each of them carried had caused mean and hurtful words. She decided to intervene.

"Me 'n my granddaughter, Cherie, was watching movies last night, all curled up cozy in my bed. One of 'em was called *The Bucket List*. You know the one about the two old geezers who make a list of all the things they want to do before they die." She turned her eyes up from the moccasin she was working on and glanced around the table. All the women were working on their projects, and although they didn't make eye contact with her, she knew it didn't mean they weren't listening.

"Well, it got me thinkin', you know with my tummy scare and all, 'bout the things I want to do before I pass over to the other side." Sarah hadn't told anyone, but the bone-weary exhaustion had crept its way back into her life. The same exhaustion that had led to the cancer diagnosis last year. She was scared.

Lucy looked up from the sock she was knitting and asked, "Like what?"

"Oh, there's lotsa things!" Sarah put the moccasin down for a moment, looked at Lucy and said, "That's what I realized." As she inhaled, a rattle escaped her lungs, causing everyone to turn and look at her. In a bleak tone, Sarah divulged, "I realized how little I've done with my life."

"That's not true, Sarah," Rose snapped in her usual harsh tone. She gave a quick shake of her head. "And don't be thinkin' like that."

"It is true. I'm not sayin' it so you feel sorry for me, but all those days lyin' in bed with my tummy thing, and then that movie last night got me thinkin' about all the things I'd hoped to have done." She picked up the moccasin. "And which ones I still want to do."

Mabel removed her reading glasses. The beaded granny string allowed them to fall safely on her chest. She looked across the table at Sarah. "Well, since you've been thinking about it, what's on your bucket list?"

Sarah wasn't sure she wanted to tell them. While she had known most of them for longer than she hadn't, it never seemed to get any easier to open up to them. Or to anyone for that matter. But the events of the last year had forced her to ask for help and, to her surprise, she was even learning to share her thoughts and feelings.

"Well, I've always wanted to see Rod Stewart in concert." She was about to continue when Lucy butted in.

"Oh, you just want him to sing your favorite song." Lucy stood up and jiggled her chest as she sang. "Do you think I'm sexy? Come on sugar let me know."

The table roared with laughter, and once she'd caught her breath Sarah teased back, "You know me too well." She winked at her friend. "Seriously though, I wanna see one of my grandchildren graduate from high school, and I, oh, I always wanted to go to Hawaii."

"Ditto to Hawaii!" interjected Lucy as she plopped herself back down in her chair.

"But the real big one that I've always wanted to do..." She inhaled again, the crackle of her lungs filling the now silent room. "Is to dance at the Gathering of Nations Pow Wow." Without raising her head, she looked around the table to see everyone's reactions. When there were no reactions, Sarah added, "You know, the World Pow Wow."

Still, no response.

Annoyed that she had to spell it out for them. "The one down in Albuquerque."

"Oh, *that* Pow Wow," said Lucy. "Geez, you dream big, don't ya girl?"

"Yup. Guess so." Sarah's cheeks flushed and her eyes turned down. She reached with her needle for a bead, assuming that was the end of the conversation.

And her dream.

The room fell silent and remained so until one voice stated, "I'll go with you."

Slowly, Sarah's eyes rose to look across the table at her friend Mabel, who tilted her head slightly and nodded, confirming what Sarah had heard.

Just over a year ago, Mabel had lost her sister to cancer and Sarah's recent battle with the same tortuous disease had called on Mabel's faith in ways she'd never experienced before. Through it all, she'd come to learn that life really is precious and she had best go after what she wanted because she never knew when she'd get another chance.

Or, *if* she'd get another chance.

It was this lesson that prompted her to look across the table and reiterate, "I'll go with you."

Sarah's voice was faint, "Really?"

"Yes, really." Mabel beamed at Sarah for a couple of seconds and then turned her gaze around the table. "As a matter of fact, we could all go."

The women had stopped working on their projects and were looking at Mabel. "We'd have to raise a lot of money, but I think we could do it." She paused for a moment and then lifted her shoulder contemplatively. "Maybe the Band could help us out. You know, let us use one of their vans."

Rose butted in, "They're not vans. They're more like small buses and I'm pretty sure someone has to have that special license thingy."

"Rose, why you always gotta go do that?" asked Lucy.

"What?" she replied snarkily and raised her left eyebrow at her best friend. Usually this tone and look silenced whoever was on the receiving end, but not Lucy.

"You always gotta go and be a Negative Nellie and shoot down ideas."

"I'm not being a Negative Nellie." Rose pointed around the table with her lips. "As usual, I'm being the only realistic voice in this group." She turned to face Lucy square on. "Tell me, who's gonna drive us? In case you didn't know, Albuquerque is a heck of a long way from here."

"I can drive," declared Mabel.

"Yeah, but you can't drive all the time. We'd need at least one more driver."

Lucy giggled and her glasses bounced up and down on the end of her nose as she said, "And we need someone to take care of us crazy elders."

As Lucy's laughter subsided, the room grew quiet. The women were accustomed to unfulfilled dreams. So why would this time be different? Not Mabel though. She looked down the table at each woman and knew this time had to be different. "Leave it to me. I know just the person to call."

"Call for what?" asked Rose. She'd already dismissed the idea as a possibility, thinking her point about one more driver had put an end to this ridiculous conversation. "Didn't anyone hear me?" Rose gave no time for a response and in her curt way asked again, "Call for what?"

Sarah's head didn't move, but her eyes looked across to Mabel. This time Sarah didn't dare breathe. "You mean," she paused, "to go to the Pow Wow?"

It had been a long time since Mabel had been this certain of anything. She couldn't help it. A slow smile developed across her face. "Yes, Sarah, go to the Pow Wow."

As if orchestrated, all the women responded at the same time, "Really?"

There was a slight pause before Mabel nodded.

The women glanced around the table at each other. No one knew quite how to respond to what had just happened. This most certainly was not their usual Stitch 'n Bitch meeting.

When one doesn't know what to do, they do what is familiar…what feels safe. For the elders that was working, so they went back to working on their projects. Each lost in a state of shock and disbelief. After a few minutes, Lucy piped up, "So if we're really gonna do this and since we're talkin' bucket lists, well, I'm just wondering...do you think we could stop in Vegas?"

Rose's tone rippled with judgment, "Vegas?"

"Yes, Vegas! You know I've always wanted to go to Las Vegas." Lucy's eyes roamed upwards, as if she was dreaming of something glorious.

Mabel looked down the table at Lucy. "I think a stop in Las Vegas is a great idea."

Lucy raised her arm in the air triumphantly. "Yes!"

With one decision, the potential of dreams becoming reality swept into their January meeting like a warm summer breeze, and with it took the harshness of more than just the winter away.

2

Aftermath

Sarah

STANDING IN FRONT of her bedroom closet, Sarah reached in and pulled out the green suitcase that was tucked in the far corner. She set it on her bed, popped the two clasps open, and lifted the top. Inside was her regalia. Sarah closed her eyes and inhaled deeply as the sweet smell of buckskin filled her. She smiled. Slowly she opened her eyes and ran her fingers over the beads.

With care, Sarah removed her dress from the suitcase and held it up in front of herself. She turned to look in the mirror. The white buckskin with brown beaded bear paws was still in gorgeous condition, even though it had been packed away for years. As Sarah inspected her dress in the mirror, the reflection of a young woman appeared. Sarah blinked her eyes hard and closed them. When she opened her eyes, the young woman was still in the mirror. She was wearing the regalia of a Fancy Dancer, her hair pulled back in a tight braid. Her face was striking. She had rich brown skin, high cheekbones, coffee-colored eyes, and supple lips. The young woman gave a slight nod of her head, acknowledging to Sarah that she was in fact seeing her. Then the young woman looked at the dress Sarah was holding and at the rest of the contents in Sarah's suitcase and back to Sarah. She moved her head up and down a couple of times and then bit by bit, her image faded from the mirror.

Sarah inhaled deeply and shook her head. "Now that was weird," she muttered to herself as she turned away from the mirror and laid her dress out on the bed. Sarah sat beside the open suitcase and one by one, pulled out the remaining pieces of her regalia. First her moccasins, then her shawl, then her headband. She ran her fingers over the attached eagle feather.

Time lapsed and as Sarah sat there surrounded by her regalia, she wondered if she'd ever wear it again. Or, as the old people used to say, "If she'd ever dance it again."

Anne

Anne flicked on the light and closed the door behind her. She's made the tiny room at the end of the hall cozy. Her books, mostly biographies and novels by yet to be discovered Canadian writers, adorned the shelves, dresser, and bedside table. There was even a large stack neatly piled beside her bed in alphabetical order, of course. She had battery-lit candles strewn about the room and had recently added an aromatherapy diffuser. Anne hadn't quite gotten accustomed to the smell of fry bread that lingered in Sarah's house. It wasn't that she didn't like the smell, she did. Just not all the time.

It had been just over a month since she'd come out from Toronto to help care for her sister, Sarah, who was recovering from chemotherapy. Anne had agreed to stay until the end of March, and some days those two more months seemed like an eternity. Especially when she was missing her Liz. Like tonight.

The clock read 9:36 p.m. That meant it was almost one in the morning back home in Toronto. Anne reached for the cell phone in her purse and looked at it for a moment, then back at the clock. Now 9:37. Liz had always been a night owl, but when she went through "the change" it got even worse. The chances were better that she'd be up than in bed, so Anne called home.

On the first ring, Liz answered, "Hello, my love."

"How'd you know it was me?"

"Because I know things and I've been waiting for your call."

"Waiting?" asked Anne. She could hear Liz smile as she teased, "Sure. I know things, remember?"

"You'd think I'd know that by now, since you've been reminding me for more years than I can count." Anne replied as she sat on the bed. She reached up with her free hand and undid the tight bun from atop her head. Her salt-and-pepper hair fell down her back. She ran her fingers through it.

Liz asked, "So, how was your Stich 'n Bitch?" But before Anne could answer, Liz chuckled and continued, "Gawd how I love saying that."

Anne smiled, half at the Stitch 'n Bitch and half at how good it was to hear Liz laugh.

Liz continued, "Whoever decided to call the group that is brilliant."

Anne had never considered where the name came from. Not only was it brilliant, but it was true! She lay down and pulled the quilted afghan from the end of the bed up over herself. Once settled, she proceeded to tell Liz about the evening, Sarah's bucket list idea, and how the idea of the trip unfolded.

"I think you should go."

"Go?"

"Yeah, go!" Liz paused for a moment. "You were invited, weren't you?"

"I suppose, but that's when I'm supposed to be coming home."

"But just think, my love. The red rocks, the New Mexico sun, the crickets, the Pow Wow, not to mention a trip with your sister. It would be good for the two of you."

It was one of the things Anne loved about her Liz. The way she could make almost anything sound enticing. Liz was always good at helping Anne sort herself out, and Anne did have to admit that the trip intrigued her, but not as much as going home.

Rose

As Rose settled into her La-Z-Boy chair to watch the evening news, her husband, Poncho, asked, "How was Stitch 'n Bitch?" He grinned every time he said it, he couldn't help himself.

She rolled her eyes. "You'll never guess what cockamamie idea they've come up with now."

"Well, if I ain't never gonna guess, why not just tell me?"

Rose told Poncho about Sarah's bucket list idea and how, all of a sudden, they were talking about going to the World Pow Wow.

"The one down in Albuquerque?" His eyes widened and his eyebrows raised.

She looked over at her husband of almost fifty years and replied, "Yep, that'd be the one."

"Well, I'll be."

They both turned and went back to watching the news. After a few moments, Poncho hit the mute button and turned to Rose. "So, you think it's gonna happen?"

Her eyebrows furrowed and she shook her head. "No! I don't think it's gonna happen. Think about it." Rose used the thumb on her right hand to begin counting off the reasons why. "Where are we gonna get the money? How we gonna get there? How'd we get those passport thingies you need and besides…" Rose paused to catch her breath. "Can you imagine all of us women in one bus for all those hours an all those miles? Somebody's sure to end up dead."

Poncho looked at his wife as if he was considering what she'd just said. Eventually he raised a shoulder and dropped it before replying, "Too bad. This ol' cowboy could use a road trip."

"Who said you woulda been invited anyways?" Rose snipped.

"I woulda invited myself." Poncho grinned at her. "I could've been the peacekeeper and made sure everyone made it home alive." Poncho snickered, but he was only half joking.

Bea

When she arrived home, Bea was surprised to find her daughter, Liv, still up. "Whaddya still doing up, my girl?" Bea asked as she kissed Liv on her forehead.

"I was lying in bed reading and the leftover fry bread kept calling me. 'Liv. Liv. Come eat us.'" Both women giggled. "Can I warm up a piece for you, Mom?"

"Please."

"Anything interesting happen at Stitch 'n Bitch tonight?" her daughter asked as she popped a piece of fry bread into the microwave.

Bea settled in at the kitchen table, opened the margarine container, and answered, "Funny you should ask that." Ding went the microwave and Liv placed the fry bread on a plate, grabbed the jam from the fridge, and sat down across from her mom.

"You ever seen some movie called *The Bucket List*?" Bea asked her daughter.

"Yeah, why?"

As Bea munched on her jam-covered snack, she shared the events of the evening.

"Really? You're going to go to the World Pow Wow?" said Liv. "Jealous! I've always wanted to go!"

"Well, I don't know just yet. There's a lot to sort out." Before Bea could finish, Liv butted in. "Oh, I believe it. Mabel makes shi..." Liv caught herself. She knew her Mom didn't like swearing. Bea barely tolerated the name of their group. Liv continued, "Mabel makes things happen, Mom! You know that." Liv nodded her head emphatically and then with a coy smile added, "I think you and your ladies are about to go road trip'n."

Mabel

Mabel stoked the wood stove, made herself a cup of chamomile tea, and settled into her comfy chair. She was far too wound up to even consider sleeping, so instead, she began to create a budget of what a trip to Albuquerque might cost.

Finally, at about two in the morning, she dozed off with the laptop still on her knees.

It was the ringing of the telephone that woke her.

She reached for the phone. "Hello?"

"Morning, Mabel. It's Chuck here."

"Chuck, how are you?" She was trying not to sound like he had just woken her.

"I'm good, but hey, what's this I hear you're organizing a trip for elders to go to New Mexico and the big Pow Wow they have down there?"

Mabel shook her head. In all her years, the moccasin telegraph had never worked this fast. "What?"

Chuck realized he had just jumped in, maybe had even woken Mabel up. No wonder she sounded all confused. "Let me start from the beginning. My daughter told me her mom, you know my ex-wife, Bea, was at her Stitch 'n Bitch meeting last night, and that you're organizing a big trip. And...well...I'd like to come along."

"Come along?"

"Yeah, I'd like to come along."

"Oh, Chuck. I don't even know if it's going to happen. There is a lot to sort out and that doesn't even include all the money we have to raise." All the reasons why the trip couldn't happen had begun to seep in last night as she worked on the budget and this morning they seemed to have developed deep roots.

"That's not the Mabel I know. The Mabel I know always finds a way. Always." He let the last word hang in the air for a few moments before continuing. "Let me help you."

"I'll think about it, Chuck."

No sooner had she hung up when the phone rang again. This time it was Lucy.

Lucy

Lucy made herself a cup of hot cocoa and even added a few of the mini marshmallows she kept tucked away in the cupboard for her grandchildren. She settled in at the table with her iPad. She mostly used it to play games, but tonight she pushed the little square at the bottom of the screen. The one that said Safari, just like her grandson had shown her. Again and again.

The bucket list conversation earlier had her thinking, mostly about Las Vegas but also about Sarah, and how she had noticed that her skin looked different tonight. Gray. Maybe it was just the poor lighting? Or maybe? Lucy didn't want to think about the other maybe, so in the space at the top of her iPad she typed Las Vegas. She spent a good portion of the night learning about all the things to do in Las Vegas and then spent the rest of the night dreaming about it.

The next morning as Lucy opened her living room drapes, the sun sparkled on the snow and she decided to take matters into her own hands. Lucy walked to the kitchen, lifted the receiver and dialed Mabel.

"Hello."

"Mabel, it's Lucy. Listen. I want to go."

"Go?"

"To Las Vegas. To the Pow Wow. The whole bucket list trip. I want to go. So, tell me what I gotta do and I'll do it."

3

The Phone Call

PEEKING INTO THE oven at the bannock she was making for dinner, Tilly was surprised when she heard the phone ring. Such a rare sound these days, the home phone ringing. Before answering, she took a momentary look at the call display, making sure it wasn't a telemarketer.

To her relief, it was her friend Mabel calling from Kamloops.

"Hi Mabel," she said, settling on the window bench that overlooked their backyard. She could see Grayson and Piper bouncing on the trampoline.

"Tilly, have you become telepathic since I last saw you?"

"No." A smile crossed her face. "It's 'Call Display.' It's nice to hear your voice, Mabel."

"You okay, Tilly?"

Tilly played with a pillow tassel, pausing for a moment before responding. She wasn't really sure how she was, so she chose to go with the easy answer. "Yeah, Mabel. I'm okay."

"Tilly, I know you. Better than you think, and I'd say by your tone and the fact that you haven't called me in weeks..." She wasn't sure how far to push it. Something was awry with Tilly, but she also knew that Tilly didn't always respond well to being pushed. After all, who does? But this time Mabel decided to push, just a bit. "And you haven't returned any of my calls for that matter, so, no, I don't think you're okay."

Tilly softly closed her eyes. All the times she'd meant to call Mabel back and then something always seemed to come up. She began to apologize, but Mabel cut in, "Listen, I'm coming to Vancouver next weekend and we can talk then." Tilly chewed on her lip, wishing she didn't feel trepidation at the thought of Mabel coming to visit her. Mabel would see through any mask she put on and would drill her about what was going on.

"In the meantime, go and smudge," Mabel told her.

Smudge? It had been so long that Tilly wasn't even sure where her medicine bundle was.

"I have a proposition for you," continued Mabel.

"A proposition?" Tilly was suddenly aware of the wall against her spine. She sat up straighter. "Now that's the most intriguing thing I've heard in a long time."

Mabel dove in. "Last night at Stitch 'n Bitch we decided we're going to the World Pow Wow." This was the first time Mabel had said these words out loud and was struck by how ludicrous the idea of driving to Albuquerque sounded.

"Really? You mean the one in New Mexico?"

"Yeah, really. And yeah, that one. We're all gonna go. Or at least that's the plan," Mabel said, and Tilly chuckled. "Plus," Mabel hesitated, "we need another driver." Her voice raised a few notches. "Aaaaand, that's where you come in."

There was a pause. Like the world stopped rotating on its axis for a moment.

"What do you mean?" Tilly blinked, and her eyes narrowed. "Where I come in?"

"I need you to be my other driver." Mabel waited a moment. "To come to New Mexico with us. Don't answer me right now. Think about it. Discuss it with Mick. We can talk next weekend when I come to visit. Love you and see you soon." Just as she was about to hang up, Mabel said one final thing, "And, Tilly, remember what I said about smudging."

Before Tilly could say anything, the dial tone filled the air. She stared at the phone and thought to herself, *A trip. An adventure. By myself. With Mabel. With elders. To the sun. To the Pow Wow. Might be just what I need to get out of this funk.*

By the time she stood, she had decided two things.

One, she'd look for her medicine bundle after dinner and smudge.

Two, she wanted to go on the trip.

4

The Catalyst

TILLY FOUND HER medicine bundle in the first place she looked, on the top shelf of her side of the bedroom closet. As she pulled it down, something fell to the floor. Tilly picked it up and held it out. A silk nightshirt.

It had been a splurge one day, over a year ago, when she and her best friend, Bette, were shopping. It wasn't really new anymore, except it had never been worn. It had been set aside for a special occasion. But there never seemed to be a special occasion.

Tilly closed the bedroom door and prepared to smudge. She sat on the floor, tucked her feet under her bum, laid a piece of red cloth out in front of her, and then placed her medicine bundle in the middle. Purposefully, she unwrapped her smudge bowl. A beautiful abalone shell that had been a gift from Bea on the day Tilly had completed her six weeks at Round Lake Treatment Centre. Although she was now over twenty years sober, some days it felt like only yesterday. She continued to unpack: a bag full of sage, a braid of sweetgrass, an eagle feather, matches, and her tobacco. Each item held a story and memories.

Tonight, she chose to light the sweetgrass, to bring in the positive energy and healing. As the first waves of smoke filled the air, Tilly closed her eyes and inhaled deeply. Every cell in her body seemed to stir, began to pulse to a different beat. She smudged herself and began to pray.

"Great Spirit, Creator of all things, Grandfathers and Grandmothers of the four sacred directions. My name is Beautiful Light Woman and I come before you in a humble manner. I offer thanksgiving for the safe passage through the night and the safe passage of those I love. I offer thanksgiving for watching over, guiding, protecting, and keeping my family safe, healthy, and vibrant. I know I have set my bundle, my prayers, and ceremony aside for a while now, but I sit here again, reconnecting." She paused for a moment. "I have an important decision to make, Creator. I am grateful for any guidance or messages you can send my way. I know this decision will not only affect me, but also my family, so I seek your help. All my relations."

Tilly opened her eyes and watched as the last remnants of smoke were released from the sweetgrass. When she was sure it was out, Tilly carefully wrapped up her medicine bundle and this time, instead of tucking it back up in the closet, she put it in her bedside table.

She walked down the hall to Mick's office. The door was open, but she still felt inclined to knock softly. When he looked away from his computer, she said, "I'm off to bed. You coming soon?" He gave a slight nod of his head. "Please don't be too long."

"'Kay." He turned back to his computer.

She stood there for a moment, wondering when he'd become a man of so few words. When they'd become a couple of so few words. Tilly craved more. More of every aspect of their marriage. She watched him for a few moments. His shoulders broad and strong, his wavy brown hair now adorned with gray strands and a small, but noticeable, roll had begun to seep over his belt.

She wondered what he saw when he looked at her. Or did he look at her?

She turned and headed back to their bedroom. On the dresser lay the silk nightshirt. She undressed and slid it on. Not only did it feel amazing on her body, but it was like it had been made for her, fitting snug in all the right places. Tilly thought tonight was as good as any night to wear it and try to create a special evening with Mick. She stood in front of the full-length mirror, buttoning and unbuttoning the top two buttons. She couldn't figure out why she felt so nervous. This was her husband after all. Eventually, she decided to leave them both undone, revealing the soft line between her breasts. Mick used to love when she came to bed like this, he'd kiss her collarbone and neck with precise attention before venturing further. Not only did she miss that, but she longed for it. Tilly couldn't remember the last time he'd kissed her with any hint of passion.

As she rubbed lotion on her freshly shaven legs, the draft of the bedroom door swept over her. Tilly stood as Mick closed the door behind him. Their eyes met and she held her breath, hoping he would say something about her nightie. About how she looked. Or anything. Or in the very least, pause and take her in.

Instead, he walked past her to the bathroom. She stood motionless, except for the slow blinking of her eyelids as she watched the bathroom door close behind him.

Her head fell forward as she lowered herself onto their bed. A deep exhale escaped her lips. No longer able to look at the closed door, Tilly closed her eyes. After a few moments of trying to regain her composure, she walked over to the closet and slipped the nightie over her head. Folding it with care, she tucked it into the back of her undergarment drawer and slipped into her usual pyjamas.

Hot tears of rage and rejection spilled down her cheeks as she crawled into bed, settling as far on her side without falling out as possible. Tilly pulled the covers up tight, closed her eyes and thought to herself, *Damn you, Mick. I'm going on this trip*

5

Feeling Sure

THE NEXT MORNING, Tilly watched as Mick sat at the kitchen table sipping his coffee and reading the paper. The sting of last night's rejection still fresh in her heart. She waited until the twins had left for school and then leaned against the fridge with her head slightly turned toward him. She watched him, like an eagle waiting for the exact moment to make its move. When he lifted the mug to his lips and took the last sip of his coffee, she knew it was time. "Mabel called last night."

Mick's eyes remained on the paper, but his stomach tightened.

Tilly took a deep breath and decided to launch in. "She's going to Albuquerque for the Gathering of Nations Pow Wow with a group of elders and she asked me to go along. You know, to help with the driving and also to take care of everyone. I've thought about it." She paused only long enough to exhale the air she'd just taken in and to watch him fold his newspaper. She looked at the kitchen floor, crossed one leg over the other, and informed him, "And I'm going to go."

This time when she glanced up and at him, she knew he'd been listening. Mick's eyes had become a darker shade of brown, almost black, and the wrinkles on his brow were more pronounced.

He removed his reading glasses, tossed them on the table, and thumped back in his chair, causing it to hit the wall. She hated it when he did that. It made her think of a teenager who wasn't getting his way. Mick shook his head and closed his eyes. "What!?"

"Mabel called and asked…"

He raised his hands. "Yeah, yeah I got it. But, just like that, you're going to Albuquerque?"

18

Tilly crossed her arms, raised her eyebrows, and with her lips pursed slowly nodded her head up and down.

He knew that look. He had come to despise it. It meant his wife had made up her mind. And once Tilly made up her mind, there was no going back.

"Fine," he said, spit flying out of his mouth.

"Fine." Tilly turned on her heels, grabbed her purse, and marched out of the house, slamming the door behind her.

Even in all her bravado, she felt unsettled by what had just happened. With shaky hands, she tried to unlock the car door, but dropped the keys. She bent down to pick them up and as she stood she found herself directly facing their house. Their home.

Her shoulders dropped, her head tilted to the side, and for a moment she considered going back in.

Maybe he has a right to be pissed. I did spring this on him, she thought. Tilly wasn't usually a door slammer and not accustomed to walking out on Mick. She also wasn't used to making decisions without talking to him first. But, lately, well, lately everything in their relationship had been different. Tilly got in the car and drove to work, dialing Mabel as soon as she got to the office.

Mabel answered on the fourth ring. "I'm in!" Tilly said with certainty as she settled at her desk. Mabel knew exactly what Tilly meant.

"Fantastic. So, Mick's on board?"

"It doesn't really matter if Mick's on board or not, Mabel." Tilly caught herself and softened her tone, remembering who she was talking to. "You need me. The elders need me. So there. It's done."

"All right, Tilly. If you're sure." It was more of a statement than a question.

Tilly's attention turned to the photos on her desk: school pictures of her twins, Mick and her on their wedding day, and an old photo with her best friend, Bette, taken almost twenty years ago when they were traveling through Mexico. She picked up the photo of herself and Bette. Leaning back in her chair she ran her forefinger over the photo. Tilly missed the spark she had in this photo. She missed the woman looking back at her. *Where'd she go?* Tears pooled in Tilly's eyes.

"You still there, Tilly?" Mabel asked.

"Yep, I'm here." Her voice was barely a whisper.

"You sure about this?" Mabel asked, tenderness wrapped around each word.

Tilly put the picture back on her desk and responded, "Haven't felt this sure about anything for a very long time, Mabel."

6

Divine Support

IT HAD BEEN four weeks since the big decision to go to the Pow Wow. During that time, Mabel had noticed a tinge seeping into Sarah's face. The color was indescribable, somewhere between gray and ash. It haunted her. She'd seen it once before, near the end of her sister, Millie's, battle with cancer. Mabel knew they needed to make this trip happen sooner rather than later.

She and Tilly had created a plan and had applied for every possible funding grant they could find.

The elders had gathered to see what money-making ideas they could come up with. In the end, they decided on organizing weekly movie nights at the community hall. They sewed together white sheets and created a screen that they hung on one of the walls. Their grandchildren helped set up the chairs, Lucy was in charge of selling 50/50 tickets, and the rest of the Stitch 'n Bitch women worked the concession. Chuck and Poncho, the two brave men who were going on the trip, took tickets at the door. Mostly, they teased everyone who came in, their way of making folks feel welcome.

They all knew they needed to draw a crowd for the first night, so they chose the legendary movie *Smoke Signals*. To their amazement and relief, the hall overflowed with people.

As the lights went down, Lucy and Rose stood at the back of the hall and watched as the movie began to play. Lucy reached over for Rose's hand and whispered, "I think this might just happen."

"Of course it's happening. The movie's playing right in front of us, Lucy." Rose shook her head and clicked her tongue.

"No! Not the movie. The trip." Lucy let go of Rose's hand and did a little jig.

"Don't go gettin' yourself all worked up, Lucy. This is just one movie. We have to raise a whole helluva lota money to make this trip happen."

Lucy stopped dancing. She snapped her head toward her friend, narrowed her eyes and tightened her lips. Raising her finger up to Rose's face, Lucy declared, "Oh, it's gonna happen!" Lucy's head moved up and down a couple times. "Mark my words, Rose. This trip *is* happening!" She turned and looked out at the hall. Not an empty seat. Awe rippled through her and this time her words were softer. "There's no way the Creator would send all these people here tonight to support us if we weren't meant to go on this trip."

Rose's eyes moved from the full hall to her little friend. Secretly, she wished she had even an ounce of Lucy's optimism and hope, but Residential school had taken all that away from Rose. No matter how hard she tried or what she did, she couldn't get it back. She never understood how it was that she and Lucy had experienced the same abuses at school, *and* Lucy had lost her only daughter. Yet, somehow, it was Rose who had become a crusty, curmudgeonly old lady.

As the movie ended and the credits began to roll, the audience clapped and whooped and hollered. The evening had been a bigger success than the elders could've ever dreamt. A community member stood and yelled out loud, "What's playing next week?" The elders all glanced at each other, not sure how to answer as they hadn't anticipated this response.

It was Chuck who responded. "Well, you'll just have to come and find out, but you might want to come early. We're sure to sell out again." His comments created the exact response he was looking for. A buzz amongst the moviegoers.

When the last chair was put away, the gym floor swept, and everything cleaned, they sat around the table in the kitchen and counted their money. They'd known the evening had gone smashingly, but they hadn't realized just how much money they had raised. With movie ticket sales, concession sales, and 50/50 tickets, they'd raised close to two thousand dollars.

In the dead of a dark, cold winter, the movie nights became a spark for the community. Every Tuesday night, the hall was full and bursting with energy and the elders loved every single minute of it.

7

Bucket List

AS THE WEEKS unfolded, the blanket of the brutally long winter began to lift and a renewed energy came over the elders. They began taking steps to get ready and Chuck had been chosen to make sure everyone had their paperwork in order: passports, status card renewals, travel insurance, etc.

Something new began to happen as a part of their regular Stitch 'n Bitch meetings—celebration. Sure they'd celebrated before, events like birthdays or when one of them had a grandchild, but now it seemed it was a weekly occurrence. Now, they'd celebrate when one of them got their passport in the mail, or when they'd gone with Chuck to get travel insurance, but the biggest celebration came near the end of March.

Mabel had an announcement to make and everyone who was going on the trip needed to hear it, including Tilly.

While Chuck and Bea had seen each other at the movie nights, they'd pretty much managed to avoid each other. But not that night.

That night, the stars aligned and had them sitting directly across from each other.

Bea leaned back in her chair, turned her coffee cup between her thumb and forefinger and did what she could to avoid looking across the table at her ex-husband. She *could not* believe he was coming on this trip. The thought had crossed her mind not to go, but that's what she always used to do in their relationship. Give up what she wanted so he could have what he wanted. Not this time!

As Mabel began, she shared the exciting news that they had raised enough money with their grant applications and movie nights to go on their trip. Not only had they raised enough money to cover all costs, but they had some spending money as well. The elders sat there dumbfounded. They knew that Mabel and Tilly had been working hard on funding and that their movie nights were a big hit, but they had no idea just how successful the fundraising had been. It was almost like there was divine intervention helping them make their trip a reality.

It was Lucy who finally broke the shocked silence. She stood abruptly, knocking over a chair, and then proceeded to break out in a jig and sing, "Woohoo! Woohoo! I'm goin' to Vegas, to Vegas. I'm goin' to Vegas." She lifted her head to the ceiling, arms spread wide and yelled, "Look out Las Vegas. Lucy's on her way."

Everyone giggled as they watched Lucy's performance and it didn't take long for the giggling to turn into fits of uncontrollable laughter.

For the rest of the evening, they gathered around Chuck and his laptop. They explored possible routes from Vancouver to Albuquerque and back and what potential attractions, scenery, and activities might be of interest to them along the different routes.

Tilly sat back and watched. She could see the delight and excitement in their faces as they explored the possibilities.

Most of them had never traveled outside of British Columbia, let alone on a trip like this. Their village was close to the city, but not close enough that any of them felt comfortable there. Their comfort lay in the vast open spaces nestled between the mountains, where the stories of their Ancestors lived in the sap of the trees and the smell of sage filled the air.

As the evening came to a close, Mabel reminded everyone, "This is our bucket list trip and time is ticking." Before Mabel could continue, Poncho butted in with a chuckle. "In more ways than one."

Mabel smiled at him. "Ain't that the truth." Her gaze turned down the table to Sarah. Their eyes met and Sarah produced a forced smile. Mabel carried on. "Right, so we need to get our little selves organized. Each of you has to figure out what's the one thing you want to see or do on this trip and bring that with you to next week's meeting. Chuck and Tilly, why don't you e-mail me your choice? And why don't you send your choice with Rose," Mabel said as she looked at Poncho. He tipped his cowboy hat in agreement.

"Once I have everyone's choice, then Tilly and I will figure out our trip."

As it turned out, their decision-making was easier than anticipated. Mabel gathered the following list:

LUCY: Las Vegas...anything VEGAS
SARAH: Dance at the Gathering of Nations Pow Wow, Albuquerque
CHUCK: Visit the pawnshop in Las Vegas where the television show Pawn Stars is filmed
BEA: Go to the Grand Canyon
MABEL: Have a ceremony amongst the red rocks of Sedona and spread my sister's ashes
ANNE: Walk through the tulips at the Tulip Festival
PONCHO: Hug a "Grandfather" tree in the Redwood Forest
TILLY: Spend two weeks with elders
ROSE:

Nothing came from Rose. She'd never really been a dreamer, so this whole bucket list idea was new to her. Besides, Rose still wasn't convinced the trip would actually happen. She wasn't about to let herself get all excited, only to be disappointed.

Stitch 'n Bitch Trip to
Gathering of Nations Pow Wow

Here is an itinerary for our trip. In a couple weeks, I will send a more detailed copy with hotels, contact phone #'s. etc. Please make sure your family has a copy. Mabel.

Day 1: Leave home and drive to Vancouver
Day 2: Leave Vancouver and travel to Mount Vernon and Tulip Town and spend night in Pendleton, Oregon
Day 3: Begin the journey to Las Vegas, with hopes to get as far as Twin Falls, Idaho and then the rest of the way to Vegas the following day
Day 3: Arrive in Las Vegas (possibly late at night)
Days 5–7: Las Vegas
Day 8: Travel to Sedona
Days 9 & 10: Sedona
Day 11: Travel to Albuquerque

Day 12-14: Pow Wow (Sarah Grand Entry Friday night 7:00 p.m.)
Day 15: Travel toward California (see how far we get)
Day 16: Travel toward California Coast
Day 17: Redwood Forest
Day 18: Begin to head home—maybe take us 2-3 days.

****Still waiting to hear from Rose about her bucket list item, so plans might change a bit. For emergencies: Mabel cell (250) 333-1260

8

Preparation

RECEIVING THE ITINERARY propelled everyone into action.

Anne

To be truthful, Anne hadn't gotten her hopes up about the trip because raising that much money had seemed damn near impossible to her. Plus, she'd been away from Toronto now for three months and was more than eager to get home. However, when Anne received the itinerary, something stirred deep inside her.

With her phone, she took a photo of the itinerary and wrote a text to Liz before attaching the photo. "Seems this bucket list trip is actually going to happen. See photo. I'll get Sarah ready for the trip and then I'll be home." Anne added a happy face emoji before hitting send.

It wasn't even two minutes later when her phone rang. Intuitively, she knew it was Liz, and before she even had a chance to say hello Liz started in.

"What do you mean you'll be home? I thought you were going to go on the trip?"

"Yes but…"

Liz didn't let her finish. "I want you to go. Don't get me wrong, I want you to come home, too. But, love," her voice softened, "this trip could be a chance for you to have some fun. Make some good memories with Sarah. Especially after everything you two have been through."

"I don't know." Anne slipped out to the back deck and settled into a comfortable chair. She had to be honest with herself, the trip appealed to her. And since she'd recently retired, there was no job to rush back to. But she missed Liz something fierce and the thought of not seeing her for a few more weeks…

Anne's thoughts were interrupted by Liz. "Listen, I'm not going anywhere, darling, so why not go on the trip? I'm not sure how, but I think I can manage not seeing you for a couple more weeks."

"But it's been so long, Liz. We've barely spent a night apart in the last four decades and now it's been almost three months." Tears blurred her vision and she added, "I miss you."

"I miss you too," replied Liz. They were both quiet for a few moments. "Don't decide right now, but promise me you'll think about it?"

"Okay. I'll think about it."

"See, there's my girl."

"I'm not saying I'm going." Defiance tinged Anne's voice.

"I know, but you're thinking about it." Anne could hear Liz smiling through her words. "I'll be here. Whether you come home tomorrow or in a month, I'll be here."

"I know."

When they finished their call, Anne leaned her head back against the chair and thought about Liz. She'd been a bright light in Anne's life since the day she'd walked into the library. Liz had come to the desk asking for help and it was Anne who led her to the book she was looking for. They'd become fast friends, but over time that friendship turned into something much deeper.

It all changed one night when they had gone to a Buffy Sainte-Marie concert at The Purple Onion Coffeehouse. Liz had reached across the table and taken Anne's hand in hers, sending shivers down Anne's spine. "I don't know when or where or how it happened, Anne, but I've fallen deeply and madly in love with you."

Anne's face had shown the surprise she felt at what Liz had just said and even more so, surprise that Liz was having the same feelings as she was. "You have?"

"Yes. I have." Liz nodded and a beautiful, radiant smile came over her face.

"I have too," Anne said. "Fallen in love with you, that is."

They'd pretty much been inseparable since.

Lucy

As soon as Lucy got in the door and set her purse down on the chair, she called Rose. "I got myself a permanent for the trip."

Rose, in her usual abrupt tone asked, "A permanent?"

"Yeah, you know where they put those tight little curlers in your hair and then they pour some kind of liquid on your head and it smells to high heaven."

"Yes, Lucy. I know what a permanent is."

"Then why'd you ask?"

"Because nobody calls them permanents anymore?"

"Well then." Lucy paused, put her finger to her lips and glanced around the room. "I know. I got a new do," she said defiantly.

"A new what?" Rose asked, with sarcasm embedded in her question. Lucy could imagine Rose's face.

"A new do." She paused for a moment to see if Rose would say anything, but she didn't. Lucy was beginning to wish she hadn't called Rose. Her excitement was almost gone. "Fine then, Rose, you ol' battle-ax! I went and got my hair done for the trip. There. How's that? Make you happy?"

It didn't make Rose happy. She felt miserable. She could never figure out why she could be mean to Lucy. After all, Lucy had been her best friend for almost sixty years. They'd been five when they met the first day of Residential school.

Rose looked out her kitchen window across the rolling hills. The only good thing that had happened at that school was Lucy. Thank goodness she was so easy going and forgiving.

Bea

Bea thought it would be easiest to tell her family all at once, so she'd invited her daughters and grandchildren over for dinner. Halfway through the meal, she was buttering her second piece of bannock and began to share her news. "I've got a little something to tell you all." Everyone stopped eating and looked at her, even the baby.

"Our Stitch 'n," she stopped, looked at the children, "well, you know, my sewing group?" Heads moved up and down. "We've raised enough money, so we're going on our trip." She paused long enough to make eye contact with her eldest daughter. "To Albuquerque, for the World Pow Wow."

Everyone, except her oldest daughter, stared at her blankly. They were surprised the trip was happening and wondered if Bea even owned a suit-case, let alone a passport.

Bea's youngest daughter's eyes grew large, her brows furrowed. She enunciated her words carefully: "Is this the *same trip* that *Dad's* going on?"

All of Bea's children looked at their sibling with varying degrees of surprise on their faces. Then, they looked back to Bea.

Bea avoided the question. Instead, she fed a small piece of fry bread to the baby.

"Mom?" Liv asked.

Bea continued to focus on the baby, avoiding the shocked looks on all of her children's faces. She fed the baby another tiny piece of fry bread before responding, "Yep, it's the same trip."

A weird sound escaped her youngest daughter's mouth, somewhere between a choke and a laugh. "No way." She looked directly at her mom, who had turned her gaze away from the baby and back to the table. "You and Dad? On the same trip?" She crossed her arms and laughed again. "Gawd, that should be interesting when you two can barely stand being in the same room."

Bea shot her daughter a look. Even at thirty-five, she knew her moth-er's look meant "That's enough."

It was Bea's eight-year-old grandson who eased the tension, his eyes wide as he asked, "Really Grams? You're going to the biggest Pow Wow in the whole wide world?"

Sitting straighter in her chair, she responded, "Yes, my boy. I am."

"Wowwww." His eyes got even bigger and he flashed a smile. Bea could look at that smile, with the two front teeth missing, all night long.

"I think it's pretty wow, too," she said as she reached over and tousled his hair. "Grams might need everyone's help getting ready. She's never done anything like this before."

Mabel

Preparing came easy for Mabel, especially since she had only herself to consider. She had never married. Sure, there had been love interests over the years, but none that she ever considered a "keeper." Her family consisted of her siblings, nieces and nephews, and Tilly. Tilly's twins were probably the closest Mabel would ever get to having grandchildren. She frequently traveled to Vancouver to spend weekends and family holidays with them.

As it turned out, the most difficult part of preparing for the trip was emotional.

A couple of years earlier, Mabel and her sister, Millie, had traveled to Sedona, back when they were both healthy and vibrant...and alive. It was still hard for Mabel to believe that it was only six months after that trip that Millie passed away from cancer. Thinking about it brought on the all too familiar feeling of being punched in the stomach.

Mabel wasn't sure if she was ready or had the strength for spreading Millie's ashes in Sedona. But, hopefully, with Tilly there and the support of her Stitch 'n Bitch sisters, maybe, just maybe she'd have the courage to honor her sister's wish.

Sarah

It had been a successful night at Bingo with Sarah winning seventy-five dollars on the four corners game. Now, as she sat in the passenger seat of her daughter's car, the exhilaration of the win was still buzzing through her. The money would be a welcome addition to her savings for the upcoming trip.

"Mom, are you sure you should be doing this?"

"Doing what?" Sarah asked as she looked over at her daughter.

"Going on this trip." Her daughter turned to make eye contact with her. "Are you sure you should be going on this trip?"

Sarah moved her head so she was looking out the passenger side window and considered her response. Finally, she answered, "Nope."

"Then *why* are you going?"

"You'd never understand."

"Try me."

"All my life I've done everythin' for everyone and nothin' for me. I was okay with it, till now. Now I want to do some things for me. Your daddy dyin' started me thinking about how life can be gone so quick, and then with my tummy problems…" Sarah never used the word cancer. "I never told any of you kids this," Sarah turned from looking out the window to her daughter, "but this whole trip was my idea."

"Seriously?"

Sarah nodded and began to giggle, which then turned into a full-blown belly laugh. Her daughter looked over at her like she wasn't sure who this was sitting beside her because she sure wasn't acting like her mother.

When Sarah finally stopped laughing and caught her breath, her daughter asked, "You done?"

"For now, but yup, this whole trip started with me. I brought up watching that *Bucket List* movie with Cherie, you know the one with the two old men, and how it got me thinkin'. Then Mabel was askin' me if I was serious about wanting to dance at the World Pow Wow." Sarah tipped her head toward her daughter and shook it a couple times. "There's no lyin' to Mabel, so I told her the truth. Next thing I know we were puttin' on movie nights an' her and that girl Tilly started writing to people to give us money and now we're off in a couple weeks." Sarah stopped talking for a few moments and looked out her window again. "So, yeah, it all started with lil' ol' me."

"Wow, Mom. Never thought you had it in you."

"I know, right? Me either, but here we are. I'm leavin' in a couple weeks for the only trip I've ever taken. I sure could use your help gettin' ready. Think you can do that?"

"Sure. What do you need?"

Following that simple conversation on the way home from the Bingo hall, Sarah's family got on board to get Sarah ready for the trip. Cherie replaced missing beads on her grandma's regalia and helped smudge it and prepare it for being danced again. Her daughter helped her get everything ready for the passport application, her son took her down to Walmart and they picked out a new suitcase. She was thrilled when they brought it home. "Look, Annie. The wheels turn every which way and it rolls real easy." Anne broke into fits of laughter as she watched her big sister dance around the kitchen twirling her suitcase.

On a cold Saturday in early April, Sarah's children held a garage sale. She and Anne stopped by and indulged in the Rice Krispie squares her grandchildren were selling. Later that evening Sarah's family came to visit and her youngest grandchild presented her with a gift. The card attached simply said, "Pocket money for you, from us, 'cuz we luv you." Inside was a new wallet containing the $347.40 they had raised at the garage sale.

Sarah blinked hard to hold back the tears, but when her youngest grandson said, "I even sold my Legos, Granny," the tears could not be contained. Her family came over one by one and hugged her.

Sarah was ready.

9

My Girl, Are You Prepared?

ON THE NIGHT before they were to leave, Grandma Tilly visited Tilly in her dreams. It had been a long time since this had happened. Actually, Tilly couldn't remember the last time Grandma had visited her like this. It was soothing to be with her again.

In the dream, Tilly was back in Grandma's barn in Saskatchewan. Grandma Tilly looked at her for a long time before reaching over and tucking a few wisps of hair behind Tilly's ear. "Are you prepared, my girl?"

Tilly tilted her head and looked at her Grandma, knowing she didn't mean prepared as in, "Do you have your toothbrush? Underwear? Deodorant?" Rather, something more meaningful.

As Grandma Tilly reached over and ran her weathered brown hand along Tilly's jawline, Tilly leaned her head into her Grandma's hand and closed her eyes.

"My girl, are you prepared?"

With that question, the comforting feeling of the dream was yanked away like a warm blanket on a chilly night. Tilly's eyes sprung open, her chest heaved, sweat broke out above her upper lip, and her body tingled. She was no longer in the dream. She pulled the covers up close to her face. Grandma's question flooded every ounce of her being. "Are you prepared?"

After a few moments of attempting to calm herself, Tilly slid out of bed, opened her bedside table, and removed her medicine bundle.

Mick turned on the bedside light. "Till? What are you doing?" He looked over at the clock. "It's four in the morning."

Her response was hasty, "I have to make tobacco ties. For the trip. I dreamt about Grandma Tilly." How could she explain to him the trepidation she felt as a result of Grandma's question? There was no way to explain the panic rising in her chest. "I need to make tobacco ties."

Mick sat up, saw that his wife was clearly unnerved. "Would you like some help? Or do you want me to come sit with you? I could make you some tea."

Great, now he's decided to be caring, ran through Tilly's head as she responded, "No." She shook her head in short, quick movements. The last thing she needed now was Mick to get up and help. "No, no thanks. I..." she pulled the bundle close to her chest, "I think I need to do this by myself."

"'Kay, but if you change your mind, come and wake me."

"Thanks." She turned away from him, closed the door behind her, and headed downstairs to the kitchen table.

She laid out the red material, tobacco, and white ribbon, then unwrapped her smudge bowl and sweetgrass. She removed her rings and, in the palm of her hand, held her wedding band and the ring Mick and the twins had given her to honor her twenty years of sobriety. Tilly closed her fingers over them for a moment before placing them on the material.

She lit the sweetgrass and allowed the smoke to fill her lungs and envelope her. After four deep breaths, Tilly could feel the change, every cell in her body was vibrating at a higher level. She began to pray, "Great Spirit, creator of all things, my name is Beautiful Light Woman and I come before you in a humble manner. I offer thanksgiving for the safe passage through the night and for the gift of living another day."

Tilly moved the braid around her head, asking for good and clear thoughts, around her ears so that she might hear what she needed to hear, around her mouth so she would say kind words that are medicine to those who hear them, and along the length of her body so that she might walk the earth in a good and respectful way. She smudged her rings and then the material, tobacco, and ribbon. The smudge left a trail of sweet-smelling, prayer-filled gray smoke weaving its way through the kitchen, into the family room, and upstairs toward the bedrooms. Tilly placed the sweetgrass in her smudge bowl and got to work making the ties.

With each tie, Tilly placed a pinch of tobacco in the center of the red material and offered the same prayer. A prayer of gratitude. "Thank you for watching over me, guiding me, protecting me, and for keeping my family safe and healthy." Tilly made a tie for each of the days they were to be away and placed them into a baggie.

"There." She took a deep breath and let it out with a long slow sigh that caused her cheeks to puff out. "Now I'm prepared," she whispered.

However, the queasiness in her stomach came rushing back as soon as she remembered Grandma Tilly's question "My girl, are you prepared?"

10

Road Trip Rules

EARLIER THAT MORNING, Tilly had said good-bye to her family. Her mother's guilt was already pumping through her blood like a raging river and she wasn't sure she was strong enough for a public good-bye.

Tilly had offered to take the first driving shift of the trip and she was adjusting the rear-view mirror when Chuck opened the passenger door and heaved himself into the seat beside her. "Don't you know, Tilly, there is no word in any of our languages for good-bye? Only 'see you.'"

Tilly looked over at him, lifted the corners of her mouth and thought to herself. *Well there it is, the first teaching of the trip.*

He pulled a pouch of tobacco out of his chest pocket and opened the glove box. Just before putting the tobacco in, he motioned toward Tilly. "Want some to make an offering?"

She wasn't sure what Chuck was talking about.

"You know, take a pinch, hold it in your hand, and offer a prayer of thanksgiving for a safe journey for us and all others who are traveling today. Then as we drive, let it fall from your hand out the window." Chuck unfolded the pouch and held it open for Tilly.

She reached in and removed a small amount of tobacco and held it in her palm. She remembered now how she'd seen her dad make offerings like this whenever they drove to Saskatchewan.

"You know how sometimes you get an uneasy feeling in the pit of your stomach?" Chuck asked.

Tilly nodded. She was all too familiar with that uneasy feeling. Somewhere over the last year, it seemed to have taken up permanent residence. She wondered if any amount of tobacco or prayers would provide relief.

Chuck's voice brought her back. "Sometimes when I get an uneasy feeling about a trip, I'll put a pinch of tobacco on each of the four tires."

Tilly looked over at Chuck, the tobacco now warming in her palm, and wondered how she could put tobacco on the four tires of her life.

"'Scuse me, 'scuse me," Poncho said as he made his way to the front of the bus. "Before we leave, I need to hang this from the rearview mirror. I always travel with sweetgrass in my truck. Keeps me protected." The braid of sweetgrass had been folded into a circle with the two ends wrapped together with red string. Poncho hung it around the rearview mirror. "There, now our bus is protected too."

Tilly smiled at him, "Thanks, Poncho."

"You betchya," he replied as he turned to make his way to the back of the bus and the seat he shared with Rose.

"Before we head out, I have a something for everyone," announced Rose. She leaned forward and reached into her purse, pulling out eight packages of antiseptic wipes.

"Oh my gawd, Rose. You didn't!" Lucy was exasperated.

"Yes, I did..." replied Rose, jutting her shoulders back and her chin forward. "Now listen everybody..." She scanned the bus to make sure she had everyone's attention before continuing, "...these are wipes for your hands and for the hotel rooms."

"Hotel rooms?" inquired Sarah.

"Yes, hotel rooms. Use them to wipe things down when you first get in. Like the door handles and, most importantly, the remote control. Don't even get me started on what's on those remote controls." A look of disgust came over her face.

"Eeewwww," came the chorus from the bus.

"Yes. Ew. That's exactly my point. And since we are stuck on this bus together for the next two weeks, if one of us gets sick, we're all going to get sick. So take precautions. Use...the...wipes."

Rose passed the wipes forward and back for everyone to receive a package. "I have plenty more where those came from, so if you run out don't be afraid to ask for more."

Lucy stuffed hers in her fanny pack. "Thanks, Rose, for takin' care of us, in your own weird way. But we aren't really *stuck* on this bus together. We've all made a choice to go on this trip, even you."

"Whatever, Lucy," snarked Rose in response, "just use your wipes."

Poncho piped up, "Speaking of this trip, what ya say, driver? Let's get this show on the road."

"Yes, sir," Tilly responded. She tucked the wipes into her backpack and started the bus. Slowly they merged onto East Hastings Street and headed toward the Trans-Canada Highway. Once on the highway they followed it out to Abbotsford where they turned off and made their way to the Peace Arch border crossing. The sun shone brightly and steam from the previous day's rain still floated in the fields. Before long the smell of cow manure seeped into the bus.

"What is that stench?" asked Anne as she covered her nose with her cardigan.

"That'd be cow..." Lucy's voice trailed off as she considered what to say. After all, Anne was not like all the rest of them. She was from the city. "That'd be cow poo."

Poncho inhaled deeply. "Ahh, that has got to be one of my most favorite smells in the world."

As they neared the border crossing, Tilly could feel tension fill the bus. She wasn't sure why. Perhaps it was that many of the elders had never been into the United States and were uncertain what to expect. Perhaps it was the history of fearing those in power, or perhaps it was the unknown. Whatever it was, it heightened as they eased along in the slow-moving line toward the border.

Tilly followed the lane specifically for buses. It was then that Mabel announced, "'Kay, listen up everyone. They're going to make us all get off the bus and go in. It's what they always do, so don't worry. Just make sure you take your passport in with you." She looked around the bus and could see the fear on almost every elder's face. "It will be okay. We have nothing to hide," she paused for a moment, "and we've done nothing wrong."

As it turned out, crossing the border was a breeze. It was one of the first signs they were being watched over. The border security officer they were assigned to had been to the Gathering of Nations Pow Wow the year before and understood their reason for traveling.

When they got back on the bus, Poncho removed his cowboy hat, wiped his sweat-laden brow, plopped down in his seat, and let out a big sigh. "Whew! Funny how even if I ain't got no reason to be afraid, authority figures still get to me. Cops and guys like those ones back there, they stress me out."

"Me too," added Chuck.

"Me three," chimed in Lucy.

11

Kindred Spirits

AS THE ELDERS disembarked from the bus and prepared to explore Tulip Town in Mt. Vernon, Washington, Mabel said, "What do you say we all meet back here at one?" Before anyone had a chance to respond, Mabel looked directly at Anne, since this was her bucket list stop, and asked, "Do you think three hours will give you enough time to see everything?"

"I think so," replied Anne.

"Good enough then. Everyone have a good morning and remember Tilly's booked us motel rooms in Pendleton, Oregon for tonight, so we're going to have to leave on time. Today and tomorrow are long travel days, but then we've got three days to rest in Las Vegas."

Lucy inhaled loudly and everyone turned to see why. "Rest and Vegas do not belong in the same sentence, Mabel Billy."

Mabel chuckled. "Right." She was in the midst of doing up her fanny pack when she remembered one more thing. "You're on your own for an early lunch today."

"Geez. We've only been traveling for two hours and already we're on our own for lunch," Poncho teased.

"You betchya, Poncho ol' man. You're on your own for lunch and if you give me any more sass, you'll be on your own for dinner, too."

Poncho laughed, reached for Rose's hand, and said, "Let's go see us some flowers, wifey."

"I'm coming too," Lucy piped in, and off the three of them went.

Tilly pulled her phone out, hit the message app, and wrote a text message to Piper and Grayson. "Miss you already, Love Momma, xo" She also sent a reminder text to Mick, "our turn 4 oranges at Piper's b-ball 2night." She looked at the completed message and wondered if she should add "Love Tilly," or "I love you," or at least "xxo." Instead, her forefinger pushed send. She knew Mick would take her text as her being bossy and sending him more instructions.

She leaned her head back against the seat, trying to figure out when she'd become such a cold wife. It wasn't like there was one incident or occasion, at least not that she could pinpoint. Maybe Mick could tell her, but that wasn't going to happen because she wasn't about to ask him. Tilly exhaled deeply and rubbed the inside of her eyes with her thumb and middle finger. She looked out the side window and saw Poncho standing there. He tipped his cowboy hat to her and grinned. Tilly raised her hand and gave him a slight wave. Poncho motioned with his arm for Tilly to join him.

She opened the door and climbed out of the bus, hopeful some fresh air and a walk amongst the tulips would help get her out of this pity party. She tucked her hands into the pockets of her Levis and made her way over to Poncho.

"Care to walk with me, Miss Tilly?" Before she had a chance to answer, he took her hand and tucked it under his arm, leading them off to explore the tulips.

"I thought you were with Rose and Lucy," Tilly said.

Poncho looked at her. "Oh, I get to spend plenty a time with those two, but you, I don't know you yet, so thought I'd come walk with you."

Tilly cocked her head. "Thanks." She'd only met Poncho once, but had instantly felt his protective, loving, teasing uncle ways.

After meandering for a bit and talking about the flowers, Poncho looked over at Tilly. "So, Miss Tilly, why don't you tell me about yourself."

"Mmm, well I'm a mom. I have twins who are ten."

"Boys? Girls?"

"One of each."

"You got lucky there, didn't ya?" Poncho teased and squeezed her hand.

"Totally." She leaned into him affectionately. He was familiar in a way that words couldn't describe. She loved that he always wore his black cowboy hat with the turquoise band and eagle feather hanging from it, except at the table—he was a gentleman after all. Poncho was a cowboy through and through. He proudly wore polished cowboy boots, ironed cowboy shirts, and a big silver belt buckle that helped hold up his Wranglers, which had a permanent line down the front where Rose ironed them. His face displayed years of working outside in harsh weather conditions. When he smiled, which was often, the lines around his mouth formed crescent moon-like crevices on his cheeks. Poncho's deep brown eyes had a cloudy film over the lens, a result of living with diabetes for twenty years.

"Any other kids?" he asked.

"Nope." Tilly remembered how desperately she and Mick had wanted children. All their plans about the future revolved around having a family. A big family. But that wasn't in the cards. The miscarriages had been beyond painful. Each time, they named the child and held a ceremony. Each time, it felt like they buried a piece of themselves, of each other, and of their relationship.

Tilly was always surprised how the grief hung about, not quite ready to leave. It sat at the table with them like an unfamiliar and unwanted dinner guest. Their grief caused them to choose their words cautiously, or not at all. It always seemed to Tilly that Mick was afraid to ask her how she was because she'd start crying and she was afraid to ask him how he was for fear of being dismissed.

But Poncho didn't need to know all this, so Tilly filtered what she shared. "We had some challenges getting pregnant. Piper and Grayson are our little miracles." She could feel him listening to her, really listening, so she continued. "They are, without question, Poncho, the greatest gifts I've ever been blessed with."

Poncho looked at Tilly and beamed. "That's how our children should always be talked about, Tilly. As gifts. Gifts from the Creator. Each and every child is a gift from the Creator."

He let Tilly sit with his words for a few moments before continuing. "My grandma told me once that when a child is conceived, four ancestors from the mother's side and four ancestors from the father's side must come together in the spirit world and agree that now is the best time for this child to come into the world."

Tilly hooked her arm through Poncho's and laid her head on his shoulder, like she might have if she was walking with her dad. If she had had that kind of a relationship with her dad.

"Love that, Poncho." She squeezed his arm. "Thanks."

"Seems to me, Miss Tilly, that everybody's so busy worrying about themselves. You know always lookin' at their phones and other gadgets. Few seem to remember that everything we do affects the next generations. Everything belongs to those not yet born." He looked up to the sky. "The ones that are still stars."

Tilly had heard elders talk before about spirits being stars and how when it's time for them to come to earth, they do so in the form of a human being. A baby.

Tilly began to share, "I've been thinking lately about how it feels like someone is missing from our dinner table. Which seems really odd to say because my husband and I..." Her voice trailed off and she swallowed hard, surprised by the stinging at the back of her eyes.

They walked a few more steps before Poncho said, "Rose and me, we've been married going on fifty years now and I understand what you're not saying, Tilly." He looked over at her for a second. He knew more about what she wasn't saying than he'd ever care to remember. "It'll either get better or it'll get worse. Half of that's up to you and half is up to him. You just need to decide what your half is gonna be."

Tilly sucked in her lips. She couldn't believe Poncho knew what she hadn't said. And as far as things with Mick were concerned, she wasn't ready to decide. Not yet anyway.

"What's your real name, Miss Tilly?" Poncho's question brought her out of her melancholy.

Although she'd never been asked it like this before, Tilly knew what Poncho meant. She'd heard many ways of being asked about names: ancestral name, traditional name, spirit name, Indian name, but she'd never been asked about it as her real name. She liked it.

"I'm Beautiful Light Woman." It had been many moons since Tilly had shared her name with anyone. So long, she'd almost forgotten the sense of power that overcame her when she used it, like she was no longer alone.

"Yes." Poncho nodded and flashed his dimples at Tilly. "Yes, you are Beautiful Light Woman." He squeezed her hand. "Time you remember who you are."

Tilly's gaze turned to the path that unfolded before them and the colorful bounty of tulips. "And you, Poncho? What's your real name?"

"Grateful-hearted one."

"Mmm." Tilly nodded and smiled. She was always in awe of how people's traditional names captured their essence in a way that English names weren't able to.

They walked for a long time, sharing stories and learning about each other. She learned that Poncho grew up all over British Columbia and Washington State because his family moved to wherever there was work when he was a kid. That's how he'd avoided Residential school, he explained: "Just before I turned five, my dad got a job picking berries in Washington, not far from here, actually. So, we moved. The farmer, he really liked my dad, so he set us up in a house and we lived there till I was twelve. I stayed back home on the rez until I was fifteen then came back down this way. That's when I met my Rose."

Rose's dad was working on the same farm as Poncho and he met her at a dance, Poncho explained. All evening he had watched her from afar, admiring her beauty and how graceful she was on the dance floor. Finally, he mustered up enough courage to ask her to dance. "That was fifty years ago," he told Tilly with a chuckle.

In the first twenty years of their marriage, Poncho worked on a ranch in the Interior. He was a well-respected, hardworking, and admired rancher who seemed to have a special connection with the animals and the land. When the owner of the ranch was preparing to retire, he sat down with Poncho and offered him the first chance to buy. He knew that Poncho had been instrumental in the success of the ranch, so not only did he provide him first dibs on the ranch, but at a generously discounted rate. Unbeknownst to everyone except Rose, Poncho had been saving his money for years, hoping that one day he'd be able to buy a small parcel of land for he and Rose. Never in his wildest dreams did he think he'd own a ranch.

But life works in mysterious ways, and in the fall of 1985, Poncho and Rose bought the ranch and moved into the main house. In the first few years, he and Rose worked excruciatingly long days. For Poncho, being on the land was one of the times he felt most alive. Even though his son now ran the ranch, Poncho still worked every single day...but to him, it wasn't work.

"My Rose and I, we had six children." His squinted his eyes as he looked out over the sea of tulips. His voice softened, "But now we have five."

Tilly looked up at him as he continued to gaze out at the tulips. "One of our boys died in a car crash. He was eighteen. Worst pain of my life, Miss Tilly. Didn't think I'd ever get rid of the feeling that I'd been kicked in the stomach. Didn't know if I'd ever smile again. And my Rose, well, she went into our bedroom and didn't come out for a long time. Almost saw two winters go by before she came out." He held up his middle finger and index finger, as to emphasize the two years. "I never thought she'd come back to me, but she did. I still thank the Creator for that every day. I sure was lost without her."

Just at that moment, Rose and Lucy suddenly came around a corner and were now on the same path as Poncho and Tilly.

"Hey, we've been looking for you, Poncho," Lucy called out.

"Well, now you found me."

Lucy was part of the package when Poncho married Rose, and over the years he'd come to love her like a sister, although he had never really understood the women's friendship. They were about as opposite as two women could be, but Lucy was one of the few people who saw past Rose's harsh exterior to the beautiful woman she was inside. For that reason alone, Poncho loved Lucy.

Lucy's eyes were wide with excitement and her voice had a hint of teasing to it. "They've got one of those fake horses that you put a quarter in and you can ride it. Thought it would be fun to get a picture of you 'n Rose on it."

Rose made no attempt to hide her judgment or disdain for what she saw as Lucy's childish behaviors and ideas. "Oh, my gawd, Lucy! When are you going to grow up?"

Lucy placed her hands on her hips and announced, "Nevaah."

Rose made a laughing sound deep in her throat and shook her head. "I shoulda known better than to have even asked such a stupid question." She looked at Lucy. "And for the record, I ain't gettin' on no horse! Poncho might, but I ain't."

Lucy began to snap her fingers and jiggled her bum a bit as she began to dance in a circle. Right there on the path she danced and sang. "Party-pooper. Party-pooper. Rose is a party-pooper. A great big party-pooper."

"Oh, that's real mature, Lucy." Rose lifted her nose in the air and pushed out her chest. "I have my dignity to uphold."

Lucy stopped her dance, scrunched up her face, squinted her eyes, and tilted her head to the side, as she said with sarcasm, "Whatever. You do what you gonna do, me an' Poncho gonna have some fun!" She grabbed Poncho's hand, and the two of them made their way toward the children's horse ride.

Rose watched them walk away, thinking, as she often did, that they were a much more natural fit as a couple than she and Poncho. He was such a gentle, kind, free-spirited man and most certainly not like most of the men she knew.

Tilly and Rose were left standing there. The awkwardness swirled around them, neither saying anything for a few moments. This was not the first time, and it wouldn't be the last time, that Tilly felt intimidated by Rose. Tilly motioned toward the parking lot and said, "Uh, well, I'd better get back to the bus. You know, in case anyone wants to get in."

Rose said nothing as she continued to watch Lucy and Poncho meander down the path.

Tilly glanced at her and wondered what she was thinking. "'Kay, well, I'll see you at the bus."

Rose gave a slight nod of her head.

As she walked back to the bus, Tilly heard Grandma Tilly's voice in her head, "Sometimes our greatest teachers are those who most frighten us."

12

Secrets Revealed

SARAH AND ANNE had been meandering through the tulips for about an hour when Sarah motioned with her head and pointed ahead. "There's a concession up there. I need a snack and a sit down."

When Sarah went to pay for Anne's bag of potato chips, Anne pushed Sarah's wallet out of the way. "You don't have to pay for my chips, and, while you're at it, you can stop being the big sister anytime."

"It's my job to take care of you, Annie," Sarah declared. Sarah was the only one who called her Annie and this tone she used, rippling with the superiority of an older sister, annoyed her.

"What's that supposed to mean?" Anne asked, but didn't give Sarah time to answer before she continued. "I've just turned sixty-five and I think I've done a pretty good job of taking care of myself. Thank you very much."

"I'm the older sister. It's my responsibility to protect you 'n take care of you." Sarah lifted her right shoulder and turned to look at Anne. "Always have 'n always will."

Anne's tone softened as she put her hand on Sarah's forearm. "But don't you see, Sarah, we're sisters. That means we take care of each other, not just you taking care of me."

"Do you have any idea how hard it was for me to ask you to come out and help me?" Sarah whispered sharply. Both women became keenly aware that the young woman behind the till was listening to their every word.

This wasn't a question Anne had expected, nor had she thought about it before. What it must have been like for Sarah to not only ask for help, but to ask Anne to come out and take care of her during her cancer treatment.

"No. I never thought about it," Anne replied honestly.

"Well, ain't that the truth! You never think about me. For what it's worth, hardest thing, other than battlin' this stomach business, that I've ever had to do."

"What's that supposed to mean?" Anne asked a second time.

"Nothin'." Sarah shook her head back and forth.

"No, Sarah. It means something. I can tell. Your face, it changed, and your eyes." Before Anne could finish, Sarah grabbed their snacks off the counter and stormed out.

Anne gave a fake smile to the woman behind the counter and then turned on her heels and walked briskly after her sister, calling, "Sarah. Sarah, wait."

When Anne finally caught up to her, she gently took Sarah by the arm and turned her around. Sarah's face was wet with tears.

Anne hadn't seen her sister cry since they were little girls. Sarah was always the stoic one. Not even during her cancer treatment or all the tests Sarah had endured, not even then did Anne see her cry. But now, standing before her, Sarah was crying, and Anne was desperate to know why.

"Sarah, what is it?"

Sarah pulled her arm away and muttered, "Nothin'."

"It has to be something, Sarah."

Sarah dug in her purse to find a Kleenex, desperate to push down the memories and the swell of emotion that was accompanying them. Finally, she found a tissue and hastily wiped her tears away.

"Just bad memories from Residential school, that's all," she said as she dabbed at her cheeks, unable to stop the tears that were seeping out of her eyes. Her embarrassment at the outpouring of emotion caused her to snap at her little sister, "Forget about it. You wouldn't understand."

Anne tilted her head to look at her sister, not sure she was ready to hear what Sarah had to say. "What do you mean? I wouldn't understand?"

"Things that happened there." Sarah's body quivered. "I'm sure you've heard the stories by now." Anne closed her eyes for a moment and nodded. Unfortunately, she knew the stories far too well.

Sarah lowered her head, looked at her sister from the corner of her squinted eye and in a defiant tone said, "But I made sure those awful things didn't happen to you."

Anne jolted back, her stomach constricting and her face turning ashen. She pulled her cardigan tight across her chest and folded her arms in front of her.

They stood quietly, Sarah looking down at the ground and Anne looking around the parking lot. It was Anne who found words first. "I think we should go somewhere and talk about this, Sarah."

Sarah shook her head vehemently. "I don't want to talk about it."

Anne knew that if she waited a few minutes, her sister would come around, so she took Sarah by the elbow and led her to a picnic table. Once Sarah was settled, her words tumbled out. "I thought I'd buried it deep, but this trip and being with everyone, hearing all the stories, well," she looked across the table at Anne, "it's bringing it all up again."

Anne nodded slowly, knowing exactly what Sarah meant. The two women looked at each other for a moment, then both their gazes dropped to the table. Eventually Anne asked, "Do you want to go first or you want me to?"

"What d'ya mean?" Sarah's eyes shot up from the table and blazed at her sister. "Nothing bad happened to you at that school. I made damn sure of it." Her tone was that of a big sister who had done the unthinkable to protect her baby sister.

Anne's eyes welled with tears. Her chest hurt to breathe. She hoped she was doing the right thing, telling what had been a secret for decades. "Actually," she said, inhaling deeply, "something did happen." Anne couldn't look at her sister. She breathed in deep between clenched teeth and began. "I was ten, in grade five." She paused and glanced at her sister, who was tearing off small pieces of Kleenex and dropping them on the table. Looking over Sarah's shoulder, Anne continued, "I was in the laundry room working, alone, when…" She stopped. This was hard. Harder than she'd ever imagined. She took a deep breath and allowed the words to release. "…Father Murphy came in. He closed the door behind him and then locked it. I can still hear the clink of that lock." Anne tucked a wisp of hair behind her ear and placed her hands in the lap of her skirt. "I'd heard girls talk about what he'd done to them, so I knew. I tried hiding in one of the dryers, but I wasn't fast enough. He caught me and then…"

"No," Sarah interrupted her sister with an audible breath, "No, that can't be." She shook her head back and forth, back and forth. They sat looking at each other. Sarah desperately tried to understand what Anne had just revealed.

When Sarah finally spoke, sorrow rolled off her tongue. "I thought I kept you safe." She looked across the table at her baby sister and her eyes burst with tears. Choking on the words, she forced them out. "I took all the abuse, so you would be protected. The nuns, they were to watch out for you. That was our agreement."

Sarah's upper lip trembled. "Oh, Annie." She buried her face in her hands and began to sob.

Anne moved around the table to sit beside her sister. She put her arm around her and rested Sarah's head on her shoulder. Between Sarah's sobs, Anne heard her sister whispering, "I was supposed to protect you. I was supposed to keep you safe."

Anne held her sister tight. "No, Sarah. It's not your fault."

When Sarah's sobbing eased, Anne cupped her sister's face with her hands. "Don't you see, Sarah? It's not either of our faults. We were children." Anne blinked away tears. "We were children. At school. We were supposed to be safe. None of that horrific stuff was supposed to happen. None of it. Not to me. Not to you. Not to any of us!" She pulled Sarah into a hug and held her as Sarah released more tears and anguish.

Eventually, the tears dried up. Sarah wiped her face, looked at her sister, and then down at her hands. Neither of them spoke for a while, each lost in her own thoughts.

"I've never told you this, Sarah, but I had a breakdown about twenty years ago." Anne glanced over as her sister's eyes got big. "I know. Shocking. Annie, who's always got it together, lost her marbles." She laughed softly, although at the time, it had been no laughing matter.

"What happened?" Sarah asked.

"You know what, Sarah?"

"Mmm?"

"I need a cup of tea. Would you like one?" asked Anne.

Sarah nodded.

"I'll be right back." Anne eased herself up, heading toward the concession where this story all began unfolding. Coming back a few minutes later, she set down two cups of tea and sat across from Sarah. Almost in unison, they removed the lids and blew on their tea. Finally, Anne began. "It all started when I got assigned the children's section in the library. Being around all those children and their parents, well, before long, all my memories were coming back. I didn't know what to do. I couldn't cope. Which is strange for us Fraser women, because we can cope with anything."

Sarah nodded as she lifted her cup for a sip. "Ain't that the truth."

"But it got real bad, Sarah." She inhaled deeply, hardly believing she was telling all this to her sister. "I wasn't sleeping or eating. It got so bad that some days Liz had to feed *and* bathe me." Anne remembered how she'd felt like a shell, like nothing or no one mattered, least of all herself. "I just didn't care. I think Liz was afraid I was going to hurt myself, so she dragged me to see a counselor. Literally, the first time I went she pretty much carried me into the room, but that's when my healing began."

Sarah couldn't believe what she was hearing. How was it that her sister had gone through all of this and she hadn't known?

"I was on medical leave from work for almost a year, diagnosed with Post Traumatic Stress Disorder. On her days off, Liz would take me to the lake and we'd spend all day there. She'd pack all this healthy food for us and we'd have a picnic. When she was working, she'd leave me cassette tapes of beautiful, uplifting music to listen to on my Walkman. And, she learned how to make me my candied salmon."

"Was always your favorite," Sarah said. "Remember Mom 'n Dad used to hide it from you or you'd have a fish all to yourself." They both smiled fondly at the memory.

Anne looked down at her teacup and turned it between her hands. "When I think of all that Liz did for me back then, I think she saved my life."

"You're lucky to have someone love you like that."

Anne slowly nodded, thinking of how grateful she was for Liz.

"What was it like, you know, the counseling thing?"

"Mmm, at first, I didn't say anything, just stared off into space, but, after a while, I began talking to the counselor, telling her what had happened. And to my surprise, she believed me." Anne blew on her tea before taking a long pepperminty sip. "I mean really, Sarah, I was this Indian woman talking about being abused by a priest at a time when Residential schools weren't really being talked about yet. But, she believed me. Never once questioned me. I think that helped me heal more than anything. Well, that, and forgiveness."

Sarah's eyebrow furrowed and her voice rose just a bit, "Forgiveness?"

Anne nodded. "After seeing the counselor for a year or so, she brought up the subject of forgiveness. I outright refused." She smiled at the thought of that session. She'd been so defiant, convinced that she'd never forgive Father Murphy or the nuns. However, over time the counselor helped her understand that it was more painful to live with such hatred and deep, deep sadness than it was to forgive.

"Trust me. It wasn't easy. I spent a whole year of my therapy learning to forgive Father Murphy and the nuns." Anne paused, knowing what she was about to say was not going to sit well with Sarah. "And Mom and Dad."

"Mom 'n Dad. Why?"

Anne looked at her big sister, uncertain how to explain this. "I know it might not make sense, Sarah, but none of what happened makes sense."

Anne proceeded cautiously. "I know Mom and Dad didn't have a choice in sending us to that school. I remember the Indian Agent in the kitchen, telling them that if they didn't give him us kids that they would arrest Mom and Dad and still take us."

Sarah was stunned. "I thought I was the only one who heard that."

Anne shook her head no.

"I don't know if I'll ever be ready to forgive those people, Annie," Sarah said.

"I know," Anne whispered. She ran her thumb over Sarah's hand, "it's not that we forget." Her eyes got a bit bigger and her eyebrows rose. "Trust me. I don't think I'll ever forget, but what I learned in counseling is that forgiveness is the only way to be in charge of your own life. Otherwise, we're still the little children they have control over. And I don't want that." Anne squeezed Sarah's hand. "And I don't want that for you either."

"But I don't know how to forgive, and now that I know they hurt you, too," Sarah inhaled sharply and shook her head, "I don't think I can ever forgive."

13

Those Eyes

BEA HAD SEEN enough tulips to last her a lifetime and was trying to pass the time by meandering through the gift shop when Chuck called to her. "Hey, Bea. Over here." She looked in the direction his voice was coming from. He was grinning from ear to ear and began to walk toward her.

"Look what I found." He held up a silver necklace with a tulip pendant on it. "I'm buying it for Liv."

Bea knew she'd hate it. Liv never wore jewellery and flowers only reminded her of funerals, so it wasn't likely she'd wear a flower necklace. Bea smirked and replied, "Obviously you don't know our daughter very well." Chuck lurched backward.

As soon as she had said the words, Bea wanted to take them back. She would have given anything to take them back, knowing they'd been like poison to him. His head dropped and he reached over to put the necklace on the shelf beside him.

"Yeah, you're right. She wouldn't like it." He moved his eyes back to Bea, but she looked away. It had been years since she'd seen that pain in his eyes and yet, it was all too familiar. He turned and began to walk away. "Chuck," she called to him, but he kept walking. She stood there, infuriated with herself. How was it that she could still be so mean to him? After all, it was at least thirty years since their relationship had ended. Bea was surprised at how deep her hurt still was. The worst of it was that most of the time she wasn't even aware of it, until she said some jackass thing like she'd just done. She gathered her thoughts while she wandered the aisles of items that tourists would take home to someone they cared about.

Eventually she summoned enough courage to find Chuck. He was outside, sitting on the fender of the bus, drinking a root beer.

When he looked up, she motioned her head toward the empty space beside him and raised her eyebrows. Chuck shrugged and took a sip of his pop. Bea didn't move. He looked at her again and thought, *Damn! This woman still gets under my skin.* Chuck reached over and wiped off the fender with his hand, looked up at Bea, and tipped his head toward the space he'd just cleaned. Neither of them seemed to notice that they still knew each other well enough to have a whole conversation without saying a word.

Bea sat down and rested her palms on her knees. She inhaled deeply and looked down at the gravel. "I'm sorry, Chuck. That was mean, what I said back there in the store. And not fair." She felt his body relax.

"No, Bea. It was fair." He looked over at her. "You're right. I don't know my children very well." In a strained voice he continued, "I only have two regrets in life, and that's one of them. But I'm trying to change that, and I..." he paused to wipe a tear away with the back of his hand, "I could really use your help."

She knew how vulnerable he was in this moment and what it was taking him to ask her for help.

Bea reached into her purse and pulled out a package of tissues. She removed one and placed it in Chuck's hand, pausing just for a moment to rest her hand on his. The familiarity of moments like this still reminded her of a lifetime ago. Of a time before the drinking, the fights, and subsequent heartbreak. She gave his hand a squeeze and let her hand linger for a moment before removing it and looking away.

He wiped his cheeks with the tissue. "So, whaddya say, Bea?" He looked over at her. "Will you help me?"

She looked back at him. Those eyes. She could get lost in those eyes if she wasn't careful. "Yeah. What the heck? I'll help you, Chuck."

14

Germophobe

MABEL GUIDED THE bus off Highway 84 and into a gas station. It had been a full day, and they still had a long stretch of highway before they reached their motel in Pendleton. A break was needed by all. Mabel hopped out and began to fuel up the bus while everyone unloaded.

Lucy and Rose went to the washrooms and as they stood outside the stalls washing their hands, Lucy pointed to the sign on the wall in front of them. It was of a Sherriff with his finger pointing out at them: "WASH YOUR HANDS OR ELSE!"

Lucy turned to Rose. "You should have a sign like that in your house, Rose. You know, you're sorta like the Sherriff."

"What's that supposed to mean?"

"Means you always worried 'bout germs. Givin' everyone their own packs of wipes. I bet you have a whole purseful." Lucy reached over and opened Rose's purse.

Rose quickly snatched it closed. "Get out of my purse, Lucy!"

"I saw them in there, the red packs of wipes." Lucy was taunting her friend now. "How many packs you got in there, huh? Five? Six? Ten?"

"Not that it's any of your business, but I have two. Only because one is almost done." Rose couldn't help but blush. "The rest are in my suitcase."

"See, that's what I'm sayin," Lucy said as she pointed to the plaque. "If I had a screwdriver with me, I'd unscrew that thing an' give it to Poncho to hang in your house."

The last comment caused Rose's eyes to narrow and her lips to tighten. "Luuucy."

Lucy didn't give her friend a chance to finish. She reached across her to open the bathroom door. "C'mon. Let's go see if they have any different kinds of gum here. Best so far was that mint chocolate chip gum I got at the last stop." Lucy walked past Rose and out the door toward the convenience store.

Rose stood with her foot holding the door open, seething as she watched her friend walk away. She couldn't help it if she was a germophobe. That's what her kids all called her. She never talked to them about Residential school or why she was the way she was.

More times than Rose cared to remember, the nuns had called her a dirty Indian and made her scrub her hands with bleach and a potato scrubber, often until they were raw and bleeding. Being clean had been drilled into her in that damn school and she'd never been able to undrill it.

Try as she might.

15

Crazy Eights

ON THEIR WAY back out to the highway, they stopped at a red light. Lucy asked if anyone knew how to play the fire drill game. Tilly smiled with fondness as she remembered this from her high school days, but none of the others seem to know what Lucy was talking about.

"What's the fire drill game?" asked Sarah.

Lucy explained that the next time the bus came to a red light or stop sign, if someone yelled "Fire drill," then everyone had to get out of the bus, run around it, and get back in, but when they got back in they had to sit in a different seat.

"Well, that's just crazy," said Rose, shaking her head in revulsion. "Not to mention dangerous."

"Well, *duh*, Rose! That's why it's so much fun," Lucy snapped back at her friend.

Poncho wasn't fazed by the tension their comments created; he was an expert at navigating their friendship. "What about the driver?" he asked.

"Drivers have to find a different seat, too," Lucy said as she turned to Poncho. "When the bus starts going again, it has to be a new driver."

"Well I'll be," said Poncho, nudging Rose's arm with mischief in his eyes. She slapped his leg, saying, "Oh, don't go getting all excited Poncho. It ain't ever gonna happen."

"What? The fire drill or you n' me?" He put his hand on her knee, leaned over, and kissed her on the cheek.

"Poncho, stop." She pushed him away playfully, but secretly she loved it when he teased her.

They drove for a few minutes and just before merging onto the highway, the bus came to a stop sign. Lucy took this opportunity to yell, "Fire drill!"

Mabel glanced in the rearview mirror. There were no vehicles behind them, so she shifted the bus into park and looked over at Sarah in the co-pilot seat. They both giggled as they opened their doors and climbed out. Being slightly competitive, Mabel took off as fast as her little legs could take her around the bus. Meanwhile, Sarah eased herself out, stepping on the sidebar and hanging onto the door as she lowered herself to the ground.

Poncho opened the main bus door and everyone piled out, except Rose, who sat with her nose in the air in the middle seat. Poncho looked back at her, but she shook her head. He shrugged and manoeuvred himself off the bus one step at a time.

Fits of laughter erupted as they almost ran into each other trying to get around the bus, some going in opposite directions. Sarah and Anne almost collided. They fell into each other's arms laughing. This was just what they needed after their heavy conversation a few hours ago. They gently pushed off each other, still laughing, and made their way to the other side and climbed back in.

Tilly being the only other driver hopped up front and Chuck hitched himself to the copilot seat. Two cars were now behind them, the first with a group of young women who were in hysterics laughing at the elders running around the bus. The second car's driver was honking and yelling out the window, "Come on! Move it! I haven't got all day!" Just before Lucy climbed back into the bus, she turned to the two cars and blew them a kiss.

Poncho, the last to climb in, also turned to the cars and tipped his cowboy hat and gave a slight bow before disappearing onto the bus. He flopped into the last empty seat. "Whew, that was almost as much fun as going eight seconds on a bull."

Despite Rose's stern upper lip, watching them all run around the bus bumping into each other had her smiling. Lucy slid in beside her and yelled, "That, my friends, is how the fire drill works."

Chuck whistled, Mabel let out a loud hoot, and Anne and Sarah were laughing so hard they both began to snort, which led to more laughter.

"You're all crazy!" Rose yelled to be heard above the laughter. But with joy rippling through the bus, she found it hard to contain her smile.

After they were back on the highway and had caught their breaths, Sarah piped up, "You know how you called us all crazy, Rose?"

"Yeah, well, you all are." Rose shook her head in defiance.

Knowing she was about to take on the "dragon lady," Sarah looked at Anne for moral support. Anne raised her eyebrows, impressed with her sister. Sarah took this as a sign of support and continued, "I was thinking that next time, if you joined us in the fire drill, then all eight of us would be crazy and we could call ourselves the Crazy Eights."

Before Rose had a chance to respond, Lucy let out a shriek, "That's it! I've got it!" Lucy was belted in so she couldn't stand to make her announcement. Instead, she raised her arms in the air and proclaimed, "We're Tilly and the Crazy Eights."

16

Lucy's Excellent Adventure

A HUSH FELL over the bus as they descended upon Las Vegas. The elders were all lost in their own thoughts as they stared out the windows. The lights glittered and shone and reflected so brightly it almost seemed that night turned to day the closer they got. As they pulled into the driveway of the hotel Lucy said, "Wow! This is a fancy shmancy hotel."

Tilly knew most of the elders weren't used to staying in motels, let alone hotels like this. Suddenly, she felt uncomfortable and blurted out. "I got a really good deal on the Internet."

"Don't matter none to me, Tilly, where you got the deal. I'm just so happy you takin' such good care of all of us," said Lucy.

A couple of bellmen came to the bus pushing luggage carts. Mabel gave one of them the keys to the bus and all the elders followed her into the hotel. As they entered the lobby, they stopped and looked around. Poncho put his hand on the small of Rose's back, causing her to turn to him with her eyes wide and her eyebrows peaked into her forehead. The sides of her mouth raised and he leaned over to kiss her cheek, whispering in her ear, "Quite a step up from our place on the ranch, eh, Rose?"

"I'll say."

"Do you actually think they're gonna let this Indian cowboy camp out here for the next few nights?" Although Rose knew his words were meant as a joke, she also knew they hinted at his insecurity in fitting into the white world.

Rose leaned into her husband and put her head on his shoulder. "They better," she said as she raised her fist, "or they'll have the wrath of Rose to deal with." They both laughed and Poncho kissed her temple. Her humor was the bridge he'd needed to feel comfortable in the hotel.

As Bea walked into the lobby she became acutely aware of the runners on her feet, her track pants, and the T-shirt she was wearing that had been through the wash at least a hundred times. Her eyes darted to Chuck. He always looked so put together and this time was no different. She was annoyed with herself. Tilly had told her they'd be staying at a fancy hotel on the strip, so why hadn't she taken a moment that morning to choose her clothes more carefully? She hated feeling like an imposter in these kinds of settings, but she hated looking like an imposter even more.

Chuck had been scanning the lobby when he noticed Bea. She stood with her weight resting on one leg and her arms folded over top of each other. He knew she wasn't comfortable in fancy hotels, and, truth be told, he wasn't either at first. But after years of staying in places like this for work, he'd come to enjoy the luxuries and comfort they provided. Chuck made his way over to Bea and stood beside her. He leaned down and out of the side of his mouth, softly said, "For what it's worth, I think you look…"

Bea raised her left eyebrow and pursed her lips as she looked up at him. Even after all these years, that look scared him. "Well," he shifted his weight, lifted his shoulders and pushed his head forward, "what I meant is, you look okay." The scowl on Bea's face and the daggers coming out of her eyes made it clear his words had not helped. "Damn, Bea MacArthur. You make me so nervous I never say anything right around you. What I mean is, you look pretty. There, I said it. You're pretty." His voice filled with tenderness. "So, stop caring what anyone else in this damn hotel thinks about what you're wearing or how you look."

I make him nervous? He thinks I'm pretty? Bea thought with surprise. Suddenly she no longer cared about people at the hotel. Chuck felt nervous around her and he'd just said she was pretty and in that moment, that was all Bea cared about.

After everyone was checked in and had their room keys, Mabel gathered them and handed out pieces of paper with the name of the hotel and her cell phone number. It had been a long travel day and everyone was exhausted. As a group, they decided to call it an early night and meet for lunch the next day.

Each of them headed off to their rooms with their assigned roommates. Once Lucy and Mable had unpacked and washed up they tucked into bed for the night. But sleep was the last thing Lucy wanted to do. Her dream, Las Vegas, was just outside the door. This was, after all, her bucket list item! Lying in bed waiting for Mabel to fall asleep was excruciating. Finally, when she was sure Mabel was asleep, Lucy slid on her clothes, tucked a twenty-dollar bill into the back pocket of her jeans, and snuck out, forgetting her key on the TV stand.

Lucy took the elevator down and followed the signs to the casino. Standing at its entrance, she closed her eyes for a moment and listened to the sounds. The whir of the machines spinning, the clanking of money in the slot trays, the waitress asking someone close by if they'd like a drink, and somewhere in the background Bruce Springsteen was singing "Glory Days." Lucy was acutely aware of the ginormous smile across her face. She found a Lucky 7 slot machine in the five-cent section. Putting her twenty-dollar bill into the slot, she got four hundred credits and thought to herself, *Why not?* Lucy hit the maximum bet button. The machine went crazy and Lucy watched as her first spin netted a hundred and fifty dollars. She did a little dance, singing to herself, "Oh yeah, oh yeah, Lucy's in Vegas and she's winnin'! Lucy's in Vegas and she's winnin'!" She didn't care who might be watching—actually, she rarely cared who was watching. Lucy continued to play the same machine until her small winnings stopped. At this point she had no idea how long she had been sitting there. Thrilled with her luck, she decided to cash out and tucked her one hundred and ninety-two dollar winnings into her pocket. She began to wander through the casino and, before she knew it, she was out on the street amongst the crowd.

After going with the flow of people for a while, Lucy noticed a Subway and Cinnabon sign. Cinnabon was her favorite. She followed the sign into a casino and through a maze of machines, smoke hanging heavy in the air. The sign led her past a larger than average machine with a fancy red velvet chair. She couldn't resist taking a seat. Lucy dug into her pocket for a couple of quarters and put them into the machine, but they fell through to the change container. She gathered them and tried again, and again. "Damn machine," she said under her breath.

A woman came to stand beside her. Lucy looked her over, all too familiar with big city women like this. She was wearing a tight white blouse with her boobs popping out, a skirt that was far too short to wear in public, and heels like Lucy had only ever seen on TV. Lucy tried one more time to put her quarters in, but they came out again. That's when the woman, speaking with a Southern twang, said, "You and your little quarters need to go somewhere else. This is a twenty-five-dollar machine."

"Oh," Lucy said in a snarky tone, "I knew that." She grabbed her quarters and tried to slide gracefully off the red velvet chair. Walking away as fast as she could, she stopped momentarily to turn around and stick her tongue out at the back of the snooty lady. She hated how people like that made her feel. Small, inferior, lesser than, all of that and more. She could hear Mabel's voice in her head, "Nobody can make you feel anything, Lucy." She knew this, but for some reason at times like this she didn't believe it.

After walking through the casino for a few minutes, Lucy realized she was lost. *Shit, which direction did I come from?* As she continued to walk, her chest tightened. She couldn't find an exit to the street, but she did find a wall with telephones. Staring at them for a long time, she realized that she must do what she least wanted to do. Call her daughter.

When she felt prepared for her daughter's lecture, Lucy dialed 0.

"This is the operator, how can I help you?"

"I have to phone home. Collect."

"Okay, Ma'am. What's your name?"

"Lucy."

"Well, Lucy. What's the number you'd like to call?"

Lucy gave him her daughter Cheryl's number and held her breath while the phone rang. Cheryl answered groggily, "Hello?"

"Hello, Ma'am. I have a collect call from Lucy. Will you accept?"

It took her daughter a moment to answer, "Yeah, sure."

"I'll connect you now," said the operator.

Cheryl sat up in bed, startled awake by the call. "Ma, is everything okay?"

"Yeah, everything's okay."

"Then why are you calling me collect at four in the morning?"

Lucy took a deep breath. "I'm lost."

"Lost?" Cheryl slid out of bed, put on her slippers and wrapped her housecoat around her as a shiver ran through her body. "Where are you lost, Ma?"

"Well if I knew that I wouldn't be lost now, would I?" Lucy snapped at her daughter.

"I mean *where* are you? Like what city?"

"Las Vegas." Lucy held the phone out and braced herself for Cheryl's response.

"Oh, Ma. Really? Your first night in Vegas and you're lost?"

This was exactly why Lucy had not wanted to call. "But I won a hundred and ninety-two dollars," she said.

She heard Cheryl sigh. "Are you in a hotel?"

"I don't know."

"What do you mean you don't know?"

"Well, I'm in a casino and most of those are in hotels, aren't they?"

Cheryl didn't have time for this. She was working the early shift and her alarm would soon be going off. "What does the casino look like?"

"Well, there's lots of machines and bright lights and loud music playing."

"Ma, you've just described every casino in Vegas."

"Oh." Lucy giggled.

"Do you see anything else?"

Lucy scanned the area around the phones. "Nope."

"'Kay, this is what we're gonna do, Ma. You need to ask someone walking by what hotel you're at."

"They're all white people and the last white woman I talked to wasn't very nice to me."

Exasperated and exhausted, Cheryl didn't have patience for her mom. "Help me to help you, Ma." Then a pause between every word, "Just. Ask. Some. One."

"Fine." Then under her breath Lucy muttered, "Betty Bossy-boots."

The first person to walk by was a man.

"'Scuse me, can you help me?"

"Depending what kind of help you lookin' for, young lady." He smiled and winked at her. Lucy blushed, raised her shoulder like a school girl and playfully said to him, "You know, I'm not young."

Cheryl could not believe what she was hearing. "Ma, I can hear you. Stop flirting and ask him where you are."

"Oh yeah." She turned to look back up at the gentleman. "What hotel is this?"

"This here is the Treasure Island Hotel."

Lucy smiled at him coyly. "Thank you."

"Anytime for you and those dimples, sweetheart," he replied as he sauntered away.

Lucy giggled. Her daughter's voice brought her back from her flirtation.

"Ma, was that all necessary?"

"What? I did as you asked. I found out what hotel I'm at. It's Treasure Island."

"I'm going to call Rose and she'll send someone to get you. Keep asking people to direct you to the lobby of the hotel and stay there. Do not move!"

Lucy scanned the signs above her to see if any of them directed her to the lobby. One did, and she felt a sense of relief.

"Ma, did you hear me?" Cheryl repeated, "Do. Not. Move!"

"Yes, dear." Lucy hung up and shook her head. She loved her daughter, but sometimes she was so damn pushy.

Cheryl called Rose, but there was no answer. That's when she remembered that Mabel had given the families a list of phone numbers. She turned on the light and headed to the kitchen to find it.

The ringing cell phone woke Mabel from a deep sleep. As she opened her eyes and saw the empty bed beside her, she knew exactly why it was ringing.

17

Mr. Chucky to the Rescue

CHUCK HAD NEVER been one to sleep in and, as he got older, his early mornings had become middle of the nights. Today was no exception, but he hadn't been prepared for his phone ringing shortly after four in the morning. He looked at the call display. Mabel Billy.

"Mabel? Everything okay?"

Her voice groggy, "Course not, Chuck. I'm not calling you at some ungodly hour in the morning just to visit."

Grouchy pants! Mabel is definitely not a morning person, Chuck thought to himself. He dared not say anything like that out loud though.

"Lucy's gone missing."

"What?"

"Well, she's not really missing. She's in the lobby of the Treasure Island Hotel."

"Treasure Island. What's she doing there? At this time of the morning?"

"She snuck out." Mabel paused, thinking it sounded like she was talking about a schoolgirl and not a sixty-four-year-old woman. "And then went and got herself lost."

"Oh."

"I knew you'd be awake so I'm wondering if you'll go and collect her?"

"Sure. I'll text you when I find her."

"Thanks, Chuck." Mabel knew Bea wasn't thrilled that Chuck was on the trip, but in this moment, Mabel was grateful that he was.

Chuck found Lucy exactly where she was supposed to be, in the lobby of the Treasure Island Hotel. She was sound asleep in a chair with head back and mouth gaping open. Deciding to let Lucy sleep for a bit, Chuck settled into the chair beside her. Even this early in the morning, the lobby was busy. His mind began to wander to Bea, reflecting on their interactions on the trip so far. He was surprised that the time they were spending together was causing all his old feelings for her to resurface. He thought he'd buried them deep enough that they'd never be accessible again. Some of his exes had told him that in burying his love for Bea he'd also buried his ability to love anyone else.

It always seemed to come back to Bea.

Chuck wondered if there would ever come a day when he wouldn't love her. Or, if there was any remote chance she had any feelings left for him. He closed his eyes, put his head on the back of the chair, and exhaled loudly, thinking, *There's no way she'll ever love me again. I hurt her too many times.*

Lucy's voice startled him. "Chuck! You found me!" She heaved herself out of her chair and leaned down to hug him, her little arms tightly squeezing his neck. "I'm real happy to see you." When she let go, he stood and laughed a bit. "I bet you are, Lucy. I bet you are."

Lucy giggled.

"So, what do you say Lucy, you hungry?"

"I'm always hungry," she said, patting her belly and smiling at him. "And geez, this ol' lady's had a long night. Let me buy you breakfast. I won tonight, or I guess it was last night now." Lucy laughed at herself and Chuck put his arm around her shoulder like a big brother.

At breakfast, Lucy started right in. "So, tell me, Mr. Chucky. How is it a good catch like you doesn't have a woman?"

Chuck was caught off guard and almost spit out his coffee.

Lucy casually ate a bit of bacon before continuing, "Cuz I see the way you been lookin' at Bea. You know," she looked at him over her glasses, as if she was about to share something important with him, "you can only say a name once too often in a certain way and anyone who's payin' attention will begin to wonder." She tipped her head, wiped her bacon hand on a napkin, and continued. "So, let's just say, I been payin' attention." Lucy looked at him again, saw that his eyes had never left her. "What's stopin' you from making a move?"

"Wow!" Chuck put his coffee down, wiped his mouth with his napkin, and leaned back against the booth. "You sure don't beat around the bush, do you, Lucy?"

"Chuck, do you see me? I'm sixty-four years old. I have no time for beatin' around the bush. So, give me the skinny. What's the story with you and Bea?"

Chuck took a long swig of his coffee, not sure he really wanted to do this, but this little lady was so adorable it was almost impossible to say no to her.

"We have a long history." He ran his finger around the rim of his coffee cup. "Mostly of me hurting her." Chuck took a deep breath and then resumed, "I'm pretty sure she's not up for it again."

"Well, you never know until you ask."

Lucy told him she'd been a widow for twenty-two years and that second chances are hard to come by. "You've got yourself a second chance here and I think you should go for it. Life for us, me more than you, is gettin' short. We have to make the most of it." She leaned across the table, as if telling him a secret. "That's what I was doin' when I headed out last night. Livin' life to the fullest." She lifted her shoulders and gave the trademark tip of her head. "I just happened to get lost along the way." They both cracked up laughing.

Meanwhile, back at the hotel, Bea was up early and had already been down to the lobby to get brochures of trips to the Grand Canyon. Knowing Chuck was an early riser too, she decided to see if he wanted to go for breakfast. She knocked on his door, and knocked again, but there was no answer. Her hunger pangs were getting the best of her and she took his not answering as a sign that it was not meant to be. She decided to head downstairs and have breakfast alone. As she got off the elevator, there stood Chuck and Lucy.

"Oh, there you are. I was looking for you," she said to Chuck.

Chuck was taken aback. "You were looking? For *me*?"

Lucy took this as her cue to leave. "Thanks for rescuin' me, Mr. Chucky. I'm gonna go to bed now." Chuck nodded slightly at Lucy, but was still reeling from Bea's words.

"You were looking for me?"

She nodded her head, trying to be nonchalant. "I was wondering if you wanted to go for breakfast?"

"Uh, sure. I'd love to go for breakfast."

As the elevator door closed, Lucy watched the two of them and giggled to herself.

18

An Olive Branch

ONCE THEY'D SETTLED into the booth and placed their order, there was nothing left to distract them. It was just the two of them, out for breakfast.

Bea broke the ice. "Remember when we were kids, Chuck?"

"You mean just a couple years ago?" His whole face smiled at her.

"Yeah right, a couple years ago." She blushed. She missed *that* look. She missed his humor. And, over the last few days, Bea had begun to realize just how much she missed *him*. She continued, "Remember how we always talked about going to the Grand Canyon?"

"Mm-hmm." He dug around in his fruit salad looking for the grapes.

Bea tried to hide the deep breath she needed to take in order to ask what she was about to ask. "Well, I was wondering," she laid her fork down and looked up at Chuck again, "you know, since it's on my bucket list. I'm wondering, if you might want to go with me?"

Chuck leaned forward, looked at Bea with one eyebrow raised, and asked, "To the Grand Canyon?"

Bea averted his eyes while nodding her head and adding a sugar to her coffee, even though she drank it black. She'd forgotten his one eyebrow gesture, remembering now how that was his way of asking "Are you serious?"

He'd wanted to say yes before she'd even finished asking, but was afraid his excitement might scare her away, so he decided to play it safe. It was surprising to have her so close again and the last thing he wanted was to risk that. No matter how many years pass, there are tender aspects about a person you once loved that you always remember. Chuck knew the courage it had taken for Bea to invite him to the Grand Canyon and how vulnerable she was feeling sitting across from him. He gauged his response with this in mind.

"Yes." He moved his head up and down a few times. "I'd, um…I'd love to go to the Grand Canyon with you, Bea."

She reached into her purse and tried to silently let out the breath she'd been holding. "I picked these brochures up in the lobby," she said as she placed them on the table. Chuck moved his plate to the side, grateful to have a legitimate excuse not to have to eat any more. After all, it was his second breakfast.

"Here, I'll show you the one I was thinking of." Bea scanned them until she found the one she wanted. As she passed it to Chuck, their hands touched. He extended a couple of fingers to gently wrap around her hand. Surprised by the electricity she felt at his touch, she looked up. Their eyes locked. With each blink Bea felt another brick in the wall she'd built around her heart coming down.

"Thank you." Chuck swallowed. "For inviting me to come with you, Bea. I think the one you picked is just fine."

His voice brought her back and she let go of his hand.

"I like the idea of flying there instead of going on a bus. Don't get me wrong. I'm loving this trip, but all those hours in the bus are giving me sore butt syndrome." He reached his hand behind him and gave his butt a rub. It was just enough humor to ease the tension.

"So, tomorrow then, to the Grand Canyon," said Bea, as she put all the extra brochures in her purse.

"Yes, the Grand Canyon. Just you and me." Chuck tried to hide his delight, but he was beaming like a schoolboy.

Bea couldn't say it out loud, but thought to herself, *Yes, just like we dreamed…all those years ago.*

Bea was remembering what a good man Chuck was. The qualities that had drawn her to him in the first place were attracting her again. Bea loved watching how he took care of the elders on this trip. Getting the stepping stool out for them to get in and out of the bus, bringing every-one's luggage out for them and loading it, holding the doors for the ladies. She had been surprised the first time she saw him placing tobacco on each of the tires. Even though she knew what he was doing, she had asked him anyway. "I'm making an offering of thanksgiving for a safe journey today. For us and all the other travelers today."

He was a kind man. A respectful man. A good man. She was allowing herself to believe in him again.

19

YOLO

AS AGREED, EVERYONE met for lunch and began planning the three days they were spending in Las Vegas. Bea and Chuck announced that they were going on a trip to the Grand Canyon the next day. Lucy asked if she could come with them and then noticed the quick glance Bea and Chuck gave each other.

"Nah. I'm too scared of heights," Lucy said suddenly. "Probably pee my pants."

"Lucy," Rose said in a sharp, scolding tone.

Lucy coyly smiled and got up to leave the table. She shrugged her shoulders playfully and said, "YOLO."

"YOLO?" asked Rose.

"Yeah, my granddaughter taught it to me. It means, 'You only live once.' Get it?" She looked at the elders sitting at the table staring back at her.

Chuck said, "You mean *carpe diem*? That's what the white people, or at least the white people of our generation, say."

"Yeah, but it sounds so stuffy, Mr. Chucky." Lucy put her nose in the air and pursed her lips. "YOLO is way more fun. So that's what I'm gonna do, YOLO!" She danced out of the restaurant, calling back to Anne, "Come on, we got some explorin' to do." Anne quickly gathered her belongings and followed Lucy out the door.

"So, what's everyone up to this afternoon?" asked Chuck.

"Mabel and I are going on the Big Bus Tour," Sarah announced.

Mabel glanced around the table and explained, "You know, the one where you can hop on and off whenever you want."

Sarah forced a smile at Mabel. "I think this afternoon we have to do a bit more *on* the bus than hopping off, if that's okay with you."

"Sure, Sarah, on is good for me too." Mabel didn't like the weird feeling Sarah's comment gave her. She turned to Bea and asked, "How about you? Want to come along for the ride?"

"Nope. No more sitting for me. My butt's killin' me so I'm going to walk the strip and people watch."

"I'm heading to the Gold and Silver Pawnshop," Chuck said.

Poncho jumped in. "You mean the pawnshop I see on TV? What do they call it?" He snapped his fingers quickly to help him remember. Everyone watched to see if his little memory tactic worked. A couple of seconds later he said, "Pawn Stars. That's it. I love that show!"

"I have a great idea, Chuck," Rose said. "Why don't you an' Poncho go together, and besides, I need Tilly's help with something this afternoon."

Tilly had plans to spend the afternoon reading her book by the pool, so she hadn't really been paying attention to the conversation. She was a bit startled to hear her name, especially coming from Rose. "My help?" she said more out of confusion than as a question. The only elder Tilly hadn't been able to connect with was Rose. Not only had she not been able to connect with her, but Rose's words had cut Tilly more than once.

"Yeah. I need your help with something," was all Rose was willing to say. Any more than that would have given her surprise away.

Tilly glanced at Mabel, but Mabel lifted her shoulders and eyebrows in unison. She had no idea what Rose was talking about.

"Oh. Okay." Tilly was both cautious and curious.

At this point Chuck looked over at Poncho. "Well, whaddya say, pardner? Shall we leave these ladies to their planning and get on down to the pawnshop?"

"You betchya." Poncho took one last sip of his coffee, removed his cowboy hat from where it had been resting on his knee, and placed it on his head. He kissed Rose on the cheek and pushed himself out of his chair. With one last glance at the table and a tip of his hat, he said, "See y'all later."

Not long after, Sarah and Mabel headed off for their bus tour, leaving Rose and Tilly alone at opposite ends of the table. Tilly played with the creamers, flipping them over and over on the table. She was acutely aware of how uncomfortable she felt with Rose. Finally Rose spoke, "You know that tiny machine you have that plays music? What do you call it? A Nemo?"

"It's a Nano," Tilly gently corrected Rose.

"Yeah, Nano, thanks." Rose looked at Tilly quickly and then back to the table. "I couldn't remember."

Tilly felt herself soften.

Rose continued, "Can you come shopping with me? I want to buy one of those for Poncho. As a gift." She glanced sideways at Tilly. "An' I suppose I'm probably gonna need your help putting music on it."

Tilly saw another side of Rose. A side usually reserved for Poncho, their family, and sometimes Lucy. A loving side. She found it endearing that Rose was doing something sweet for Poncho. "Sure, I'd be happy to help you, Rose."

"You would?" Rose was surprised because she'd been anything but friendly or kind to Tilly. She knew it was her way to keep people from getting too close so they couldn't hurt her, but she hadn't yet figured out how to change this behavior.

"Yeah, I would."

They spent a short time at the Apple store buying Poncho his iPod Nano and then hunkered down in Tilly's hotel room to set it up. Together, they huddled over her laptop as Tilly introduced Rose to the wealth of music available on the Internet. They were able to get all of Poncho's favorite songs and before they knew it, Poncho's Nano was full of music from Elvis, Willie Nelson, Dolly Parton, Johnny Cash, and Tammy Wynette.

"I need one more song," said Rose.

"What's that?" asked Tilly

"'Unforgettable,'" responded Rose, but she wasn't sure Tilly would know it, so she added, "Nat King Cole sang it."

"Oh, I know that song," Tilly said and began searching for it online. "Friends of mine used it as their first dance song when they got married."

Rose looked at Tilly for a few seconds before she spoke. "That was me an' Poncho's wedding song, too."

Tilly looked from the screen to Rose, noticing how her cheeks had flushed.

"Look, Rose. I found a video of Nat King Cole singing it. Want me to play it for you?" Rose nodded. Tilly clicked the play button and sat back in her chair while Rose leaned forward and watched.

When the song ended, Rose spoke almost in a whisper. "He has the voice of an angel. To see him sing that song." She looked back at Tilly and their eyes met. "Thank you."

Tilly lifted the corners of her mouth slightly. If there was one thing she'd learned over the last few days, it was to not make a big scene of anything with Rose. "I think I saw there was a version of his daughter singing with him. Want to see that one, too?"

Rose nodded with rare enthusiasm.

While Rose requested more songs to load on Poncho's Nano, Tilly tried to remember the last time she had done something thoughtful for Mick.

Something kind.

Something that showed her love for him.

No matter how hard she wracked her brain, she couldn't remember.

20

Pawnshop

CHUCK WAS SITTING in the front seat of the taxi as it pulled into the pawnshop parking lot when he noticed it. The Graceland Wedding Chapel. It made him think of Bea. She knew him better than he knew himself. Each time she smiled at him, another piece of his heart and his past mended. He could hardly believe that tomorrow they would be going to the Grand Canyon, just the two of them.

He remembered how Bea's hand had felt in his earlier at breakfast. His heart flipped again, just as it had then. Bea could've asked any of the elders or Tilly to go with her, but, no. She chose him. Even after all these years and all that had gone on between them, she wanted to go with him. He shook his head in awe.

From the back seat of the taxi, Poncho paid the taxi driver and then shook Chuck's shoulder. "Are you comin', pardner?"

"Yeah." Chuck reached for the door handle and thanked the driver.

Since the Gold and Silver Pawnshop became so popular on The History Channel, it had become more fondly known as Pawn Stars, and there was almost always a line of people waiting to get in. Today was no exception. As Poncho and Chuck joined the line, Poncho asked Chuck, "Might be none of my business, but what were you thinkin' about back there in the taxi?"

Chuck looked at him quizzically and tucked his hands into the pocket of his khaki shorts. Poncho continued, "You had this big funny grin on your face. I kept talkin' to you, but you didn't hear nothin' I was sayin'."

The two men looked at each other for a couple seconds. Chuck didn't know what to do. Should he tell Poncho that he couldn't remember what he was thinking about? Or, tell him the truth? That he was daydreaming about the only woman he had ever really loved—Bea.

Poncho stepped off the sidewalk and onto the street so he could peek around a few people and see how far it was to the front of the line. "Whatever it was you were thinkin' about, well, it sure seemed to make ya happy. You had the same kind o' silly grin my grandson has when I take him to the candy store." He looked back at Chuck. "But don't be tellin' my Rose I take him to the candy store. That'd get me in biiiiig trouble."

Chuck smiled at him. "Don't worry. Your secret's safe with me." They stood in line for a few minutes. "Since we're sharing secrets and all," Chuck kicked at a few pebbles on the sidewalk, "back there in the taxi, I was thinking about Bea."

"Bea?"

Chuck simply gave his head one nod.

"Well I'll be knee-high to a grasshopper."

"Please don't say anything to anyone. No one knows. Well, Lucy knows and…" Chuck placed his thumb and forefinger above his upper lip and ran them down the sides of his chin, then added, "…and, I think Bea knows."

"So almost half the bus knows. Quite the secret you got they, Chuck." Poncho snickered and bopped him in the arm. "Have you thought bout the fact that we're the only two men on that bus?" He lifted his eyebrows at Chuck. "Women. You know they know things, right?"

Chuck nodded.

The line began to move and the next thing they knew they were inside and quickly became lost in their own world of navigating the shop. Poncho spent most of his time looking in the sports section. Chuck perused the entire store and found himself leaning over the jewelery counter. To be more specific, the ring counter. He noticed a beautiful set of gold wedding bands with a West Coast native design on them. He asked to see them and realized on looking closer that the design was of two eagles coming together and a diamond joining their beaks.

"There's an engagement ring that goes with these as well," the salesman said. "The diamond was a bit loose so our jeweller is just fixin' it, but I can get it if you want to see it." Chuck didn't respond. He was holding the rings between his fingers, swirling them about. He slid the man's ring on. It fit perfectly. He hastily removed it. *Crazy. You're thinking crazy thoughts, Chuck. She'd never marry you.* He handed the rings back to the guy behind the counter.

"Rings like this," the salesman said, holding them in front of Chuck, "they don't usually last very long around here." He lifted one shoulder, hesitating before putting the rings back under the counter. "Just sayin'."

"That's okay." He couldn't help but wonder if the woman's ring would fit Bea. "I'm just looking." Chuck straightened up, tapped the glass with his forefinger and walked away. Almost as if he was saying, "I'll be back."

21

Choosing Joy

IT WAS AFTER Lucy and Anne had been shopping for a couple hours that Anne suddenly noticed Lucy was no longer beside her. She looked back and saw her friend standing motionless. The shopping bags Lucy had been carrying now lay in a heap at her feet.

Anne's eyes tried to follow where Lucy was looking. If she had it right, Lucy was watching a young woman in her early twenties. Her black hair was pulled back in a braid that lay flat along her back, almost to her buttocks. Her eyes were big, round, and the color of dark chocolate. Her cheeks were also big and round and when she smiled, dimples popped out on both cheeks. She was wearing a white tank top, frayed cut-off jean shorts, and flip-flops.

Anne turned to walk back toward Lucy. She noticed that the color had drained from her friend's face and that in those few moments, Lucy had aged. She seemed shorter, more hunched over, her wrinkles more pronounced, and her bifocal glasses had inched their way down her nose. Her black purse had slipped from the crook of her arm and was barely hanging on her wrist.

Anne walked back urgently and gathered up Lucy's bags. She stood beside her friend, who remained mesmerized by the young woman. When the young woman walked out of sight, Anne reached over and ever so gently touched Lucy's arm. "I'm here, Lucy."

"Sit down, I need…to sit…down," Lucy said weakly.

Anne quickly glanced around and found an empty bench in the shade. She guided Lucy to the bench and helped her sit down. Lucy removed her glasses and looked at Anne, who saw something different in her friend's face. An indescribable sadness. Lucy motioned her head to where the young woman had been and said in a broken voice, "She looks just like my daughter." Tears began to stream down Lucy's face and her lips trembled.

Anne was puzzled. She'd seen pictures of Lucy's daughter and she thought the woman they'd just seen looked nothing like her.

She moved closer and put her arm around Lucy's shoulders. With her free hand she dug into her bag, pulled out a package of Kleenex and handed it to Lucy. They sat quietly for a long time, Lucy lost in the thoughts that were causing her tears and Anne, content to simply be present with her friend.

"Usually, I follow them for as long as I can. I think of them as a gift. But today," Lucy moved her head from side to side, "I couldn't move. My feet wouldn't move." She blew her nose hard and wiped her tear-stained cheeks.

Her words began to roll off her tongue. "It reminded me of when she first went missing. I couldn't get out of bed. No matter how I tried, I just couldn't get out of bed." Lucy looked at Anne. "Then one day, I did. That's when I started calling the police to find out what was happening. They told me they hadn't opened a file for her because they didn't consider her missing. The officer said to me, 'Your people always go stay with family and never let each other know.' But I knew, Anne. I knew when she didn't arrive at her cousins' that night that something terrible had happened to her." A shiver ran through Lucy's body and she whispered, "A mother knows."

Anne was beginning to understand what Lucy was talking about.

"It was almost a year before they found her body. Not far from where she was last seen." Lucy inhaled and gulped. "Hitchhiking on Highway 16." Lucy turned to look at Anne. "The one they call the Highway of Tears."

Anne nodded. Even though she lived in Toronto, she was familiar with the segment of highway in northern British Columbia.

As the tears rolled down her cheeks, Lucy continued to share. "For years, I was surrounded by blackness. I didn't want to live. I wanted to be with her and if that meant dying so I could be with her on the other side, then that's what I wanted. Those feelin's scared me. Real bad, cuz I still had my boys and grandchildren to live for. So, the counselor at the band office who was helpin' me told me about a place I could go and get help with my greavin'. I wanted to go. But I didn't want to go too." Lucy looked at Anne. "If that makes any sense."

Anne nodded.

Lucy wiped her eyes. "Rose, well she pretty much talked me into goin'." Lucy looked at Anne and forced a smile. "You know how bossy she can be."

Anne raised her eyebrows and her lips raised into a slight smile.

Lucy continued, "Tsa Kwa Luten Lodge is where they sent me. It was hard. Almost harder than those first days when she was missing." Lucy's voice seized, she took a couple of deep breaths and played with the Kleenex in her hand. "My girl, she was always such a happy, bright girl. I often wished I'd named her Joy instead of Jenny. Joy suited her better. That was her, bringin' joy to my life and everyone she met. Just like that young woman I saw, she looked like my Jenny. She had that same special glow as my Jenny."

Lucy blew her nose before continuing. "Near the end of my time at Tsa Kwa Luten, I began to feel a tad more like my ol' self." She looked at Anne and shook her head. "But, I'll never be who I was before..." her voice trailed off.

After a while, Lucy looked up and out to the shoppers that milled around. "One afternoon, we had some free time, so I went for a walk down to the ocean. It was so pretty, you know when the sun dances on the ocean and makes it look like it's covered in stars?"

Anne nodded.

"I sat down on a log thought about how much Jenny would've liked sittin' there and before I knew it, the tears were rolling down my face. I just let 'em, didn't wipe 'em away or anythin' and then outa the blue, a hummingbird came and fluttered in front of me." As she recalled the memory, a smile slowly emerged on Lucy's face and she looked back to Anne. "I know it might sound a bit crazy, and I never told anyone this, but I think it was her. My Jenny."

"I don't think that's crazy at all, Lucy."

"No? You don't think me thinkin' my daughter came to visit me as a hummingbird is just a little weird?"

"No." Anne shook her head. "Not at all, actually. I think we get visited by those who have gone to the other side all the time. Most people don't pay attention though, you know, to the whispers."

"That's just what it was like. Like that hummingbird looked me right in the eye and said, 'Look, Ma. I'm free and I'm fast and I make people happy.'"

Lucy wiped the last remnants of tears from under her eyes and sat in comforting silence for a few moments. Then she described to Anne how the hummingbird had flown a full circle around her and then fluttered in front of her again before flying off. "I don't know how long I sat there, long time though cuz I missed dinner and the staff came lookin' for me."

Anne smiled at her friend, her tone tender as she said, "That sort of seems to be a theme in your life, Lucy."

Lucy giggled. "I suppose, eh?"

Lucy tilted her head, closed her eyes, and let the Las Vegas sun warm her. "I thought about suicide every single day after she went missing," Lucy whispered with her eyes closed. "But that day with the humming-bird, it was the first day I didn't. I decided to live. To honor the memory of my beautiful Jenny by living." She slowly opened her eyes and looked out to the shoppers. "Doesn't mean I don't miss her. Gawd, I miss her so much. Every minute of every day I could be crying, but that ain't gonna bring my Jenny back. So instead, I look for joy. I know there's lots of people who think I'm a bit crazy. And I am. Ain't no way as a parent you can go through what I been through and not be a bit crazy. How else do you cope? Some days it feels like I been punched in the gut, but it always seems like on those days, the hardest days, I get visited by a humming-bird." Lucy looked over at her friend and grinned.

"Funny how that is."

"I know, right? Creator and those Ancestors of ours work in mysteri-ous ways."

The two women adjusted themselves on the bench. They sat in silence as they watched the shoppers move in and out of the stores.

After awhile, Lucy turned to Anne and frowned. "Sorry to ruin our fun day. So much for YOLO."

"Oh, Lucy. You haven't ruined anything." Anne tenderly pulled Lucy in for a hug.

When they were done hugging, Lucy let out a deep sigh. "I think I'm done shopping for today, Anne. With my late night at the casino and this little boohoo, ol' Lucy here is in need of a nap."

"Sure, Lucy. Let's head back."

The women stood, collected their bags, and headed to where they could catch a bus back to the hotel.

22

A Chance to Love

ROSE KNEW PONCHO better than she knew herself and this went far beyond his likes and dislikes. She knew that he had the kindest heart of anyone she'd ever met. She knew he was wiser than most ever took the time to discover. She knew, before he even opened his eyes in the morning, that he started his day with the same seventeen words, "Thank you for the safe passage through the night and for the gift of living another day."

Rose also knew his peculiarities. That's how she knew that when they returned to the hotel that afternoon, Poncho would slip off his cowboy boots, remove his hat, and crawl onto the bed. He'd fold the pillow in half and tuck his left hand under it before laying his head down. Rose decided to surprise him and tuck his new Nano under the pillow, right where his hand would find it.

Just as predicated, Poncho was barely in the door when his cowboy boots were off and his routine unfolded, except when he slid his hand under the pillow, it hit the box. He sat up as fast as his old body would allow, looked at his wife with wide eyes and said, "Rose, there's somethin' under my pillow."

"Mm-hmm," she responded as she hung her sweater in the closet.

"Not the time to be uninterested, Rose."

She could tell by his tone that he was unnerved. They weren't accustomed to staying in hotel rooms and who knows what he thought was under his pillow. "Why don't you lift the pillow and see what it is?"

"Nu-uh." Poncho moved down the bed and stared at the pillow.

Rose walked over, lifted the pillow, and revealed the wrapped box underneath. He looked at her puzzled. "How'd that get there?"

"I put it there."

"You?"

"Yes, me!"

"Why?"

"It's for you, you big dummy. I knew you'd come in here, slip off your boots, and crawl right into bed to watch the sports channel, so I put it under the pillow." Rose looked dejected and her voice went a few octaves lower. "It was meant to be a surprise."

"Oh." His eyes wandered from Rose to the box and back to Rose. "What is it?"

At that moment Rose wanted to take the box, rap him over the head with it, and take the damn Nano back to the store. Her husband could be so infuriating!

Instead, she leaned over, picked it up, and held it toward Poncho. She placed it in his hand and sat down on the bed directly across from him.

He looked at his wife and asked, "You're not sick or somethin' are you, Rose?"

"No, I'm not sick! Why can't I surprise my husband?"

"Well, you can." He smiled wide. "You just never done it before."

Her eyes lowered to the floor, she placed her hands on her lap and spoke. "Being on this trip's made me remember how much I love you and," she lifted one shoulder and let it fall, "I just wanted to show you, cuz like you said, I never do."

When she looked up and over at Poncho, a solitary tear was rolling down his cheek.

After a few moments of their eyes connecting, he looked down at the box in his hand. "Guess I'd better open it then, eh?"

There was a small note hanging from the ribbon that read:

> For my Poncho,
> Thank you for giving me the chance to love.
> Your Rose, always.

"Aw, Rose." He took a breath, pulled the handkerchief from his back pocket and wiped the tears that were leaking from his eyes. Poncho opened his gift. He had no idea what it was at first, turning it over and then over again. Finally, he lifted his eyes to Rose, eyebrows raised and smile lurking. "Is this like that thingy that Tilly listens to her music on?"

"Yep, open it all the way." She came to sit beside him on the bed. "We even put music on it, all your favorites." Rose could no longer contain herself, she was beaming.

They spent the rest of the afternoon lying side by side on the bed, each with one ear bud, listening to the songs Rose had chosen.

After the last song played, Poncho turned on his side and looked at his wife. He ran his weathered hand along her jawline and before kissing her whispered, "Thank you, Rose. Besides our children, this is the best gift you've ever given me."

23

Exploring Again

LATER THAT EVENING, several of the elders headed down to Freemont Street. They started with watching the light show and then meandered down a few steps to where an Elvis impersonator was singing, "Can't Help Falling in Love with You." It had been the first song Chuck and Bea had ever danced to and for years she hadn't been able to listen it. But tonight, she closed her eyes and allowed her body to surrender to the music.

Bea felt someone come and stand beside her. She knew it was him. She smelled him. Felt him. Remembered him. When the song ended and the clapping had quieted down, he leaned over and whispered in her ear, "Tell me, Bea. How do I unlove you?"

Before her brain could censor her response, her heart's words flew out of her mouth, "Maybe you don't have to." Her stomach flipped and her body tingled as Chuck took a step closer. Standing so their shoulders touched, he wove his fingers into hers. Instinctively, she tightened her fingers around his, just as they'd done thousands of times…many, many full moons ago.

Bea was letting her melancholy get the best of her and was about to let go of Chuck's hand when he let out a nervous giggle, almost like a snort, and she couldn't help but laugh. He squeezed her hand gently. He turned his head to look at Bea. The love and tenderness in his eyes caused Bea's body to explode with goosebumps.

"Is this okay?" he asked, as he squeezed her hand.

"Yes." She smiled, suddenly feeling shy.

***

As Bea waited for Chuck the next morning, she tried to get the butterflies in her stomach to go away. Or at least fly in alignment. She stood staring out the hotel window at the pool below, watching the young people move their bodies to the pumping music. She tried moving her hips like that, sort of sexy-like, but it hurt her back. *What am I thinking? Chuck and I? Back together? Having sex again...after all these years. That's crazy.* She shook her head. Whispering to herself, as if the walls were listening, "I don't even know if my body works that way anymore. Maybe everything's all dried up."

The knock at the door startled her back to reality. She took a deep breath. *It's only a trip to the Grand Canyon, Bea. Nothing else! Get yourself together, woman!* She wiped her sweaty palms on the front of her jeans and opened the door. Chuck was standing there smiling at her, his eyes deep pools of brown. Bea thought, *I could get lost in those eyes again if I'm not careful. I know I'm staring at him, but I can't help it.*

The gray hair at his temples was brushed into place, not a whisker was to be found on his skin. She noticed he'd even trimmed his nose hairs. He smelled of a powerful mixture of Head and Shoulders, Old Spice, and too much deodorant. Bea found this both endearing and attractive. She knew she should just grab her purse and leave. Inviting him in would put them in this small room together. Who knows what might happen then.

"Ready, Bea?"

Her inner dialogue continued. *Am I ready? Ready for what? For what I want to happen, but I'm terrified of?* Her heart pounded in her head. Her hand had become slippery on the door handle.

She heard what sounded like her voice. It was saying, "Why don't you come in?"

He looked at her for a few moments. "Are you sure, Bea?"

They both knew what her question meant.

Bea nodded her head.

The door closed behind him and they stood face to face, their bodies now inches apart.

"I know this sounds crazy, Bea." He brought his hand up to her cheek, gently running it down to her chin. "But I love you. I always have and always will." He leaned in and placed a feathery soft kiss on Bea's lips. Her lips instinctively responded and she lifted her arms around his neck.

The Grand Canyon would have to wait. They had other, more important exploring to do.

24

Missing Roommate

IT WAS LATE when Tilly got back from Bingo and she was surprised to find that Bea wasn't in their room. She should be back from the Grand Canyon by now. Tilly waited about fifteen minutes before she called Bea. No answer. She texted her. After waiting a few minutes and receiving no return text from Bea, Tilly started to get concerned.

This was not typical Bea behavior.

Tilly went to Mabel and Lucy's room to see if they knew where Bea might be. Lucy took Tilly by the hand and headed toward the door. "Come with me, Tilly. I have a good ol' Indian hunch where she might be."

Tilly couldn't help herself and a crooked smile came over her. This Lucy was something else. She followed her to the elevator, where they rode up to the eighteenth floor.

They stepped off the elevator and Tilly asked, "What are we doing here?"

Lucy took her by the hand. "Just come with me."

They wandered the hall for a few moments until Lucy stopped in front of a door.

"Here it is. The room I've been looking for." She looked down and noticed a Do Not Disturb sign hanging from the door handle. Lucy pumped her fist beside her in jubilation and stated, "I knew it."

Tilly looked at the sign and then stared at Lucy, trying to put the pieces of the puzzle together in her head. "Is this...?" Her voice trailed off.

Lucy's eyes got big and a gigantic smile came over her face. "Yep."

Tilly pulled Lucy in close to her, almost nose to nose. She looked around to make sure no one was watching them and whispered, "This is Chuck's room?"

Lucy's head moved up and down in excitement and her curls bounced on her little head. Everything about Lucy was little, except her personality.

Tilly crossed her arms and began to slowly nod her head up and down. A smile came over her. "Well I'll be."

"I know, right?" They both turned and gazed at the Do Not Disturb sign. Lucy's voice softened, "Second chances. Sometimes they really do work."

They scurried down the hall to the elevator with Lucy giggling all the way. By the time the elevator came they were both in hysterics.

***

The next morning Tilly heard the door unlock. It was 7:03. She quickly closed her eyes and pretended to be asleep.

Bea ducked into the washroom and after a few moments emerged wrapped in the plush hotel housecoat, her hair damp. She sat down on Tilly's bed and shook her shoulder. "Tilly, wake up. I need to talk to you."

Tilly sat up and leaned against the headrest. She reached over to the nightstand to grab her glasses and asked, "What is it, Bea?"

Bea avoided Tilly's eyes for the time being. "I did something last night." Her face lit up as she recalled the night with Chuck. "I don't regret it. Not at all. But now, I don't know what to do." She turned to look at Tilly. "You see Chuck and me, well, we..."

Tilly put her hand on Bea's forearm. "I know, Bea."

"What do you mean, *you know*?"

Tilly leaned her head back against the headrest, wishing now she hadn't let Lucy lead her astray. She exhaled deeply, feeling like she had invaded Bea's privacy. She lowered her eyes for a moment before looking at Bea. "Last night when you weren't here," she motioned to Bea's bed, "I went looking for you. Well, Lucy and I went looking for you and we went to Chuck's room and saw the Do Not Disturb sign hanging from the door. And, well, we put two and two together and..." her voice trailed off.

Bea's head fell back. "So you *do* know."

Tilly turned her head to try and make eye contact with Bea. "Just so you know, Bea, I think it's marvelous."

"Marvelous?" Bea asked.

Tilly nodded and thought how Bea looked different. Younger, joyful, and more vibrant than she'd ever seen her.

"Well, it was." Bashfully Bea tilted her head, looked at Tilly and continued. "It was marvelous." She slowly sounded out the last word.

Tilly pulled her in for a hug. "Oh, Bea. I'm so happy for you."

"I'm happy for me too, Tilly," Bea whispered into Tilly's hair.

25

We *Are* Adults

IT HAD BEEN a late night or rather an early morning for almost everyone. They gathered at Denny's for breakfast and to sort out their day. They had just ordered when Lucy asked, "So Mr. Chucky, how are those second chances working out?"

Chuck's head snapped down the table to where Lucy was sitting. His mouth fell open and his brown cheeks were instantly tinged with red.

Bea hadn't had a chance to let him know that Tilly and Lucy had seen the sign. He looked at Bea. She met his eyes, but quickly looked away.

Chuck glanced around the table. Not a single one of them would look at him. They were all smiling or trying not to laugh.

"Yes!" He threw his napkin down on the table. "We slept together. We *are* adults. So you can stop hiding behind your coffee cups."

He put his arm around Bea, but instead of returning his warmth, she glared at him and smacked his leg. She didn't want everyone to know, at least not yet. It wasn't that she was embarrassed, more that she wanted to stay in the bubble of the two of them. She'd waited over thirty years to have Chuck beside her again, and she wasn't quite ready to share that with everyone.

"Since they all know. Might as well be open with how I feel about you." Chuck pulled her into a kiss and she lingered for a moment, but remembered that everyone was watching and pulled away.

"Chuck, that's enough," Bea said, blushing.

Everyone clapped, and Lucy leaned her head back, clicking her tongue on top of her mouth.

26

Route 66

THE BUS PULLED out of the hotel at 6:53 a.m. and Mabel announced, "We are seven minutes ahead of schedule."

Poncho moved his head up and down. "Now that, my friends, is what I like to call 'Indian Time.'" They were all too familiar with the negative connotations usually put on that term, but being elders they all knew Indian time actually meant being early.

Today they were driving from Las Vegas to Sedona, another fairly long day in the bus, so they had decided on only one scheduled stop: Seligman. However, there were always additional bathroom breaks, a requirement when traveling with elders.

Within half an hour, they reached the Nevada Arizona state line and the Hoover Dam. The sight from the interstate was spectacular, causing Mabel to ask, "Y'all want me to stop?" The consensus was no. An hour later they entered the town of Kingman, which greeted them with a water tower that stated "The Heart of Historic Route 66." They stopped long enough for a quick bathroom break and then were back on the road. Tilly slept through the stop and, when she woke up, Poncho was beside her. His cowboy hat was tilted over his face and soft sounds escaped his lips on each exhalation. Tilly looked at him for a few moments. Less than a week ago, many of these elders were acquaintances to Tilly and now, they felt like family. That thought seemed to lighten the tightness she'd been feeling in her chest. She took a deep breath and released some of the constriction. Her exhalation was louder than she'd realized, jolting Poncho awake. He lifted his cowboy hat and looked over at Tilly. "Guess I fell asleep while I was waiting for you to wake up." He let out one of his snort laughs and reached down to the bag at his feet. "Got you a li'l somethin' when we stopped." He handed Tilly a can of coconut water.

"We stopped?" Tilly was disoriented. How had she slept through a stop?

"Yep, quite a while ago. You were sound asleep, but you're always on us elders 'bout being hydrated and it's an awful hot one today, so thought I'd get you one of these." He reached into the bag at his feet and pulled out a second coconut water and proceeded to open it.

Tilly was touched by his thoughtfulness. "Thanks, Poncho."

He winked at her. "Seen you drinking them all the time, so thought I'd try one, too." Poncho took his first sip, then a long drink. "Not bad, not bad, Miss Tilly. I've decided it's time to turn over a new leaf. No. More. Coke," he announced.

"No more Coke? Wow." She sat up straighter in her seat. "That's huge, Poncho."

"I know, right? But with my diabetes, I best start takin better care of myself. And this trip, my Rose and I, well, we needed this trip, Tilly." His eyes left her and looked a few seats up to where Rose was sitting. "We still got a lot of livin' to do."

Tilly tilted her head and nodded, reaching over and gently squeezing Poncho's weathered hand.

"Now, Miss Tilly, if you don't mind, I'm gonna listen to my music." He beamed. "Other than my family, this is the best gift I ever got." He still couldn't believe Rose had bought this for him and that she had even put his favorite music on it.

"What are you listening to?"

"Good ol' Willie Nelson." He offered her one of his earbuds. She welcomed an escape from her thoughts. The cord didn't quite reach so Tilly cozied up closer to Poncho. She placed the bud in her ear, closed her eyes, rested her head on Poncho's shoulder and let the music transport her to another time. A time when she and Mick would sing along to these songs while driving between Kamloops and Vancouver; a time when things were easier; a time when they were connected; a time when she knew what she wanted.

When they entered Seligman, Mabel broadcasted from the driver's seat, "Let's drive the full length and then we can decide where we want to stop and eat and what we want to do here."

As it turned out, driving the main street of Seligman took all of thirty seconds, if that. The elders stared out the windows at the eccentric displays in front of the stores.

"Are you sure we ain't still in Vegas?" asked Lucy.

"I know. It's kind of wild, isn't it?" responded Mabel.

At that moment, they pulled up to a restaurant called Roadkill Café and Poncho jumped into the conversation. "Roadkill Café. Yummy! Anyone up for a bite to eat?" he said as he glanced around the bus.

Rose shook her head vehemently. "Ugh! That's disgusting."

Anne looked at Sarah, who moved her head from side to side with wide eyes. "Us neither," Anne responded.

"Uh-uh," said Lucy with a crinkled up nose.

Tilly giggled. "It's a good day to be a vegetarian."

Poncho turned to Chuck, the only one who had not yet commented, and asked, "What d'ya think pardner? Shall we have us a li'l snack of roadkill?"

Chuck looked to Bea. She lifted her shoulders and raised her hands. "I ain't your keeper. If you want roadkill for breakfast, fill your boots. But I'm gonna find myself a muffin to eat with my Cheezies."

Chuck leaned forward and placed his hand on Poncho's shoulder and gave it a squeeze. "Count me in."

Mabel pulled into the parking lot of the Roadkill café and turned off the bus. "How about we meet back here," Mabel looked at her watch, "in an hour and a half?"

There was mutual agreement as everyone got off the bus to explore Seligman. Poncho and Chuck walked across the parking lot and entered the Roadkill Café for breakfast while the women all crossed the street.

The women were drawn to the tall green building whose sign boasted "Best Espresso on Route 66." Outside the store was an old black-and-white police car and metal tractor seats that had been set up for people to sit on. That's exactly what they did, with Anne taking photos of them in various poses.

"Sure am glad I never sat my butt in one of these," said Lucy as she ran her hand over the hood of the police car.

"Yeah, me too," said Rose.

"Me too," added Sarah.

Anne was quiet.

The three women exchanged glances and then Lucy asked, "Why you not sayin' anything, Anne?"

Anne avoided their eyes and turned to walk into the store, but Sarah stopped her. "Uh-uh. You don't get off that easy. Go on. You have to tell us, now you got us all curious."

Rose and Lucy stepped in front of Anne and blocked the path into the store, both women grinned.

Anne rolled her eyes and folded her arms across her chest. "Fine, but you have to remember I live in Toronto. And that Liz and I were quite political back in the day." She paused and brushed a stray piece of hair behind her ear. She hadn't thought about this story for years and couldn't believe she was about to tell it to these ladies. Anne looked at each of them, shook her head slightly and began. "We were at a protest in the mid 70s and things got out of control. Liz and I happened to be near the ones who started the out of control part and we got scooped up with them and shoved into a police car." Anne leaned back against the car and tipped her head. "Much like this one. Next thing I knew we were at the police station, giving our statement and spending the night in a jail cell."

"Really?" Sarah's eyes were wide. "Why is it I never heard this story?"

Anne gave her sister a look. "Because nothing ever came of it. The police realized Liz and I had nothing to do with what was going on and promptly let us go. They even apologized for the confusion."

"But you *did* get to ride in a cop car, and not just in the car, in the *baaack*." Lucy was in awe.

"Yes, I did, Lucy, and I never need to do it again." She stopped talking for a moment, her eyes narrowed. "I haven't even thought of that day for years." She took a last look at the police car and turned back to the store. "Now I really need an espresso. Come on. Let's go inside." Anne stepped between Rose and Lucy and continued into the store. She didn't wait to see if anyone followed her.

Once inside, they rummaged through the shelves overflowing with knickknacks, peculiar gifts, and some items that looked like they'd been discarded from Dollar Mart. Lucy and Rose headed down one aisle and it wasn't long before Lucy had an armful of gifts for her grandchildren. She turned to Rose and Sarah, who were exploring the items on the shelves and said, "At this rate, I'm gonna need me another suitcase."

"At this rate, you're gonna go home to the poorhouse," replied Rose without even looking up.

Sarah furrowed her eyes and shook her head. Rose was really starting to get on her nerves, and that took a lot. She sided with Lucy. "I think it's real sweet, Lucy, that you be takin' all those gifts home to your grandbabies. They're real lucky to have you thinkin' of them as much as you do."

Lucy smiled at Sarah, then glanced over at Rose and stuck her tongue out at her. When she knew Rose was watching her, she deliberately reached for another touristy snow globe.

Meanwhile, Anne was meandering by herself when she noticed a middle-aged man sitting by the cash register. She made her way over and stood there for a moment before he looked up from his crossword, nodded his head and said, "Mornin.'"

"Good morning. The sign out front says you have espresso."

"Yes Ma'am, we do. Best espresso you'll find anywhere along Route 66."

"Really? Well, in that case, make it a double."

The left side of the man's face lifted slightly. "You're going to go big time are you?"

"I suppose I am, 'going to go big time', as you say." She couldn't help it, a smile crossed her face. "Most of this trip I've been drinking brown-colored water disguised as coffee. So, yes, I like the idea of going big."

"Alrighty then." He gave Anne a wink as he stood, reached for an espresso cup off the top of the machine and began to grind the beans.

Anne remained standing at the counter. She found the store overwhelming. It was simply too much for her organized, librarian self. She closed her eyes and allowed the smell of freshly ground coffee to soothe her senses.

When the gentleman set the espresso in front of her, Anne opened her eyes to thick froth settling on the top. With her thumb and forefinger on the handle, and her pinky extended outwards, she picked up her espresso. After all, there are some things that just must be done a certain way, no matter if you are in downtown Toronto or in a small town in the heart of Arizona.

She lifted the cup close to her face, closed her eyes, and inhaled slowly, allowing the intoxicating scent to fill every cell in her body. With her eyes still closed, she took a sip.

Heaven.

Right there in that tiny town and in that tiny cup, was a piece of heaven.

This was simply the best espresso that had ever crossed her lips. It made her think of Liz and how every weekday morning, at seven o'clock sharp, Liz would place an espresso and half a grapefruit in front of Anne. She would sip her coffee as she read *The Globe and Mail* and, once she was done the paper, she would eat her grapefruit, pack up her lunch, and head to the library for her day of work.

As Anne stood relishing her great find in this quirky store in the middle of nowhere, she wondered what life would be like when the trip was over and she returned home to Toronto. Now that she'd retired, what would she do after she ate her grapefruit?

Meanwhile, Sarah had her head buried in one of the shelves when out of the corner of her eye she saw her. The young woman.

The one who had come to her the night they first discussed this trip.

The one who she could see, but was pretty sure no one else could.

Sarah stood upright and, bit by bit, turned her head fully to look at the young woman.

The young woman smiled at Sarah and tipped her head just a tad. Sarah deliberately nodded her head in return, indicating, "I see you." Then she glanced down the aisles and around the store to see if her sister or any of her friends were watching. Rose and Lucy were down another aisle nattering at each other as usual and Anne was on the other side of the store talking to the man behind the counter.

Sarah turned back to the young woman and their eyes met. She was drawn into those eyes, wide and round in the middle and narrow at the sides, as if the tiniest stroke of a paintbrush had drawn them. They reminded Sarah of teardrops, and the color was like night sky when the moon is but a sliver. A quiver pulsed through Sarah's body.

The young woman's eyes moved to the right as she scanned the shelves full of blankets. Then, purposefully, she reached up and removed a Pendleton blanket. It was dark brown, with turquoise and white designs, and was absolutely gorgeous. Sarah wondered how she had not noticed it before.

The young woman held the blanket in her right hand and tenderly ran her left hand over it four times. She then cradled the blanket in both her palms and extended it toward Sarah.

At first Sarah wasn't sure she was to take it, but, when she hesitated, the young woman nodded. Sarah reached out and took the blanket into her hands, feeling the weight of it. She looked at it and couldn't help but run her hand over it, just as the young woman had. Sarah had no idea how long she stood there like that, but when she looked up, the young woman was gone.

Sarah pulled the blanket tight to her chest, closed her eyes, and rubbed her cheek along it.

There was no question. She must buy it.

Sarah walked over to the counter where Anne was talking with the man and laid the blanket beside the till.

"Wow, Sarah! That's beautiful," remarked Anne. She took a quick glance around the store, a bit dumbfounded, and asked, "Where'd you find that?"

The man behind the counter, wide-eyed, added, "Yeah, where'd you find that? I put stuff away all day long and I've never seen a blanket like that in here before."

Sarah pointed to the back of the store.

"Hmm, well I'll be," he said as he lifted the blanket and searched for a price tag. "Forty-nine, ninety-nine. Now that's a bargain. You know what you pay in the city for a blanket like this?" he asked, raising his eyebrows.

Sarah nodded. She knew full well what a Pendleton blanket like this would normally cost. Which was why, until now, she'd never owned one.

27

Entering Sedona

WHEN THE LAST of the Crazy Eights was on the bus and Chuck had tucked away Lucy's stepping stool, Mabel announced, "No more stops. We need to get Tilly to Sedona by two o'clock cuz she's going on a tour."

"A tour? What kind of tour?" Rose asked.

"It's a Jeep tour," was all Tilly said, thinking that was enough information for them, but when she turned around she saw they were all waiting for more. Self-consciously she explained, "It's a Jeep tour to visit the vortexes. It's called Touch the Earth."

Tilly turned back to the front, hoping that was the end of it. But Mabel raised her pointer finger as if to say, "Wait," and then, almost on cue, Poncho piped up and teased, "Miss Tilly, you really going on a tour to touch the earth?" She heard him slap his leg as he laughed. "You can pay me and I'll take you out to the earth so you can touch it."

Tilly knew that elders only teased you if they liked you, but today she was feeling a bit tender, so the teasing stung. Mabel sensed this, and glanced over at her. "Don't listen to them, Tilly. Go and do something that makes you happy. You've been taking good care of all of us, so now it's time for you to go take care of you."

Rose asked, "What's a vortex anyway?"

Mabel could feel Tilly's discomfort, so answered for her, "Well, you know back home when the wind swirls about and picks up a sage brush and twists it about in the air before placing it down again?"

Even though it had been Rose who had asked, all the elders were now listening and almost in unison responded, "Mm-hmm."

Tilly was surprised at how interested they all were. "That's like a wind vortex, but Sedona is famous for energy vortexes. The spiraling isn't wind or water, it's energy. Spiritual energy. The vortexes are known as spiritual places to offer prayer, meditate, or go for healing."

Poncho's tone had changed. "Is that what you're doin', Miss Tilly? Going for healin'?"

"Yeah, I guess so." Tilly hadn't really thought about why she was going on this tour. She had seen it online as one of the "must do" things in Sedona and it had intrigued her. But Poncho's question had reminded her of the teaching of always knowing *why* you are doing something. Popular culture called it being clear on your intent.

"Good. That's good." Poncho's voice had softened. He understood the need for healing.

As they drove through Sedona and toward their hotel, Rose let out a small yelp when she saw the sign Sedona Knit Wits. In a rare tone of excitement she shouted, "Look! Look everyone." Rose pointed across the street. "Over there. That store. It was made for us."

"Oh, I think we could get into some trouble in that store," Lucy said as she rubbed her hands together.

Mabel yelled from the driver's seat, "Oh no, Lucy. You've already had your quota of trouble on this trip."

"Whaaat?" Lucy tried to look confused. "Me?"

"You already forgettin' your night out in Las Vegas, Lucy?" Sarah asked. "An' how you got lost an' had to call home an' then Chuck had to rescue you?" Sarah beamed at the memory and turned in her seat to look at Lucy. "That's a story we all gonna be tellin' for a long time."

The bus erupted with laughter and Lucy brought her hands up to her mouth trying to cover her smile. Rose rescued her friend by changing the subject and pointing back at the Sedona Knit Wits store. "That's where I want to spend my day tomorrow. Who's with me?"

All the women chimed in agreement, causing Chuck and Poncho to look at each other. They weren't sure what they were going to do, but they sure as heck weren't going to spend the day at or with the Knit Wits.

28

The Crossing Paths

WHEN TILLY CHECKED in for her tour, she was told to meet at the Jeeps in thirty minutes. She meandered out to the back of the building where tables and chairs overlooked the red rocks. The sun was at its peak and most people who were waiting for the various tours were seeking shade; however, Tilly found a seat in the sun, put on her shades and sat back, closing her eyes. She welcomed the sun and its healing energy. Her mind began to wander back home to Mick and the kids. She missed them! She missed their laughs, their hugs, holding Piper's hand while she fell asleep, and playing catch with Grayson. She thought about Mick. It was hard to pinpoint what she missed about him. It seemed like it was a lifetime ago since they had really connected. She realized, sitting in the Sedona sun, that she no longer knew the heartbeat of her husband. She used to know what made him happy, what made him laugh, what made him sad, what infuriated him, but she wasn't sure she knew any of that now.

"Excuse me." A male voice jolted Tilly out of her thoughts. "Is this seat taken?"

She opened her eyes, but, even with her sunglasses, the sun was too bright. Tilly raised her hand to shade her eyes, seeing the handsome man belonging to the voice. She sat up a bit straighter and replied, "Uh, no. No one's sitting there."

"Great." He pulled out the chair and sat down. Tilly pretended to adjust her sunglasses as she took a quick glance at him. He was lean and she could see he had the sinewy muscles of an endurance athlete. His sleek jawline was slightly covered by his dark brown, wavy hair that looked like it had been tousled by the wind. Or maybe that's how it always was.

"You waiting for the Vortex Tour?" he asked.

"Yes."

"Thought so." He lifted his sunglasses and smiled at her. She wasn't sure if it was the way his faded green shirt made his hazel eyes dance, or his dimples or the warmth that radiated from him, but something about him caused her stomach to flip.

"Oh really, what made you think so?" Tilly said nonchalantly.

He looked at her briefly. "Your shirt."

Tilly looked down and realized she was wearing her T-shirt with BE AMAZING written on it. Bette had given it to her for her birthday last year and it had been her favorite ever since. Although, lately, she had not been feeling all that amazing.

She tipped her head slightly and shrugged her shoulders. "It was a gift."

"Someone knows you well. So, what's your name, or should I just call you Amazing?" He took a quick sip from his water bottle before continuing, "Cuz you know all those crazy Hollywood types are naming their kids all kinds of names and maybe yours really is Amazing?" He looked at her playfully. There they were again, those dimples, popping right out at her.

Tilly sat speechless for a moment, wondering, *Is he flirting with me?* She swallowed hard and answered, "My name's Tilly. And you?"

He put his hand out to her and she reached across the table to shake it. "Rob, Rob Sanchez. Very nice to meet you." He gave her hand a slight squeeze before letting it go. "Where you from, Tilly?"

"Vancouver."

"You're from Canada, eh?" He teasingly placed emphasis on the *eh*.

Without pause, she teased right back, with a long drawl, "Yeh, and you?" From behind her sunglasses, Tilly raised her eyebrows at him.

"Oh, so that's how this is going to go this afternoon." He chuckled and sat up straighter in his chair, as if the games had just begun.

There was no opportunity for further bantering as a petite, red-haired woman came over to where they were sitting. "Any chance you two are waiting for the Vortex Tour?"

Rob nodded. The woman, who introduced herself as Kathi, explained that she was their tour leader. She pointed her pen at Tilly and said, "You must be Tilly."

Tilly stood and said, "That's me."

"And you're Rob?" He smiled at her and Tilly noticed that Kathi's cheeks flushed. She thought, *Good it's not just me who reacts to those dimples.*

Kathi quickly regained her composure. "Okay, well the other two couples are up at the Jeep. What say we go visit some vortexes?" She smiled at them both, turned on her heels, and headed toward the stairs. Rob motioned with his hand for Tilly to go first.

When they got to the Jeep, Kathi briefly introduced everyone and let them know that at the first stop they'd be doing a circle of introduction and sharing why they'd chosen to do this tour. Tilly noticed one of the men rolled his eyes.

"Okay. Let's pile in and get this show on the road," Kathi stated. "I need a copilot, so one of you couples will have to separate."

Tilly started, "Oh, Rob and I..." But before she could explain that they weren't a couple, she was cut off by a women named Delilah.

"I need to sit in the front, my knees are too sore to climb in and out of the back," she stated.

The Jeep had three sets of seats, each with two seatbelts. "That settles it. Delilah up front with me." Kathi pointed to the back seat: "Raoul and Alvira, you two back there, Rob and Tilly on the side seat here, and, Frank, you can sit on the other side here with the blankets."

Tilly watched as Rob helped Alvira and Raoul get into the back of the Jeep. At first, she wasn't aware that her gaze had moved from how he was helping them to how his body fit in his faded Levis.

Damn Levis! They got her every time!

As Tilly climbed into the Jeep, there was no denying it, there was something about this man that she found incredibly attractive.

29

Vortex Tour

AS THEY HEADED out through Sedona, the wind blew against Tilly's face and through her hair. With her eyes closed, she leaned her head against a bar and imagined the wind carrying away some of the negativity and hurt she was holding.

When they arrived at their first vortex, Kathi asked everyone to make their way up to the top of the small lookout and form a circle. "Great," Raoul said sarcastically and stormed off to the top of the hill. When they'd all reached the top, Kathi introduced herself further, sharing that she had been living in Sedona for over eleven years and was a Jungian therapist in her previous life. "Now I bring people to the vortexes for their healing," she explained. She asked everyone to share a bit about themselves, where they were from, and why they chose this tour.

As they went around, Tilly learned that Delilah and Frank were from Tulsa and celebrating their fortieth wedding anniversary. They had been to other energy vortexes in the world, in Maui and New Zealand and wanted to experience Sedona. Raoul went next, his accent was pronounced, but Tilly was unable to place it. "My wife, she make me come on dis tour."

Kathi playfully said to him, "Nobody in life can make us do anything. We all make our own choices."

Tilly smirked and watched as Raoul rolled his eyes.

Alvira looked at her husband. Annoyance was written all over her face. "What?" he asked.

She shook her head slightly. "Never mind." Alvira turned to Kathi and then looked at each person momentarily. The energy in the circle changed, deepened. "My husband and I are from Spain. He had to come here for a conference, so I came along. I was diagnosed with cervical cancer last year and have just come through two surgeries and chemotherapy." She took a deep breath and Raoul's eyes dropped to the ground as he delicately placed his hand on her lower back. "Even though I got the 'cancer free' from the doctor a few months ago, I'm still afraid. Afraid of so many things, but, mostly, of all the damage that's been done to my body. So, I wanted to come on this tour for healing."

There was silence in the circle, everyone transfixed by Alvira's honesty. "There's one thing I've learned over this last year, besides how much I love my husband, who behind all this toughness and sarcasm is a big teddy bear." Raoul lifted his head slightly and looked at Alvira in a way that only a man who has the deepest of affections for his wife can. Alvira continued, "I've learned that life gives us plenty of opportunities to experience the richness of being alive, it's up to us to say yes to those experiences. When Raoul told me he was coming to the US, I said, 'so am I, and we're going to Sedona.'"

It was then that Tilly noticed what a gorgeous smile Alvira had. "So that's how we got here and why we chose this tour. It's true, I did make Raoul come with me," she said as she reached for his hand. "After this past year, we are both in need of healing and positive energy." They looked at each other for a moment, Raoul lifted her hand to his lips and kissed it.

Tilly was grateful she had her sunglasses on and that the tears welling up in her eyes were not visible.

Kathi was not as self-conscious, openly wiping the tears from her cheeks. "Thank you, Alvira." She smiled at her tenderly. "I hope you find what you are seeking today, and always." There was quiet for a few moments. Tilly had lowered her head, hoping to avoid sharing for as long as possible, but the silence had become uncomfortable.

"Guess I'll go then. My name is Tilly and I'm on a road trip with a group of Native Canadian elders and we are on our way to the Gathering of Nations Pow Wow. As part of our trip, each person is doing one of their bucket list items. Sedona was on the list for one of the elders, so I looked it up online to learn more and this tour was listed as one of the things to do in Sedona." There. She'd said a lot without saying why she'd really chosen this particular tour or that she was craving healing, guidance, and clarity.

Rob was the only one left to introduce himself. "My name is Rob Sanchez. I live in the San Fernando Valley and I'm dad to three amazing girls who keep me humble and in style." He chuckled and so did everyone else in the circle. "I'm a massage and reiki therapist and so I'm fascinated with the vortexes and healing. But the real reason I chose this tour and why I've come to Sedona is that a few months ago, after almost twenty-five years of being together, my wife and I divorced."

No matter how many times he said those words, it was still incredibly difficult to hear them reverberate back and hit his heart. "I'm out here trying to remember who I was before all these roles of who I'm supposed to be took over. And to figure out who I want to be. Seems crazy at forty-five. The only thing I know for sure is that I want to be a dad. I love being a father, but any more than that right now..." he paused and his eyes landed on Tilly. She had been watching him, but quickly turned her eyes to the red soil beneath her feet. "Any more than that and I draw a blank. So that's why I came on this tour. To seek inspiration."

Tilly sneaked a peek at him from under her lashes and thought to herself, *He just said everything I didn't have the courage to say.*

"Thank you, everyone, for sharing, it helps us all understand a bit more why we are here on this tour together." Kathi smiled at Raoul. "Even if your wife made you, we're all here together for a reason." Raoul tipped his head slightly. Tilly wasn't sure if he was agreeing with her or pondering the idea. Kathi told them more about energy vortexes and the differences between the female and masculine energies. She explained that the airport was a powerful masculine energy vortex and now that she understood why everyone had come on the tour, they wouldn't be going up there. Instead, they would visit only the feminine, healing energy vortexes. She ended by saying, "So why don't you walk around a bit and we'll leave for our next stop in fifteen minutes."

Tilly went for a short stroll and revelled in the landscape surrounding her. Every direction held stunning red and orange rock formations. She stood on a cliff and overlooked the valley where Sedona lay, overwhelmed by the beauty. Removing her backpack and unzipping the front compartment, Tilly pulled out the pouch of tobacco Bette had given her for the trip. She'd told Tilly, "It's for the offerings, prayers, and gratitude that you've been missing in your life. You'll know when to use it." Tilly had used it quite a bit since the trip had started and was now moved to lay some tobacco down in gratitude. She reached into the pouch and removed enough to cover the palm of her hand. Closing her fingers around the tobacco, she offered a prayer: "Great Spirit, Creator of all things, my name is Beautiful Light Woman and I come before you in a humble manner. I offer thanksgiving for my safe passage through the night and for the safe passage for all my loved ones. I offer thanksgiving for the privilege of witnessing the beauty of this land and for the healing energy you've placed here. I have so much in my life to be grateful for, Creator, and I thank you for that. At this time, I ask for the strength and courage to release the hurt and negativity I'm carrying. May today, amid this beautiful land, be the start of that releasing. Please watch over my family back home, especially my children, my parents, and the elders I'm privileged to be traveling with. Watch over all of us, guide us, protect us, and keep us safe, healthy, and vibrant. And may we experience joy. Hiy Hiy."

Tilly gently squeezed the tobacco in her hand and placed it at the base of a juniper tree. She stood and headed back to the Jeep, noticing the tension in her neck had dissipated.

They stopped at two more vortexes. At both, Tilly said prayers and made similar tobacco offerings. Each time, she felt a bit lighter. She stuck pretty much to herself, enjoying her own company and needing the time to reflect.

Before long Kathi called everyone to the Jeep. "The last vortex we're going to visit is my favorite and I've left it for last so we could have a bit more time there. You can only get to it on foot or in 4x4 vehicles, so we're going do a bit of off-roading to get there. It's called Mystic Vista and I think you're going to really like it. Let's get going."

30

Mystic Vista

DURING THE DRIVE to Mystic Vista, especially once they turned onto the dirt road, Tilly was aware of Rob sitting beside her. Kathi explained a bit about life in Sedona. She told them that some people say one year of living in Sedona is like ten years of therapy. "There are three rules to living here." She put the Jeep into four-wheel drive and raised her forefinger. "First rule: Don't take what anyone says personally."

Rob interjected, "That's a good rule in life no matter where you live."

Kathi acknowledged that was true. She smiled at him in the rear-view mirror. "Second rule: Drink lots of water, and third rule: Get out of town at least once a week. This spot I'm taking you to, it's my spot to come to when I need to get out of town."

Over the last few moments, Tilly had become intensely aware of Rob. The bumps and tilts of the Jeep maneuvering the dirt road had her leaning and falling into him. She was embarrassed by her inability to remain on her side of the double seat and apologized.

"No worries. It's all good," he said lightheartedly. "It's like being a kid again." His easy, carefree attitude helped lessen her discomfort and enjoy the ride. Before she knew it, Tilly was smiling wider than she had for a very long time and loving every moment of the off-road experience. Even, or maybe especially, the falling into Rob.

When they reached the base of Mystic Vista, Kathi turned off the engine and asked, "How fun was that?" Almost in unison, as if it had been planned, they all responded, "Awesome!" Rob was right, it was like being a kid again, and Tilly was grateful they still had the ride back out.

"This is Mystic Vista. You can hike up to the top there, but just be careful because there are rattlesnakes and scorpions. It might be chilly so take one of these blankets to sit on or wrap around you. We're going to be here for about forty-five minutes, so please, take this time for you. You may never come back here, so make it memorable."

Everyone unloaded from the Jeep, grabbed their bags and blankets, and each went their own way. Tilly climbed to the top of the hill and gasped at the beauty that lay before her. In every direction and as far as she could see were the healing mountains and rocks of Sedona. The colors were breathtaking, like a painter's palette of oranges, reds, yellows, and golds. She searched for a private place to settle in, one where she could be absorbed in the beauty and release the heaviness in her heart. Once she found *the* spot, she scanned the area for rattlers and scorpions, knowing that Kathi had not been joking. Tilly laid her blanket down and sat cross-legged. Instantly, tears filled her eyes. The sadness and loneliness could no longer be held at bay. She cried, deeply and loudly, not caring who might hear or what they might think. She desperately needed this. After all those nights of crying silently into her pillow, it felt good to hear herself. Her thoughts led to Mick. Her heart physically ached as she thought to herself, *How did this happen? How did Mick and I get like this? How did there come to be a chasm between us?*

Tilly used to know how to reach him, how to pull him out of his shell when he turtled. But, in that moment, sitting looking out at the beauty, it occurred to her that it wasn't just Mick who had turtled. She, too, had withdrawn. Somewhere along the way she'd stopped talking *with* him and begun talking *to* him. In her mind, it was a form of self-preservation.

A few months ago, after going three days without talking to each other, Mick had suggested couples counseling, but, in her denial, Tilly had said they didn't need it. Truth was, she was terrified of having to sit with him and dissect their relationship. Even more terrified of the very real chance that, in the dissecting, they wouldn't know how to put it back together. It seemed easier at the time to remain in denial than to take that risk.

Tilly knew she could no longer live in denial. Her marriage was in serious trouble. She wasn't sure she and Mick could find their way across the chasm and back to each other.

As she sat atop that mountain, Tilly remembered how she used to be happy. She was someone who frequently felt joy, who loved adventure, and who exuded love and warmth. She wanted that woman back. She needed Beautiful Light Woman back.

Up there, overlooking the glory of Sedona, Tilly made a commitment to herself. To start taking care of *her* needs and get back to doing the things that made *her* happy.

This time as she pulled out her tobacco and offered her prayers, they were different. "Creator and Ancestors, thank you for the time alone to seek clarity and guidance. I offer thanksgiving for watching over me and protecting me. I am grateful for the opportunities you are sending me that will help me to remember what happiness and joy feels like. Please watch over my family, keep them safe, and may they feel my love all these miles away. Hiy Hiy."

She laid the tobacco on the ground in front of her. In that moment, a gust of wind blew by and swept each tiny particle of that tobacco up, spreading it far and wide on the sacred land of Mystic Vista. Tilly smiled to herself, knowing the wind was Grandma Tilly working her magic. She stood and lifted her head to the sky, letting the last of the late afternoon sun shine on her.

31

Connection

THE TRIP BACK to the tour office was fairly quiet, everyone lost in their own thoughts. When they arrived, Tilly said a quick good-bye. She grabbed her pack and headed off to find a coffee shop, seeking time and space to write and capture all that had transpired for her on the tour. Along the way, she came across a store promoting healing massages, crystals, and energy work. Tilly loved stores like this and decided the coffee shop and writing could wait.

Tilly found a heart-shaped rose quartz for Piper and a beautiful piece of hematite for Mick's office desk, but her greatest find was a necklace for herself. It was made of mala beads and had a rose quartz hanging at the end. The write-up beside it said, "When worn, it promotes self-love." *Perfect,* she thought to herself, *just what I need.* She slipped it over her head and took the tag and her gifts up to the till. On her way out, Tilly noticed Rob browsing the book section. She paused, unconsciously brushing her bangs out of her eyes and considered, *Do I?* But before she could decide, Rob turned around and his face lit up. "Hey, I was hoping I'd run into you again!"

Tilly looked away for a moment, trying to act aloof. She'd been so involved with herself on the tour that there had been very little interaction between them, but she was intrigued and most definitely attracted to him. More than she wanted to admit, actually, and it had her feeling nervous.

Tilly cinched her backpack up over her shoulder and replied, "Hey yourself."

"What a great store," he said, turning momentarily back to the bookshelf, running his hand over the books. "Always so hard to choose just one."

She knew exactly what he meant. Books were one of Tilly's few indulgences. She always had a pile beside her bed, in the living room, and in her office.

Rob turned and walked over to where Tilly was standing. "Looks like you found a few things."

Tilly lifted her shopping bag and glanced up at him. "Gifts for my daughter," she said, pausing for a moment and swallowing. She wished now that she'd shared more in the introduction circle so she could have avoided this awkward moment, but she hadn't and now, for some reason, she felt like she needed to tell him. It all came tumbling out too fast. "And my husband. Because I'm married. I'm happily married. So, so, I bought him a gift." She looked toward the door, repeated hurriedly, "Because, I'm happily married."

She could not believe she had just said that. All of that. What was it about this man that discombobulated her? Tilly took a deep breath and rubbed her lips together, avoiding Rob's eyes. She secretly wished the floor would open up and suck her into some dark abyss, away from this man who had her rambling and acting strange.

"I know you're married."

She turned her head toward him and their eyes connected. Rob spoke just loud enough for Tilly to hear. "I saw you playing with your ring up at Mystic Vista."

Just then, the store door opened, causing the chimes to go off and jarring them out of the moment. Tilly saw this as her opportunity to leave before she got herself into trouble.

"'Kay, well I'm going to go find something to eat. It was great meeting you. Take care." Tilly lifted her hand to wave, smiled at him, and began to head for the door.

He turned quickly and touched her arm. "Wait. I was about to get a bite, too. There's a great Mexican place a few miles up the road. I've got my motorbike." He pointed out the window to his bike. "And an extra helmet." He stopped for a second before asking, "Why don't you join me?"

Tilly looked out the front window where she could see his bike. Nothing fancy, but it sure looked like fun. It had been years since she'd been on a bike, before she'd even met Mick. If nothing else, Tilly was up for the thrill of being on a motorbike. And besides, had she not just offered prayers of gratitude for the happiness and joy that was on its way? She was sure this was a sign. That's all it was, right? The thrill and joy of being on a bike? Nothing to do with Rob.

She shrugged, trying her best to be nonchalant. "Sure, why not?"

Actually, there were plenty of reasons why not.

They exited the store and Rob climbed on first, straddled the seat, then handed Tilly her helmet. She stuffed her gifts into her backpack and slipped it over both shoulders, wrapped her scarf around her neck, and put the helmet on. Tilly made a quick scan of the bike, trying to assess the most graceful way to get on. As if he had read her mind, Rob stuck his arm out toward her. "Best way to get on is to swing your right leg up and over and use my arm as a balancer until you get settled."

She followed his instructions and before she knew it she was nestled in behind him on the bike. Before he put his helmet on, he turned around and said, "Sorry, no handles, have to use me to hang on." She forced herself to smile, trying to pretend this wasn't a problem for her.

As he backed out of the stall and maneuvered through the parking lot, Tilly wrapped her arms around his waist and felt the strength of Rob's body as she leaned into him. She found herself aroused and feeling sensations she had not felt for a very long time. As he started to speed up, Tilly's scarf went flying off. She squeezed his stomach to get his attention and tried to yell over the engine.

"I've lost my scarf."

"What?"

"My scarf," she yelled.

Rob pulled over, put down the kickstand and ran back to get the scarf. He wrapped it around her neck a few times and tucked it in. "There. That should work." He flashed his dimples and got back on the bike. "Ready?" he asked over his shoulder.

Tilly hesitated, knowing she should get off the bike. Right here, right now. Instead, she placed her hands on his hips. "Yes, I'm ready."

When they arrived at the restaurant, Tilly was ecstatic. Taking off her helmet and boasting a grin almost as wide as her face, she said, "I'd forgotten what a thrill it is to be on a bike. That was beyond fun! Thank you."

"Any time," Rob replied.

Once seated at the outside patio, Tilly pulled out her phone and told

Rob, "I've got to send a text to the elders I'm traveling with, they'll be wondering where I am." She paused for a moment, considering what to say to Mabel. She decided on, "Go ahead and have dinner without me. I'm going to get something quick and then go back to the room." Before hitting the send button, Tilly reconciled with herself the fact that most of what she had written was true. Then, before making sure the text had been delivered, she put her phone on airplane mode and tucked it into her pack.

Over dinner, their conversation flowed with ease and was frequently accented with bouts of laughter. Rob asked questions about her life and was sincerely interested in what she shared. Tilly was acutely aware of how good it felt to be listened to and be the focus of Rob's attention. As a result, she relaxed, opened up, and talked freely.

Meanwhile, back at the hotel, Mabel and Bea discovered that Tilly wasn't in her room and there was no sign that she had been. They both checked their phones, no messages from her either. They exchanged a look. Intuitively knowing something wasn't right, they headed back to the bus. They weren't sure where they were going, except that they were looking for Tilly.

After about an hour of driving around Sedona, Bea spotted Tilly on the restaurant patio. "There! There she is." Relief flooded her voice as she pointed for Mabel to see Tilly.

When Bea saw a man sitting across from Tilly, her tone quickly turned from relief to annoyance. "Who's that?"

"I don't know, but we're going to find out," Mabel said, trying to quell her irritation.

Mabel had barely parked the bus when Bea opened her door, ready to march over to Tilly. Mabel quickly reached over and put her hand on Bea's arm. "Slow down. Best if we don't pounce on her."

"But I want to pounce. We thought she'd be back at the hotel hours ago, it's late, no text or phone call and now she's here," Bea motioned to where the two were sitting, "with some guy."

Tilly was laughing hard and had her head tilted back. For a moment, they both watched. Tilly was happy. There was something both heart-warming and unsettling witnessing her like this.

"Who do you think that guy is?" Bea's voice softened momentarily as she was struck by the animation in Tilly's expression and the joy radiating from her. Gifted in reading people, Bea knew with one glance that this man Tilly was sitting with had a good, pure heart. It frightened her because she knew how this situation could go sideways. Real fast.

"That's not how our Tilly acts," Bea said to Mabel. "Having dinner with some stranger. Especially one how looks like him."

"Maybe not, but we don't know the whole story. So, let's go over and introduce ourselves and find out who he is."

The two climbed out of the bus and walked in unison toward the unsuspecting duo. As they got close, Tilly was leaning forward and talking. She didn't see them coming, but Rob did. He swiftly sat back in his seat, his body stiffening. Intuitively, he knew these were two of the elders Tilly had been telling him about. He saw the look in their eyes, especially the taller one with glasses, and it unsettled him. Tilly noticed the darkness come over his face and she turned to see what he was looking at.

Oh crap! Echoed in her head when she spotted Mabel and Bea. She had no chance to do or say anything before they were at the table and Mabel was saying, "There you are, Tilly. We've been looking for you."

Tilly sat straight up. "Ahh, ahh," was all that would come out.

Bea said nothing, but stood with her arms crossed waiting to see what Tilly had to say for herself. Finally, when it was obvious Tilly couldn't find words, Bea nodded her head toward the man sitting beside Tilly and said, "Who's this?" Her eyes narrowed behind her glasses and she stared at him like he was bad weather.

Rob had been taught to stand when introduced to a woman and shake her hand, but this woman, the taller one, frightened him. He remained in his chair. His legs were like Jell-O and he knew they wouldn't hold him.

"Tilly, why don't you introduce us to your friend?" Mabel said and glanced at Bea, giving her the "be gentle" look. Bea looked away and shook her head. Both Tilly and Rob saw this exchange and were grateful for Mabel's softness. Rob leaned on the table and stood, with his hand outstretched. "My name is Rob Sanchez. Tilly and I met on the Vortex Tour earlier today and were both hungry when we got back into town, so we came here for dinner." His words poured out faster than he would've liked, indicating how nervous and intimidated he was.

"Well, Mabel here—" Bea looked at Mabel and then back at Rob. "Mabel and me, we're Tilly's aunts and we've been looking for her. She told us she'd be back at the hotel, and when she wasn't, we were worried."

Tilly looked down at the table, feeling Bea's eyes burn into her. She cursed herself for having lied to them. Now here they were, having found her with Rob. And for the first time ever they had called themselves her aunts, indicating the traditional role and responsibilities they felt for her. She was mortified.

The intensity of Bea and Mabel standing there was more than Tilly could handle. "Well, now that you've found me, how 'bout we get back to the hotel?" Tilly said as she stood. "I'm exhausted from the day." She reached into her backpack for her wallet, pulled it out, and searched for some money.

"It's okay, Tilly," Rob said. "I'll get dinner." She knew he could feel her embarrassment. Even though they'd only spent a few hours together, their connection was powerful and Tilly was doing everything she could to try and hide it from Bea and Mabel. But it wasn't working.

"Thanks." She looked at him for a second, wishing Bea and Mabel would give them a moment alone so she could say what she really wanted to say. To thank him for an amazing day—for the ride on his bike and the exhilaration. To thank him for making her laugh, like really laugh. To thank him for listening to her. To thank him for waking something up in her, for igniting a spark that had been out for a long time. A real long time. To thank him for so very much. But that wasn't going to happen. Not with Bea and Mabel standing there.

Tilly tucked her wallet away and turned back to Rob. "It was nice to meet you. Enjoy the rest of your time here in Sedona." Tilly looked at him and her eyes softened.

As Bea and Mabel watched her, they began to understand why their Tilly was acting so strange. There was no denying the chemistry between their dear Tilly and this man.

Tilly continued, "and thanks again. For the visit and for dinner." Even though she had given him her cell number earlier in the evening and they had talked about doing something together tomorrow, nothing had been finalized. She wanted to say something about tomorrow, but she didn't dare in front of Bea and Mabel.

Rob stood. "Yeah, you too, Tilly." He turned to the elders. "It was nice to meet you both. Safe travels."

"Thank you," said Mabel. Bea gave him a forced grin.

Tilly slipped her pack on and glanced back at Rob. Their eyes lingered. She smiled at him one last time, raised her hand and gave a slight wave then turned to leave.

32

All Actions Have Reactions

THE THREE WOMEN drove back to the hotel in silence. A few times Tilly opened her mouth to explain to them what they had seen, but the truth was that she didn't know what they had seen. She didn't know how to describe the electricity and connection she felt with Rob. In fifteen years of marriage to Mick, not once, at least not until now, had she been this attracted to someone else. Sure, there were times she found someone physically attractive. She was human, after all, but this, this connection... it was different.

When they got back to the hotel, Bea joined Tilly and Mabel in their room. Mabel nodded her head toward the table. Tilly pulled out a chair, collapsed into it and waited for them to join her. The two elders stood over by the door. Tilly couldn't hear them, but out of the corner of her eyes she saw them talking. She was a jumble of emotions: guilt for her attraction to Rob; shame for lying to Mabel and Bea; delight in the fact that Rob found her attractive; fear about what the two women were going to say to her.

After what seemed like an eternity to Tilly, Mabel and Bea joined her at the table. It was Mabel who spoke first, in a tone Tilly had never heard before. A chill slid down Tilly's spine. "All actions have reactions, my girl. You know that." Mabel folded her arms across her chest. Tilly knew she'd crossed the line. "Your lie scared us and caused unnecessary stress. You said you'd be back after the tour and when you weren't, we got worried. But then after a few hours, when you still weren't back, we got scared."

Tilly nodded. The truth was hard to deny.

"Why did you lie to us?" Bea asked, anger apparent in her tone.

Tilly took a breath and began to answer, but Bea raised her hand. "No. Wait. You don't have to answer that. I already know."

Tilly sat back in her chair and crossed her arms. She felt the aunties staring at her. Watching her. She looked to the floor, avoiding their eyes.

Bea sighed heavily and leaned back hard in her chair. "One of the greatest things about getting old is that very little shocks you anymore." She turned her head to Tilly. "But this, your behavior, your disregard for us, and don't even get me started on the way you were looking at that man." Bea shook her head. "All of this has shocked me, Tilly. What's going on with you?" She looked at Tilly for a long time, but Tilly didn't have the words to answer or the courage to return the gaze. "Well, I guess that's that then," Bea said as she stood up. "I'm going to call it a night." She looked down at Tilly and, try as she might to remain angry with her, she also knew that Tilly must have something pretty serious going on for her to act like this. It was extremely out of character. Bea reached down and cradled Tilly's chin in her hand, gently lifting Tilly's face to look at her. Words were not needed; Bea's eyes stated her disappointment. After a long pause, Bea leaned down and kissed her on the forehead. "Good night, Tilly. Remember, I love you. I most certainly did not like your behavior tonight, but I do love you."

As Bea left, Mabel stood and walked to the bathroom. Tilly remained at the table. *What the hell is happening to me?* she wondered But there was no answer.

A few minutes later, Mabel emerged from the bathroom and said to Tilly, "Your turn."

Later, as Mabel and Tilly lay in their beds, awkward and unfamiliar silence swirled about them.

33

Trouble

TRY AS SHE might, Tilly could not fall asleep. Instead, her mind replayed and replayed the day. Knowing an attempt at sleep was futile, she got up, threw on her sweats and a hoody, and headed to the hotel lobby to call Bette. She would know what to do.

We all need one person we can rely on when the storm becomes too much to handle alone. Tilly's one person was her best friend, Bette.

Once she reached the hotel lobby, Tilly found a cozy chair and called Bette. She dialed their "I need to talk ring" that they'd started years ago, letting the phone ring twice, then hanging up and calling back in two minutes. Tilly kept looking at her phone, waiting impatiently for the two minutes to pass. When she called back, no one answered. She tried again. Just as she was about to hang up, Bette picked up, and before she could say anything, Tilly blurted, "Bette, it's me."

"Tilly?"

If Tilly had been paying attention, she'd have noticed the grogginess in Bette's voice, but she *wasn't* paying attention. She needed to talk. "Yeah, it's me."

"It's two in the morning. Is everything okay?"

"Oh, sorry, Bette." Tilly had no idea that she'd been lying in bed wide awake thinking about Rob, Mick, and her life for the last three hours. "But, I need to talk to you."

"I know, so just give me a sec." Tilly waited, wondering how or where to start when Bette came back on the line. "All right, Tilly, I'm settled in. What's up?"

"I'm in trouble, Bette. Big, big trouble."

"Trouble? Do you need me to send money?"

"No, not that kind of trouble. Worse." Tilly rubbed her hand along her forehead. "I've met someone." Hearing the words come out of her mouth made all of it even more real. Made it more intense and yet, more delicate.

"What?" Bette tried to keep her voice low, but Tilly was talking crazy. "Met someone?" Bette repositioned herself in the chair, hoping it would make her more awake. "Okay, Tilly, you have to start from the beginning. I've just woken up and the last time we talked you were in Las Vegas with the elders. I have no clue what you mean by *you met someone*."

The words came tumbling out of Tilly's mouth. "Now we're in Sedona, and I went on this Jeep trip to the vortexes and it was beautiful and healing and inspiring and life changing." She took a quick breath. "And there was this guy on the trip. Rob. He's kind and funny and interesting and... and handsome. Oh, Bette, he's hot! In the green eyes, dimples, wavy hair, Levis-that-fit-to-perfection kind of rugged hot."

"Oh," was all Bette could mutter.

Bette's minimal response at Tilly's pouring her heart out didn't stop her from continuing. "We ran into each other after the trip and he took me for a ride on his motorbike."

Bette's head fell into her hand and she muttered, "Oh no, not a motorbike."

Tilly didn't hear her. She just kept on rambling. "I felt free on the back of that bike with him. I felt alive for the first time in a long time." She paused, deciding if she should say this or not, but it was Bette, and she could tell Bette anything. "And his body!" She could feel the redness in her face, but couldn't stop herself from saying, "His body felt so damn good, Bette." She continued to purge, barely taking a breath between sentences. "And then we went for dinner and talked for like, forever. I felt like he was genuinely interested in me, like he really wanted to hear what I had to say. What I was thinking and feeling." That was when the emotions took over and Tilly choked on her words. "Do you know how long it's been, Bette, since I felt like someone was really interested in me? Besides you."

Bette hesitated for a moment, knowing what she was about to ask was going to be revealing. "Do you mean, how long it's been since Mick was interested in you?"

"Yes, Mick. We're going about our daily lives, raising our children, going to work, paying the bills, but it's like we've become roommates. Roommates, Bette." She stood and walked toward the window. "I don't know the last time we had a deep, meaningful conversation about anything that matters to either of us, besides Piper and Grayson...and..."

Bette could hear the exasperation in her best friend's voice.

Tilly stared out the window, the darkness of the night reflecting how she felt about her marriage. "...and sex, well, maybe that's why Rob's body felt so good cuz I don't remember the last time I had sex with my husband. It used to be that on Saturdays we'd turn on the TV for the kids and sneak into the bedroom, locking the door behind us. He called it our 'afternoon delight.' I know it's an old euphemism, but I loved how he had a name for it! Now Saturdays are full of soccer games, errands, meal preparations, and everything else mundane about married life." Tilly's eyes began to fill and she managed to squeak out, "No more sexy Saturdays," before she began to cry. The kind of crying where your eyes and nose leak, but no sound comes out.

Bette sat quietly on the other end, knowing Tilly would continue when she was ready. "And today, on the back of Rob's bike and over dinner, I felt a stirring that I'd forgotten I even had."

"*Diiiiid* anything happen?" Bea couldn't believe she was asking this of Tilly. "Did you act on that stirring?"

"No. Luckily Mabel and Bea saved me. We were just finishing our four-hour dinner when they found me."

Bette interrupted, "Four hours?"

"See, that's what I mean. We talked for four hours and it felt like twenty minutes." Tilly moved the phone down from her mouth for a moment, remembering how she felt sitting there with Rob.

"Are you going to see him again?" Bette asked.

"I don't know. Over dinner we had briefly talked about doing something tomorrow, and I gave him my cell number, but we never got to make any plans because Bea and Mabel showed up."

Tilly asked Bette what she should do if he called. She didn't know. She was supposed to take Mabel and the elders out on the land to have a ceremony and spread Mabel's sister's ashes. But she didn't tell Bette that, instead she lied. "There's nothing standing in my way." Even as she said it, they both knew there was plenty standing in her way of spending the day with Rob.

"Oh, Till. You need to think long and hard about this."

Tilly sat down and released a long, slow breath. "I know, Bette." She put her head back against the chair and closed her eyes. Fatigue consumed her. "I know."

"I've never heard you talk like this, so I know this is serious. Makes me think, though, that when you avoid the truth too long, it comes looking for you. Sounds like that's what's happening to you. No matter what you decide to do, I think Rob crossing your path is a blessing. If nothing else, hopefully it will inspire you and Mick to talk about what's going on in your marriage."

They both let the words hang in the air for a moment.

Bette continued, "Go get some sleep, my friend. It'll give you a fresh perspective."

"Thanks, Bette."

"Call me anytime. I love you, Tilly."

"Love you, too." Tilly pushed the end button and sank deeper into the chair. She needed a few minutes before heading back to the room.

34

A Precarious Situation

TILLY HAD ONLY been asleep a few hours when the buzzing of her phone woke her. Thinking it was one of her twins, she sat up and grabbed her phone off the bedside table before it woke Mabel. Tilly didn't recognize the number. She blinked a few times and rubbed her eyes. The few hours of sleep she'd managed to get after talking to Bette had left her eyes feeling gritty. She looked at her phone again and read the text message. "Good morning, Tilly, it's Rob. I'm wondering if you're up for an adventure?"

An adventure? Tilly thought to herself as she fell back on her pillow, closing her eyes. After talking with Bette last night, she'd decided not to see him again. But now, spending the day alone wasn't nearly as appealing as an adventure with Rob.

It was like her fingers were being operated by someone else's brain. She texted him back, "Yes. What'd you have in mind?" Her conscience kicked in for a moment, her finger hung over the Send button. Finally, she pushed it.

Almost immediately the little bubble indicating he was writing came up. The thought that he was there waiting to respond so quickly made her heart flutter. "If I told you what I had in mind, then it wouldn't be a full-on adventure." Although she barely knew him, she knew he'd be grinning mischievously when writing that. She could see another message was being written. "All you need is a swimsuit and sunglasses. I can pick you up, or we could meet somewhere."

Tilly knew Rob's motorbike would wake Mabel for sure. Although neither Bea nor Mabel had said anything directly, she knew full well where they stood on her seeing Rob again. She didn't want to have to explain to anyone where she was going or with whom she was going. Tilly texted Rob back: "I'll walk. Meet where we had dinner last night? Need a good coffee! Thirty minutes?"

Again, the bubble appeared almost immediately. She waited. "Awesome, look forward to seeing you!!!"

She stared for a moment at the three exclamation marks he used and pulled the covers up over her head. "What am I doing?" she mumbled softly to herself, causing Mabel to stir in the bed beside her. Tilly held her breath, hoping she hadn't woken her. She needed to get out of this hotel room before Mabel woke up.

Of course, Tilly knew she was putting herself in a precarious situation. Since sobering up twenty years ago, she'd always done the right thing. She was known for being wise, having integrity, and taking the high road in difficult situations. But today, today she was doing the unthinkable. She was spending the day with a man who made her heart flip. A man who wasn't her husband.

She got out of bed and tiptoed to the bathroom, turning the handle on the door as she closed it to ensure it made no sound. Tilly quickly got ready, slipping into jean shorts and a simple white T-shirt. After applying a tiny bit of makeup, quickly tweezing the few rogue eyebrow hairs and slipping her new necklace over her head, she glanced in the mirror. She stopped and looked harder at the woman in the mirror. She liked who was looking back at her. Her face had darkened from the sun, she looked healthy and vibrant, and her deep brown eyes stood out more than usual. The furrowed lines on her forehead had softened and she thought, *I look like me again.*

Tilly cautiously opened the bathroom door. Knowing she needed to leave a note for Mabel, she wrote, "Morning Mabel. After last night, I really need the day by myself to think. Hope you understand. Tilly."

She looked at the note. It was her handwriting, but it was *so* not like her. She felt ashamed and remorseful about not being honest with Mabel, but still, she slipped her backpack over her shoulder, took one last glance at the note and left.

Mabel watched as the door closed behind Tilly.

35

Sedona Synergy

BY THE TIME Tilly had reached the café, the morning sun and her quick pace had caused her cheeks to flush. Or perhaps it was the nervousness of seeing Rob again. She wiped the small beads of sweat from her forehead and above her lips, took a deep breath, and walked in. She scanned the café for Rob, but he and his big, bright smile were nowhere to be found. She knew he had to be there, his bike was parked out front.

The woman behind the counter asked her, "Are you here to meet a man?"

Tilly stopped cold. She was here to meet a man. It sounded *so bad* coming from the server like that.

"If you are and it's the one with hazel eyes and dimples," the woman gave her an approving smile, "he's waiting for you in the back. On our outside patio."

"Thanks." Tilly shifted her pack to the other shoulder and looked down the long hall that led outside. She could turn back now and no one would ever know.

She could walk out and go back to what was safe. Familiar.

She could go back to the hotel and spend the day with the elders, preparing to honor Mabel's sister.

She *should* go back to the hotel!

So many things she could do and should do. But what Tilly wanted to do was spend the day having an adventure.

She *needed* an adventure.

She chose to walk down the hall and out to the courtyard. It was gorgeous. Flowers were in bloom everywhere, there were water fountains in each of the four corners, and Cat Stevens' melodic voice streamed through the speakers. Her eyes seemed to know exactly where to find Rob. The sun washed over him as he sat at a table reading. She was about to take a step toward him when a dragonfly buzzed in front of her and lingered for a few moments. Grandma Tilly. Dragonflies always reminded her of Grandma Tilly, so much so that she'd come to think every time a dragonfly crossed her path it was her Grandma visiting her. Her heart lurched.

Tilly inhaled sharply. Nausea consumed her. She looked to where Rob was sitting, her thoughts a jumbled mess.

Temptation.

Danger.

Lust.

Longing.

Dragonfly.

Grandma Tilly.

Air. Need oxygen. Now. *Breathe, Tilly, breathe,* she said in her head, knowing if she didn't get some oxygen into her she was going to end up in a heap on the ground.

Rapid, shallow breathing.

Again…dragonfly. Grandma Tilly.

She turned, pushed past the server as her legs carried her back out the way she had come in. She shoved her arm through the dangling strap of her backpack and began to run.

Hard, breathless running. Running from what she'd *almost* done. Running for her marriage. Running to escape. Running from it all and running back to her room. Running and praying Mabel was still sleeping.

As she reached the hotel entrance, her chest was on fire. She leaned over and put her hands on her knees and with no ability to control it, spewed vomit onto the hotel lawn. Again and again, until her stomach was empty. Then came the dry heaves and the tears. Searing hot tears falling onto the earth.

When the heaving subsided, Tilly stumbled the last few steps to her hotel room, pulled her pack off, and rummaged for her key. The door opened. There stood Mabel, and then Bea emerged beside her. They both extended a hand, reaching for her elbows and helped her into the room.

The two aunties wrapped their arms around Tilly and held her until the tears subsided. Bea led her to a chair and then poured a large glass of cold water, adding a piece of lemon. She paused for a moment to pray over it. Praying for Tilly's strength, health, and that she would have the courage to come through this in a good way. Bea sat down and took Tilly's hand in hers. No words were needed. There would be plenty of time for that; right now, Tilly needed tenderness.

Meanwhile, Mabel ran a hot bath with Epsom salt, cedar, sweetgrass, and sage. When everything was ready, she emerged from the bathroom and softly said to Tilly, "Time for a cleansing bath, my girl."

Tilly opened her eyes and looked between Mabel and Bea, almost as if she didn't recognize them. Bea and Mabel exchanged a knowing glance. They'd both been to this place before. The place where the familiar is unfamiliar and the only emotion available to you is sorrow. The place it hurt to breathe and you feel almost void of caring. Especially for yourself.

Mabel told Tilly, "You need to sweat out some of the pain you're feeling and fill yourself back up with good medicine. Come on. We're putting you in the tub."

They pulled her to her feet and led her into the bathroom. The sage- and cedar-scented steam penetrated Tilly's nostrils and she breathed deeply, craving more. Mabel caught Tilly's eyes. "Do you need help?"

"No, I'm okay." In turn, Tilly looked at each of these women. She wanted to say so much to them. How important they were to her, how grateful she was they were in her life, how she revered them...but those words would have to be for another time. "Kinânskomitin." Thank you in Cree was all she could say.

When Tilly was alone in the bathroom, she sent a text to Rob. "Sorry not to have shown up for our adventure. Well, I did show up, but I had to leave. Too many feelings for you already, full day together and I would've really been in trouble. Thank you for reminding me of who I am."

She closed her eyes, leaned on the counter, and held the phone to her chest.

After a bit, Tilly eased herself into the tub and lay back so only her face was out of the water. She closed her eyes, allowing herself to seep into the peace that now surrounded her, almost immediately drifting off to sleep. The women knew the bath would have this effect, so they went back to preparing for today's ceremony, but checked on her every ten minutes to make sure she was safe.

After an hour of deep sleep, the kind of sleep that helps heal the soul, Tilly awoke. The water had gotten cold and goosebumps covered her. She added a little hot water to warm up before she got out.

When Tilly walked back into the room, she saw Bea and Mabel playing cards at the small hotel table. As she made her way over to her bed and sat down, the two women directed their gaze to her.

Bea asked, "How was your bath?"

"I fell asleep."

"Yeah, we know."

Tilly looked confused.

"We were checking on you to make sure you were okay."

Tilly suddenly felt self-conscious and pulled the housecoat tighter around her. Bea read her mind. "Don't worry. Nothing we ain't seen before." They all giggled and it was in that moment that the two women knew Tilly would be okay.

Maybe not right away, but they knew she would find her way back from this darkness.

36

Friendship

THAT DAY, LUCY and Anne had been shopping for about an hour when they came across an ice-cream shop and decided to indulge. As they sat under a large umbrella, relishing both the break from the sun and the cool, delicious treat, two young women walked by holding hands.

Anne looked at them from the corner of her eye, keenly aware of her mixed emotions. On one hand, envy at the freedom these young women had in expressing their love and on the other hand, her own discomfort at the display of public affection.

It was never like that for her and Liz. Times were different back then and it wasn't safe for them to be demonstrative in their feelings for each other. It was moments like this when Anne realized how far society had come. She turned her eyes away from the young women and looked to see if Lucy had noticed them.

Lucy's head was cranked as she watched them walk down the sidewalk. "Was it hard?" Lucy asked as she turned back to look at Anne.

"Was what hard?" Between her reminiscing and the Sedona sun, Anne's ice cream had begun to melt and she had to quickly lick the sides of her cone.

"You know, realizing you were gay."

Anne looked over at Lucy who shook her head once and responded, "You don't have to answer if you don't want to. I know I can be a Nosy Nellie sometimes, but I was just wondering, you know, what it was like for you."

Anne motioned her head up the sidewalk to where the young women had walked and asked, "Seeing those two holding hands make you think of that?"

"I suppose. I've wondered a few times before. They just weren't the right times to ask."

Anne finished off her cone, wiped her mouth, and settled in to share her story. "It wasn't realizing I was gay. It was *being* gay that was hard. When I moved to Toronto and had my first relationship with a woman, I thought it was because of what had happened to me in Residential school." She looked over at Lucy and their eyes met momentarily. Neither needed to say a word, the knowingness floated between them, a shared common experience. "But, eventually I learned that wasn't the case. That there was something inside me that felt more at home with women than men. And after a couple of awkward fumbles that I wouldn't even call relationships, I met Liz. And I just knew. I can't really describe it and I know it sounds corny, but I knew she was the one."

Lucy looked over at her friend and with tenderness, smiled. "Mmm, that's sweet. How long you been together?"

"Oh gracious. That was 1967." She let out a soft laugh. "Let's just say it's been a few years."

"Were people ever mean to you?"

Anne was taken off guard by Lucy's questions, but it didn't stop her from answering. "Yes, especially the first time I came home to the rez. I don't know how it happened. Still baffles me, but the moccasin telegraph went into action and it seemed like the whole community knew I was gay. I didn't even get to tell Sarah. That was part of why I'd come home, but she'd already heard. It was hard for her, it took a long time for her to understand. But, for others, well, that's another story."

A shiver ran down Anne's spine. Even though this was far in the past, the pain felt like yesterday. "There was a lot of gossip. Mean things said to me. About me. And about my family. As an Indian woman, or I guess we are called Indigenous Women now." She gave Lucy a wink.

Lucy rolled her eyes and shook her head. "Who can keep track? I still think I'm Indian. Doesn't really matter the fancy words people use, it's their tone and how they look at you that matters."

"Exactly! That's exactly what happened when I came home to the reserve. I'd experienced my share of hatred and bigotry in my life, but not from my own people. I think that's what hurt the most. Sadly, that's when

I realized I no longer felt like I belonged at home. That's when Toronto became home. I was young and didn't know how to deal with the ignorance, but over the years I've gotten better. Doesn't mean the remarks still don't sting at times." She looked over at Lucy. "Sometimes they downright hurt."

Lucy nodded, understanding on so many levels. "I'd like to meet your Liz one day."

"You should come visit us in Toronto. I'm sure we could find some trouble to get into." Anne nudged Lucy's arm with hers and both women laughed.

37

A Slight Delay

LATER THAT MORNING, when the elders met at the bus for their scheduled ten o'clock departure, Tilly was missing. It was Poncho who asked, "Where's Tilly?"

Mabel replied, "Um, Tilly's not feeling very well, so I think we should let her sleep a bit longer. Why don't we go in and have a coffee, then I'll wake her."

Poncho started in an annoyed voice, "What? This is supposed to be your day, Mabel." But Rose gently touched his arm and shook her head. "Oh, okay," he said, and they all headed back to the hotel.

As they sat sipping their coffees no one knew quite what to say. An uncomfortable silence swirled about them. Finally, Chuck spoke up, "I know she's not sick. I know that worried look you have, Mabel." He paused for a moment and put his hand on Bea's arm. "My Bea here, she keeps stirring her coffee, even though she takes it black. So...I'm just wondering, is Tilly okay?"

Bea and Mabel's eyes met across the table, neither knowing if it was their place to answer Chuck's question. Again, silence enfolded the table. The elders looked between Mabel and Bea. Finally, Bea gave a slight nod of her head.

Mabel jumped in, "No. She's not okay, but she will be. It's not really my place to say any more, but she needs our support and understanding."

"Got it," said Chuck.

"Got what?" asked Tilly. She had come up behind their table without anyone noticing.

"Tilly," the elders echoed in varying tones of surprise.

"Sorry I held you up, I was feeling homesick and needed to talk to my children." She looked at Bea and Mabel for a few seconds before adding, "And my husband."

"Everything okay on the home front, Tilly?" asked Bea. All three women knew there were many layers to the question Bea was asking.

"Yes, everything's okay. Piper has been busy with babysitting the kids next door and Grayson hit a triple in his game last night, so they're good. And Mick," Tilly looked between Bea and Mabel, "we had a good talk. Guess it's true what they say, distance makes your heart grow fonder."

"Oh, I don't know about that, Tilly," Poncho joked. "My Rose is right here," he leaned over and kissed Rose's cheek, "and my heart is still growing fonder." Rose playfully pushed him away, but her cheeks darkened and she gave him a coy smile. He winked at her and looked around the table at the elders. "Now that Tilly's here, whaddya say we get this show on the road?"

Mabel looked up at Tilly and gave her a look saying, "Shall we?"

Tilly nodded. "Yes, let's get the *show on the road* as you say, Poncho. I'll drive today, Mabel." Tilly knew this had the potential to be a difficult day for her dear friend, spreading her sister's ashes was another circle in Mabel's grief and letting go.

"That'd be great, Tilly," replied Mabel as she tossed her the bus keys.

38

Until We Meet Again

TILLY WAS GRATEFUL for Siri's help navigating them out of Sedona and toward the area where Mabel wanted to have the ceremony. The bus was pretty quiet for most of the drive, but when they drove across a cattle guard Chuck broke the silence.

"Now there's a sign I've never seen before," he said as he pointed out the window and read aloud, "Danger. Primitive road ahead. Be Careful."

Poncho chuckled. "We could use signs like that for the roads back home on the rez."

Laughter filled the bus as they started to bounce along the dirt road. "Good thing I put my over-the-shoulder-boulder-holder on today," joked Lucy. "Need extra help keepin' my girls in place."

"Lucy," groaned Rose.

"What? I'm just trying to keep the laughter going. I know we're on our way to a ceremony, but things don't always have to be all serious. Don't you know the sayin' 'laughter is the best medicine'?"

"Yes, I know that saying, but today..." Rose didn't finish because Mabel cut in.

"It's okay, Rose. I appreciate you thinking this is a special day, but Lucy's right, we need a bit of everything, especially laughter and especially on days like today." She then turned her eyes to the front of the bus and said to Tilly, "If I remember correctly, we are real close to where Millie asked me to spread her ashes. It's just up here on the left."

The elders were all watching out the windows. The landscape reminded them of home: the dry, rugged terrain, sparse trees, sagebrush, and the heat. They came around a corner and the land opened before them.

"Wowww," Sarah said, "not sure I've ever seen anything quite as pretty as that there right before us."

As far as they could see, the glowing sun lit up the red rocks and pillars that unfolded before them. Depending on how the sun hit the rocks they were shades of red, pink, and orange. Some of the hues were indescribable in the English language.

In a hushed tone, Mabel said, "This is it." She inhaled and almost as if talking to herself, continued, "This is the spot."

Tilly slowed the bus and pulled off the road.

"Wowza. I can see why your sister wanted this to be her final resting place," said Lucy. "I ain't ever seen anythin' as pretty as this."

Spread out before them was the beauty of creation. They overlooked a small valley. At one time, it might have been a creek bed, but now it was bone dry and the base for magnificent rock formations. The rocks varied from ten to over a hundred feet in height. Some of them took on the features of animals and birds, while others appeared to have faces embedded in them.

Mabel reached down and lifted her small suitcase to her lap. She clicked it open and removed her medicine bundle and the cedar box that held her sister's ashes. Mabel set her suitcase back on the floor, opened the bus door and stepped out. She stared out at the landscape and breathed in deeply. The hot, dry Sedona air filled her lungs.

Earlier in the year, she and her family had spread most of her sister's ashes by the river on their traditional territory, but just as she'd been asked, Mabel had kept some ashes for this spot. She looked at the box that held the ashes of what was her sister. "I'm doing just as you asked, Sis, bringing you to your final resting place." Mabel began walking. There was no rush today. Today was about bringing her sister back to this place that had filled her with such joy.

Everyone followed and before Mabel knew it, a line of elders plus Tilly were following her to a piece of land that jutted out over the landscape.

Bea carried her bundle while Chuck and Poncho both carried their drums and Tilly brought a few blankets to sit on, remembering Kathi's warning about scorpions and snakes. When Mabel stopped and everyone had caught up, they intuitively formed a circle.

Mabel removed the red cloth from around the cedar box, stepped into the center of the circle, laid the cloth down, and placed the box on top of it. She stepped back into the circle and Lucy placed a hand on the lower part of Mabel's back.

"Mabel's asked me if I'd lead us in ceremony today. She's described what Millie wanted and we've created a ceremony that honors those last wishes," Bea began. She explained that they'd begin with a smudge of the four sacred medicines—sage, cedar, tobacco, and sweetgrass—and say a prayer. After the prayer, Poncho and Chuck would sing an honor song, the cedar chest with the ashes would be opened and each person would have a chance to say what was in their heart, with Mabel being the last to share. "That's when Tilly's going to start singing the Women's Warrior Song. Mabel will walk out to the ledge and spread Millie's ashes. When the song is done and Mabel has come back into our circle, she'll say a prayer, and the ceremony will be over."

And that is exactly what happened.

Except.

Except for the eagles.

And the westerly breeze.

Just as Tilly began to sing, "Hey, hey, yuh he oh hoh, hoh," they arrived. Four bald eagles. They soared over the elders and the circle they had formed. The elders smiled at each other and Poncho gave Mabel the ol' Indian nod. They knew the Ancestors had come to be with them. To remind them they are never truly alone.

Mabel opened the box and as she began to spread the ashes with her hand, the gentle, westerly breeze carried Millie to her final resting place.

39

The Sayings We Use

THE NEXT DAY, Tilly got up a bit early to FaceTime with her family as she thought they'd likely be arriving in Albuquerque after the twins' bedtime. So far on the trip she'd been able to talk with them every day. Sometimes their visits lasted a while and sometimes they were quick catch-ups and I love you's, depending on everyone's schedules. The length of the visit didn't matter to Tilly, being able to see and talk to her most precious gifts was what mattered.

Later, as she was loading the elder's luggage into the bus, rain started to fall. Drizzle at first, but as they drove through Sedona it turned to a downpour. Mabel pulled over to the side of the road, put on her flashers, and looked across to Tilly.

"Tilly, do you think you could drive? You're more used to the rain than me and, well, after yesterday, I'm feeling..." Mabel's voice trailed off. The only sound was the rain hitting the metal roof of the bus. The elders in the back watched and waited. They all knew yesterday had been tough for Mabel.

Tilly reached across for Mabel's hand. "It's okay, Mabel. I should've thought of it earlier. I'm sorry."

Mabel's eyes swam in salty tears and she simply nodded. Undoing her seatbelt, she reached for the door handle.

"I'll go, Mabel. You slide over."

Tilly pulled her jacket up over her head, hopped out and ran in front of the bus to the driver side. She climbed in as quickly as possible, but still managed to get drenched. As she reached down to buckle her seatbelt, she noticed Mabel had rested her head against the door. Mabel's eyes were closed and tears slowly navigated their way down her face and fell onto her hoodie.

Tilly reached over and placed her hand on Mabel's. After a couple of seconds, Mabel squeezed Tilly's hand. Tilly knew this was Mabel's way of letting her know she was okay.

Grief has many layers and how one navigates those layers can be different on any given day, sometimes it even changes moment to moment. For now, Tilly knew Mabel needed time to be quiet and reflect.

After driving for a bit, Tilly looked up to the sky and said, "Feels like home."

Chuck watched the rain bounce as it hit the road. "Man, it sure is coming down."

"Yeah, like cats and dogs," remarked Poncho from a couple rows back.

Lucy twisted in her seat so she could see Poncho. "You know, I never really understood that saying, rainin' like cats 'n dogs. I mean really, cats, dogs, falling from the sky? That's just…" Lucy's voice trailed off and her eyes roamed up to the left as she tried to recall something. After a few seconds, she turned to Anne and asked, "What's that big word you taught me the other day? *Ludi…*"

"*Ludicrous*," replied Anne.

"That's right. Ludicrous. That's what that sayin' is." With one sharp movement Lucy nodded her head once, almost as if she was putting an exclamation mark at the end of her words.

"Sometimes the sayin's white people have just don't make sense," Sarah added.

"Yeah, like, can't get blood from a stone," said Lucy.

"Or, have a good chin-wag," said Sarah. "Ain't that what we all tryin' to avoid, saggy chins? Or any form of saggy body parts?"

Poncho jumped in. "How 'bout, have your cake and eat it too. Really, why would you have cake and not eat it?" Poncho looked over at Lucy and continued, "That's just ludicrous." He smacked his knee as he and Lucy cracked up laughing. Eventually Poncho caught his breath and continued, "The other one that always makes me laugh is, make hay while the sun shines. Makes it sound like they're the ones makin' the hay, but we all know it's the Creator that makes the hay."

"The one that makes me laugh is, up a creek without a paddle," shared Rose.

Her husband looked at her and responded, "Yeah, really. What're you doin' heading out on the creek without a paddle in the first place?"

As much as her seatbelt would allow her, Lucy bobbed up and down. "I know, I know, put the cart before the horse—that makes no sense."

From the front seat and to everyone's surprise, Mabel interjected, "Yeah, we just call that being contrary."

Silence and curiosity passed through the bus. Mabel could tell the term contrary wasn't familiar to everyone. "Contrary folks are uniquely gifted cuz they do things the opposite of how everyone else does it."

The bus quieted for a bit as the elders thought about what Mabel had said. She added, "You know in ceremony, they're the folks that go right instead of left, they start at what we might think is the end. They see things differently than the rest of us."

Chuck added, "Maybe some of *our* sayings are weird to non-Native people."

"Like what?" inquired Rose.

Chuck thought for a moment. "How about bannock butt?"

Rose quickly countered, "Better than sayin' 'Hey you, over there, the one with the flat ass.'"

The bus erupted with laughter.

"Oh, Rose," snickered Lucy. "You go girl."

Tilly giggled as she looked in the rearview mirror and said, "See, that's exactly why you're the Crazy Eights."

Once again, laughter filled the bus. Just the medicine Mabel needed.

40

Truck Stop

EVEN ON A good day, it was slow going up the winding road out of Sedona to Flagstaff. But today's rain required Tilly to concentrate on the unfolding road in a way she wasn't used to. She leaned forward in the seat and could feel her hands tighten on the wheel and her breath get shallow.

Finally, after about thirty minutes, the rain began to ease. As they rounded yet another corner, the sky seemed to open right before them and a double rainbow appeared over one of the largest red rock monoliths Tilly had ever seen. A smile came over her face and she heard Anne in the seat behind her say, "Wow, look at that. It's stunning."

"Mm," added Mabel.

Tilly looked over at Mabel, who looked back and gave a slight smile and a nod of her head. Each knew the other considered the rainbow to be a sign from Mabel's sister.

Due to the heavy rain, waterfalls cascaded over the red rock cliffs and in some cases, spilled out onto the road. Combined with the hoodoos and glorious red rocks, the drive out of Sedona was spectacular.

"How much longer till we get to Flagstaff?" asked Lucy.

Exasperation woven between each word, Rose responded to her friend, "Lucy, you sound like a child."

Tilly looked in the rearview mirror and saw Lucy give Rose a nasty stare. Tilly stepped in, "I think about another half hour. Why?"

"Cuz I gotta use the ladies room."

Again, Rose went after her friend. "You always gotta use the ladies' room."

"So, my bladder ain't what it used to be."

Sarah jumped in, "None of our bladders are. I need to use it, too."

At that point, the road seemed to flatten out and the red rocks began to be replaced with pine trees.

"Want me to try and find somewhere to pull over?" asked Tilly.

"Nah, I can hold it," Lucy said as she crossed her legs and gave her bum a little wiggle.

"Sarah?" Tilly asked.

"I think I can make it."

With the improved driving conditions Tilly was able to increase her pressure on the gas pedal. Within ten minutes, they approached a road sign indicating the first exit to Flagstaff was only a few miles ahead.

Tilly eased the bus into a parking spot and noticed this was much bigger than a regular gas station. It was a full-blown truck stop, with a large convenience gift store. For a group of elders, this was dangerous. Browsing, they called it. She knew their day of driving from Sedona to Albuquerque was ambitious, but it was the only way to get there and ensure Sarah would have a full day to rest before the Pow Wow began.

"Ten minutes, everyone. We still have a long drive ahead of us," said Tilly.

"Sure thing, Miss Tilly," Poncho said as the elders began to unload from the bus.

"It's not you I'm worried about, Poncho," she replied. He laughed, knowing exactly who Tilly was referring to.

Tilly took the opportunity to make a short video message and sent it to her twins. She considered calling Mick at work or texting him, but, in the end, decided against it and chose to check her e-mail instead.

When much longer than ten minutes had passed and not a single one of the elders had emerged, Tilly went inside. She found the elders, snacks in hand, at the till waiting to pay. She noted who was there and asked, "Where's Lucy?"

They all looked at each other and then glanced around the store. The shelves stood taller than Lucy, so there was no way they could see her.

"Why don't I go look for her while you all pay," Tilly stated. Without waiting for their response, she turned and said over her shoulder, "I'll be back in a moment."

Tilly began walking up and down each aisle, her pace quickening as she came close to covering the entire store. The washroom was the only place left where Lucy could be.

Tilly looked for the washroom sign and began walking in that direction. Almost there, she heard Lucy's unmistakable laugh. She followed the laugh around a corner and through an open door to what was much like a living room. It had a large screen television, leather couches, and a number of men. Long distance truck drivers. In one quick scan, Tilly tallied them. Five. Nestled in the middle of one of the couches and between two truckers was Lucy.

Lucy had her hands on her knees, her shoulders slightly raised and head tilted back, laughing.

Tilly stood in the doorway and waited until Lucy stopped. "There you are, Lucy. I've been looking for you."

"Tilly, come." Lucy motioned with her hand for Tilly to enter. "Come in and meet my new friends."

Tilly took a few steps into the room as Lucy introduced each of them by name and where they were headed. Tilly nodded and smiled at each of them and she couldn't help herself, she found it quite extraordinary that, in a few short minutes, Lucy had not only found this room, but had also gotten to know each of the men, their names, and where they were going.

"I'm sorry Lucy, but we need to get going."

One of the men butted in, "Already? She just got here."

Another one added, "Yeah. Don't you know a journey isn't only about reaching your destination, but what happens along the way? We're just getting to know little Lucy here." He smiled at Lucy and then looked back to Tilly, patting the empty space beside him. "Why don't you take a load off?"

There it was, another one of those peculiar sayings the elders were just talking about on the bus. "I'd really love to, sir, but—"

Before Tilly could finish, Lucy had scooted herself to the edge of the couch and was reaching to the two men beside her to help her out. When she was solid on her feet, Lucy addressed the room. "Sorry fellas, but Tilly's right, we gotta go. You all drive safe now, you hear?"

They nodded.

Lucy wove one arm through Tilly's and waved good-bye with her other. As they began to walk out, Lucy whispered, "That was fun, but can we keep it to ourselves?" She motioned her head toward the front door where the elders were standing, waiting, snacks in hand. "They still haven't let me live down getting lost in Las Vegas, last thing they need is more ammunition. Especially Rose. She's always after me for bein' too friendly, if you catch my drift." Lucy winked at Tilly and the smile that already beamed across her face grew.

Tilly slowly nodded her head and smiled at this tiny elder walking beside her. "Sure thing, Lucy." She reached over with her free hand and gave Lucy's arm a squeeze. "Your secret's safe with me."

41

Standin' on the Corner

EXCEPT FOR PULLING out to pass semi-trailers, Tilly's hand barely moved on the wheel. The flat, straight, open road enveloped the bus mile by mile. The clouds dotted the sky causing shadows to dance across the land. Tilly thought to herself how the landscape unfolding before them reminded her of a mixture of the sagebrush desert of Kamloops and the flat lands of Saskatchewan.

From the middle of the bus, Poncho piped up and asked, "Hey, Miss Tilly, you know how flat it is out there?"

Tilly was now used to playing along with him. She looked in the rear-view mirror to catch his eye with a smile and responded, "No, Poncho. How flat is it out there?"

"It's so flat that you can see your dog run away for three days." His eyes squeezed shut as his mouth fell open and he heaved with laughter. Tilly giggled and turned her gaze a bit to the right, to where Rose sat beside her husband. Her eyes rolled and she tilted her head back.

After the laughter subsided, Tilly and the Crazy Eights rode in silence for the next forty minutes. They passed a sign that indicated the next city was Winslow. Chuck, who was now sitting up front with Tilly asked, "Hey Tilly, you think we can stop there?"

"Where?"

"Winslow."

"Aw, Chuck. We just got back on the road." Tilly was beginning to feel like this was going to be a very long day of driving.

Lucy, who was in the seat behind Tilly, had overhead the conversation and butted in. "Why Mr. Chucky, you need to use the li'l boys' room?" She giggled.

He looked back at Lucy and shook his head. "No. No. That's not it at all." He was quiet for a moment.

Tilly looked sideways at him.

Chuck met her eyes and started sharing. "When I was first sobering up, I used to listen to The Eagles song, 'Take It Easy.'" He raised his right shoulder a bit and said, "Guess you could sorta say it was my theme song. I needed to hear the messages in that song about lightening up, not trying to understand everything and taking it easy." He looked over at Tilly, who had turned her gaze back to the road unfolding before them and then back at Lucy who was watching him. He asked them, "Do you know the song?"

Tilly nodded and Lucy responded, "'Course I do. Might be old, but I ain't ancient."

Chuck couldn't help himself, this woman always made him smile. "Then you know the line about standin' on the corner in Winslow, Arizona?"

Before either woman had a chance to respond, Chuck continued, "Here, let me play it for you." He plugged his iPhone into the bus stereo system and scrolled his thumb down his screen until he found what he was looking for.

Lucy turned to everyone, "Hey, Crazy Eights. Listen up. Chucky's gonna play us a song."

No one recognized the song until the drums kicked in, then the bus filled with a hum of recognition. Just after the lines, "Well, I'm standing on a corner in Winslow, Arizona," Chuck hit the pause button and turned to address the elders. "The next town is Winslow and I'd like to drive through."

Mabel called out from the back, "I was there with my Millie. There's actually a park called 'Standin' on the Corner Park.'"

Chuck cranked his body a bit farther so he could see Mabel. "Really?"

Mabel nodded, but added, "It's not a park like we think of a park. No trees or grass, or anything green for that matter. After all, this is Arizona, but the flatbed Ford is there."

Chuck turned his head slightly toward the driver's seat. "So what do you think, Tilly?"

Tilly inhaled deeply and let it out in a big puff of her cheeks.

Seeing her reaction, Chuck sat back in his seat. "It's okay. We don't need to stop."

She looked over at Chuck. This man had not asked for a single thing on this trip, and besides, this trip wasn't about her, it was about the elders.

Tilly smiled at him. "Sorry, Chuck. Sometimes I get caught up in the clock and forget to," she removed her hands from the wheel long enough to use her fingers like quotations in the air, "take it easy."

Chuck found this quite humorous and let out a loud belly laugh. "I still haven't mastered that one either, Tilly."

Just as Chuck said this, he added, "There it is, Exit 252. We need that one, Tilly." He pushed the play button and The Eagles song filled the bus again.

Winslow beckoned them and they responded. Tilly slowed to twenty-five miles an hour as they drove through the heart of Winslow. One-story, white-and-gray houses adorned the sides of the roads. Not a single soul was walking on the sidewalks and the front yards were vacant of any life.

"What day is it today?" asked Lucy.

"Tuesday, why?" asked Tilly.

"Cuz there's not hardly anyone on the streets, thought maybe it was Sunday."

Chuck leaned forward in his seat and pointed. "There. That must be it up there. In the center of the four way is the Highway 66 sign. The store on the left says Standin' on the Corner."

As they came to the stop sign, Lucy saw the red truck parked on the corner. Pointing and with a slightly raised voice she said, "Look! Look! Over there. It's the flatbed Ford."

"Wow. Who would've ever thunk there really was a flatbed Ford?" said Poncho, not to anyone in particular.

"Who's that guy?" Chuck asked referring to the statue of a man holding a guitar standing on the tip of his boot.

"That must be him, the guy from the song, the one who's standin' on the corner," Lucy said.

"Well I'll be…" Chuck's voice trailed off.

Tilly pushed gingerly on the gas pedal, turned left, and parked in front of the store. It took no time for the elders to get off the bus and cross the street to the truck. Before any time had passed the elders were taking photos of each other in front of the truck and beside the statue.

Tilly overhead Poncho say, "Annie, will you take a photo of me and Rose?"

"Anne, you mean Anne," her tone bordered on being harsh. "Only my family calls me Annie."

Poncho's head snapped back and his brows furrowed. After a moment, he softly said, "But, we are family. After all that time stuffed on the bus, we're family. Family isn't only about blood. It's about who you love and who loves you. I've come to love you like a sister, so I'd like to call you Annie," he paused, "if that's okay with you?"

Anne could feel the shame slide up her neck and across her face, leaving a trail of red. Why'd she react to Poncho like that? She wished she was used to such displays of love and kindness, but she wasn't. Not publicly anyways. She looked at him standing there beside his wife with his lopsided grin. She had never met a man with a bigger heart than Poncho Billy. Uncharacteristically, Anne's eyes fill with tears. "I'd like it if you called me Annie." She glanced around at all of them. It was true, they had become like family. "I'd like it if you all called me Annie."

"Alrighty then, it's settled. We shall all call you Annie. Now let's get back to the business of taking a photo of me n' my Rose."

After a couple of photos, Poncho waved Lucy into their photo and then humbly stepped out so his wife and her best friend could have their photo taken. Mabel stood next to the male statue and said through a smile, "Now I wouldn't mind myself one of these!"

Laughter erupted.

Next up were Bea and Chuck. They wrapped their arms around each other and she leaned into him, whispering in his ear, "So glad you asked to stop."

"Me too, my love." He leaned down and kissed her temple. The camera clicked, and that moment was caught forever.

Tilly sat in the bus watching them. She found their excitement amusing, not in a judgmental way, but rather in a deeply endearing way. It pleased her to watch them find such joy in this unplanned stop. She stepped out of the bus and crossed the street, saying, "Here. Let me get a photo of all of you."

The elders formed a line between the truck and the statue. There was no need for her to say smile. Their faces were already reflecting their happiness.

42

The Invitation

THE HUM OF the bus halted as Tilly turned off the ignition. It had been a long day of driving and they'd finally arrived in Albuquerque just before dinner. As Chuck stood, he banged his head on the roof of the bus. "Ouch." He rubbed his head and began to speak. "Can I have everyone's attention for a minute?"

The elders seemed oblivious to him as they packed up their belongings, eager to get off the bus.

"Hellooooo?" said Chuck, a bit louder this time. Only Lucy noticed.

She put her thumb and middle finger in her mouth and blew hard. The shrill sound silenced everyone.

Chuck turned to Lucy. "Thanks." Lucy gave a nod of her head and Chuck turned back to the elders. "Now, I know you're all used to Mabel being the one in charge, and I'm not saying I'm in charge or anything like that. But it's like a flock of geese. Sometimes, one has to fall back and let the others carry them along. And so that's what I'm doing, and what we've all been doing today. Letting one of our own fall to the back and rest."

By the way he was rambling and using metaphors out of context, Bea knew Chuck was nervous. She reached over and took his hand and pulled him close. "Just tell them about tonight."

"Right." Chuck faced the elders again. "So, I talked to Mabel about this back at the gas station and she thought it was a good idea. I'd like to offer Bea's and my room for a talking circle tonight."

The elders looked at each other, quizzical.

"Talkin' circle?" asked Rose. "For what?"

"Yeah, what we need a talkin' circle for?" Lucy probed.

Chuck looked to Bea for moral support and then to Mabel. Both women gave him a slight nod of their head.

"I feel like it would just be good to have an opportunity to talk. You know, a lot has happened on this trip."

"Yeah, like you and Bea fallin' in love again Mr. Chucky," Lucy teased.

"Well," his face darkened, "yes, Lucy, that is one of the things, but there have been others and the next few days at the Pow Wow could be emotional. In a good way, but still emotional." He glanced at Bea, seeking moral support.

This time, a slight nod of her head and a wink.

"One of the things I learned from Bea a long time ago is to trust my Indianition. So that's what I'm doing."

Lucy's head snapped back and she scrunched up her face, "*Indianition*?"

Bea explained, "It's a play on words, Lucy. You know cuz we're Indians and we have intuition, so I call it Indianition."

"Ohhhh, now I get it." Lucy let out a couple giggles. "That's a good one, Bea."

Tilly who'd been quietly observing all this unfold, smiled to herself. She remembered with fondness the first time Bea had told her about Indianition. About not listening to all the voices around us, but trusting the voice within and letting it guide us and our decisions.

Rose declared, "I ain't goin' to no touchy feely healin' circle!"

Lucy turned in her seat and snarled, "Rose."

"What? I didn't come on this trip to be part of no Indian healin' circle thingamajig."

Chuck and Mabel looked at each other for a moment and then Mabel spoke, "That's fine, Rose. You don't have to come tonight. Actually, you don't have to do anything you don't want to on this trip. But you do need to be respectful. For some of us," she lifted her fingers up near her head and imitated quotation marks as she said, "the Indian healin' circle thingamajig is important and so, just as we respect you not wanting to come, I ask you to respect those of us who find the circle helpful."

Rose folded her arms in front of her chest, blinked her eyes slowly and deliberately as she continued to look at Mabel. The temperature in the bus was on the rise. Partly because the air conditioning was no longer running and partly because of the conversation.

Chuck spoke first. "Why don't we go and check in. Let's say we'll meet in the lobby at seven tonight. Give everyone time to get a bite to eat first." Chuck looked at Rose, who was now looking out the window. "Everyone's welcome. No pressure though. Everyone's got to do what's right for them."

43

Legacies

AS THEY SETTLED into their respective rooms, each of the elders contemplated Chuck's invitation. While Rose's delivery might not have been the most graceful, she had had the courage to speak what others weren't quite ready to share.

For Anne, the thought of sitting in a talking circle caused her to feel anxious. It wasn't the sharing her feelings part, but rather that she might not know what to do.

Or when to do it.

Or how to do it.

When she left the reserve almost five decades earlier, healing circles, talking circles, and ceremonies weren't happening. At least not in her family. Instead, internalized racism, alcoholism, abuse, and violence were happening. A lot. And because of that and all she had experienced at Residential school, Annie had never engaged with the Aboriginal community in Toronto and, honestly, had never connected with her culture. As a result, she'd never been in a traditional healing or talking circle.

Sarah, too, had never been in a healing circle. Sure, she smudged at home, but that was private. After all, she was a private person. Or at least that's what she told herself.

That evening, as she unpacked, she asked Annie, "So what d'ya think, Annie? You gonna go tonight?"

Annie, who now was sitting in the lounge chair, had her feet up on the ottoman and her book *Monkey Beach* in hand. She looked across the room, made eye contact with Sarah, and then looked away, lifting her book to read. "It isn't really something I'm comfortable with."

After a few moments, Annie removed her glasses and placed them atop her head. "How about you, Sarah? Are you going to go?"

Sarah moved across the room and tucked her nighty under the hotel pillow. "Naw. It's not really my thing." The sisters looked at each other and then Annie turned back to her book and Sarah continued unpacking. When she finished zipping up her suitcase, Sarah walked over to where her sister was reading, sat in the chair opposite, and then lifted each foot onto the ottoman. She had to push Annie's feet over, which produced a furrowed brow stare.

"What? You don't need the whole foot stool."

"It's not a foot stool, it's an ottoman." As soon as the words escaped Annie's mouth she wanted to take them back. But, to her surprise, Sarah simply moved her upper body from side to side as she mocked Annie and repeated sarcastically, "It's an *ottoman*."

Annie couldn't contain herself. She started to laugh. Sarah began to laugh, too. When Annie caught her breath she said, "That's not really what I sound like." Sarah looked across at her sister, tilted her chin downwards and lifted her eyebrows. Both women sank a bit deeper into their chairs. The relaxation was welcome tonight.

With her eyes closed, Sarah quietly said, "I've been thinkin' Annie, an' I'm gonna go tonight."

"Really?"

"Yeah, really."

"I'm going to join you then." Annie sat up a bit in her chair, removed the book from her lap and set it on the table.

"Why?" asked Sarah, eyes still closed.

Annie didn't really know why.

Sarah kept speaking, "You don't have to, you know. I can take care of me and you can take care of you. 'Member, we already had this talk."

Annie swallowed. The tulips. That conversation. Residential school secrets. Unable to protect and keep safe. She swallowed again. Her mouth dry. Heart thumping. She closed her eyes and rested her head against the back of the chair.

"You okay, Annie?"

No response.

Sarah reached across and placed her hand on her sister's arm. "Annie, you okay?"

With effort, Annie moved her head up and down.

"I didn't mean to upset you," Sarah said. "I won't go. I'm tired anyway. We can stay in an' play cards."

"No." Annie inhaled. "No. I think I want to go."

"You think?"

Annie nodded and then began to share. "I'm embarrassed to tell you this, Sarah, but I've never been in a talking circle." She proceeded to tell her that she didn't know what to do and was afraid to make a mistake. Or worse, be judged by the other elders for not knowing what to do. "When I moved away to Toronto, these things, these ceremonies weren't happening. Everyone was too busy trying *not* to be Indian."

Sarah grinned at her sister and started laughing.

"Really, Sarah? I open up and share with you and this is what you do? You laugh in my face? No wonder I went away all those years ago and never came back."

"No! No wait, Annie, let me explain." Annie shrugged Sarah's hand off her arm.

"I'm laughing cuz I ain't ever been in no talkin' circle either."

44

The Circle

IT WAS 6:55 P.M. when Poncho entered the lobby where everyone had already gathered.

Chuck took a step to greet him and asked, "Rose?"

Poncho shook his head once and cast his eyes downwards. Chuck reached up and placed his hand on his friend's shoulder and gave a squeeze.

Bea led everyone back to their room where nine chairs formed a tight circle in the cramped space of the hotel room. In the middle, on the hotel coffee table, Mabel had created an altar. She'd placed an eagle feather, a smudge bowl, a blade of sweetgrass, a bowl of water, and a pouch of tobacco. There was also a plate of food with a tea bag and pinch of tobacco on it. The window and front door were wide open, and the air conditioning was on. They needed to ensure adequate airflow so that the smoke from the smudge didn't set off the fire alarm. When everyone had taken a seat, Chuck reached over to remove the empty chair.

Poncho asked, "Can we leave it?"

Chuck turned to Poncho, who kept talking. "My Momma always said there was room at the table for one more. Maybe tonight we could follow that 'n leave the chair in the circle." He paused and took a breath. "For my Rose."

"Sure, Poncho," Chuck replied, smiling at his friend before turning to address the group. "Thank you, everyone, for coming this evening, I thought it would be good to go over a few of the protocols of being in circle. Even though we are all elders, doesn't mean we all know our culture or ceremonies. Thanks to..." Chuck took a breath and was about to go on about Residential schools, the Indian act, and so much more, but Bea placed a hand on his knee and gave a slight shake of her head.

"Not the time or place?"

Bea shook her head again.

Chuck looked around the circle and continued, "Bea, Mabel, and I talked earlier and would like to suggest we smudge first, then we'll send the feather around to the left. Follow your heart. When you have the feather, you can share whatever you want or you can choose to pass. Remember that whoever has the feather is the only person to talk at that time." He paused for a moment, giving time for everyone to consider what he had said.

"So, what do you think?"

Nods up and down.

Bea stood, and the others followed her lead. She lit the blade of sweetgrass and turned to the person on her left, Tilly. Bea fanned the sweetgrass with the eagle feather and when the smoke was wafting, she held it out for Tilly to smudge herself. After Tilly was finished, Bea made her way around the circle. When she reached Annie, the last in the circle, Bea held the blade of sweetgrass and feather for her to take. Annie's hands remained by her side as she looked at Bea, unsure of what to do.

Bea softly looked at Annie. "It's okay. Just do as I did for you."

Annie reached up and took the braid of sweetgrass and eagle feather into her hands. She fanned the sweetgrass and held it out for Bea to smudge herself.

"All my relations," Bea said, indicating to Annie that the smudging was complete; however, Annie continued to look at Bea, uncertain of what to do next.

"Place the sweetgrass in the bowl and the feather facing upwards. It will continue to act as a messenger between us and the Ancestors. When the circle is over, we will turn the feather over and place it back in the feather holder."

Annie followed Bea's guidance and then stepped back into the circle. Mabel reached for the hands of those who stood beside her. "Left hand facing up, extending back to the wisdom, teachings, and guidance from our Ancestors. Right hand facing down, passing forward the wisdom of our Ancestors and the wisdom we've gained during our life."

Nervous giggles erupted from Lucy and Sarah as they attempted to sort out their hands. As serenity descended on the group, Mabel offered a prayer.

At one point in her prayer, Mabel shared, "We offer thanksgiving to the Ancestors to the left of us, the Ancestors to the right of us, the Ancestors behind us and those in front of us. Thank you for blanketing us with your love, guidance, and protection. To you, our Ancestors, who gave up so much so that we can stand here as we do today, we humbly offer thanksgiving."

Tilly had heard Mabel pray many, many times, but she'd never heard her speak of Ancestors being all around or for blanketing with love, guidance, and protection. She felt it. Their presence. Their warmth. Their love. Their adoration. Their support. Not only Grandma Tilly, but the presence of others as well. And in that moment Tilly realized she wasn't alone. She was never alone.

It was one thing to understand it in her mind. But in her heart, being able to feel the love woven into the blanket wrapped around her and knowing she was never alone caused tears of gratitude to flow down Tilly's cheeks.

Mabel stood and retrieved her drum from its bag. Out of habit, she ran her hand around the front of it, but in this New Mexico heat it didn't need to be warmed. She started with the beat of the Women's Warrior song, the same song Tilly had sung just the day before overlooking the red rocks of Sedona. This time all the women sang.

"Hey, hey, hey
Yuhi oh oh ho
Yuhi oh oh ho
Hey, hey, yuhi oh…"

45

One Less Thorn

LATER THAT EVENING, after the talking circle had ended, Tilly was sitting on her hotel balcony enjoying the warmth of the New Mexico evening when she heard music playing below. Putting down her journal she stood to see where the music was coming from. To her surprise, she saw Poncho and Rose dancing on the garden terrace, moving together like one. Not a single misstep. Almost as if Rose could anticipate Poncho's every move.

The next morning, Tilly was out on the hotel patio enjoying her morning coffee when Rose meandered out. Tilly invited Rose to join her and decided to tell Rose about seeing her and Poncho dancing the night before. "It was so beautiful to see the way the two of you moved together. Like one."

"Well, that's what happens when you been dancin' together as long as we have," Rose said. She was sensitive to growing old, never sharing any personal information that might reveal her age.

"How've you made it work, Rose? You know, dancing together for so many years?"

"Oh, the dancin'." She stared at Tilly for a few moments. "That's the easy part."

Under the intimidating glare of Rose, Tilly squirmed.

"I think I know what you're asking, Tilly," Rose said. "It's about how we make it as a couple. Right?"

"Yeah, I guess." Tilly was unaware that she was turning her wedding band around and around.

"You guess? Well, you need to get clear if that's what you're askin' me, because if it is then you need to be ready for what I have to say." Rose looked at her over her glasses. "You might not like what I have to say."

Tilly hesitated and then moved her head up and down in slow motion. "That's what I'm asking, Rose."

Rose's gaze turned down to the cup she held between her palms. "First thing you need to know is that it ain't always easy. And it ain't always hard." Rose looked up to see if Tilly was listening. "And sometimes it's downright boring."

"How do you make it work though? You know, when it's hard?" Tilly lifted her eyebrows and continued. "Or when it's boring?"

"I know this is gonna sound, what's that word?" Rose squinted her eyes and looked up to the left, searching her mind for the word. "*Cliché*. That's it." She looked at Tilly. "Bet you're surprised a crusty old lady like me knows that word."

Tilly shook her head. "No." If Tilly had learned anything on this trip so far it was to never underestimate anyone. Especially not an elder!

Rose continued, "Anyway, you have to take it one day at a time. Sometimes one hour at a time. I'm sure if you were to ask my husband he'd even say that to live with me you have to sometimes take it one minute at a time." Both women giggled. The comfort that surrounded their conversation increased. "Poncho 'n me, we've had our share of hard times, Tilly. Hard years, actually. But for some reason that no one seems to understand—not even me—he loves me."

Tilly was surprised by the depth of Rose's honesty and vulnerability. She waited as Rose considered what to say next.

"Quite a few years ago, we separated for a while. Well, we didn't officially separate, but he asked me to move outta our bedroom. That was more hurtful than if he'd kicked me out. And not for the reason you might think, Tilly. Yes, it was the place where we had our special relations."

"Special relations?" Tilly looked at Rose for a moment. The sides of Rose's mouth turned upwards, her cheeks flushed.

"Oh. Got it." Tilly looked down at the table. "Sorry."

"It's fine." A bit curt, but she carried on, "It was hard to move out of the bedroom cuz that's where we did our best talkin'. What do you young people call it?"

Tilly shook her head. She had no idea what Rose was referring to.

"I think my daughter calls it 'pillow talk'. Anyway, we could talk about anythin' lyin' there facin' each other, holdin' hands. So, when he asked me to move out of our room, I knew how much I'd hurt him."

"Can I ask what you did that hurt him?" Tilly knew she was taking a huge risk asking this, especially of Rose.

"You can ask, but doesn't mean I'm gonna tell you."

Ouch. Both women sat in the residue of Rose's snarky remark.

"Sorry, Tilly." Rose was mad at herself for her response. When was she going to learn? "Lucy's always telling me I need to be kinder," she said and looked at Tilly. "I'm trying."

"It's okay, Rose."

Rose looked straight ahead, avoiding Tilly's gaze and proceeded to tell her that she'd had a relationship outside of her marriage. "I never felt like I deserved to be loved, not the way Poncho loved me. So, I hurt him. I hurt him in ways that almost ruined him. And me. And, us. Somehow, though, over time he found it in his heart to forgive me."

Rose proceeded to share with Tilly that Poncho had asked her to go to a healing program. He thought it would be helpful if she began to deal with the negative messages and hurt that happened at Residential school. At first, she had refused, but eventually she gave in. "I hated it there, I made the staff's job *real* hard."

Tilly could only imagine.

"I learned, though, that I didn't know how to love. I thought I did, but I didn't. How could I? I went to that school when I was four and never came home till I was twelve. Not once. Not even for holidays. And the things that were done to me when I was there," Rose's voice trailed off. She sat quiet and motionless for a bit. "Only person who really knows what happened there is Lucy. And since we're bein' truthful, I don't even know why she's still my friend. I'm not as good a friend to her as she is to me." Rose paused for a moment. "But you see, Tilly, that's what happens when you been hurt real bad and you don't know what to do with all the hate in your heart. You have to share it somehow cuz it's just too much to carry. So me, I share it by bein' mean. I've been nasty to pretty much everyone." Rose took a sip of her coffee, swallowed hard, and added, "Even my kids, Tilly. Thank goodness they had Poncho to balance things out, but you know where it changed?"

Tilly shook her head from side to side.

"With my grandbabies." Rose couldn't help herself, the thought of those precious little ones and even the teenagers and their moodiness made her smile. "Those grandbabies they changed my life." Rose cleared her throat. "They're teachin' me how to love."

Tilly's eyes stung as they filled with tears. No matter how many times she listened to former students share their stories, it was always the same. Heart-wrenching.

"I know it all sounds corny. Especially coming from me." Rose raised her eyebrows while looking at Tilly. "I know people think I'm a bitch, but I've softened over the years."

Tilly couldn't help herself, a smile crossed her face.

Rose playfully swatted at her arm and Tilly coiled back.

"Really, I have."

Tilly half smiled at her. "Mm-hmm."

They sat finishing their coffees. Rose wondered if she dared continue. Things had just gotten to a sweet place with Tilly, why go wreckin' it? But it wasn't in Rose's nature to not say what needed to be said.

"I'm gonna give it to you straight, Tilly."

Tilly thought, *Oh no, here it comes. The wrath of Rose.*

Rose twisted in her chair so she faced Tilly. "I hurt Poncho real bad and almost lost the most loving and kind man that the world knows. God knows I don't deserve a man like him." She lifted her forefinger, leaned forward, and pointed at Tilly. "But listen to me when I tell you, don't do what I did. It took years for Poncho to trust me again. And even longer for me to trust myself." Rose sat back in her chair, crossed her legs, and swung the top one back and forth. The truth of what had just been said danced in and around the two women.

Eventually, Rose looked at Tilly and shook her head slowly. "Some days, I still don't think I've forgiven myself for hurting him like I did." Rose inhaled deeply, as if seeking solace in the ancient Albuquerque air.

Tilly crossed her arms, thinking of Mick and how judgmental he was about people who had extramarital affairs. He most certainly would not approve of the time she had spent with Rob, especially if he knew the feelings she had for him.

Rose looked down and motioned her head to Tilly's hand. "I see you playin' with your weddin' band and how you been mopin' about. Don't make the same mistake I did, Tilly. Not all men will invite you back to the pillow. Not all men are like my Poncho."

As if Rose read Tilly's mind, she added, "I've learned that just because you do a bad thing, doesn't necessarily make you a bad person. But I don't want you carryin' the same burden, so," she paused and waited for Tilly to look at her. "Be. Careful."

46

Arrival

IT WAS ALMOST ten o'clock on Friday morning when the bus pulled up to the drop-off zone at the Gathering of Nations Pow Wow. This was Tilly's second trip of the day to the arena where the University of New Mexico Lobos played basketball, now transformed for the Pow Wow. She had come earlier to pick up the wristbands for everyone and so she would know where drop off was for elders and dancers.

Tilly put the bus in park, leaned her head back against the seat, and released her stress with an exhalation that came from the bottom of her toes. "Whew, we made it! Sarah, we need to get you in there as registration for dancers starts in five minutes."

Silence.

Not the kind of silence that could be filled with words, but rather, a silence that penetrates one's soul. That was the kind of silence that wove through the bus that morning.

Tilly turned to Mabel in the copilot seat, but she was looking out her window. Still, no talking and no one was making a move to exit. Tilly swivelled around in her seat so she could see the elders. Each of them was looking out the window toward the arena, mesmerized. With her hand, Tilly shaded her eyes from the glowing New Mexico sun and looked out at their view.

Hundreds and hundreds of people were milling about. Most were visibly Native, including tiny infants in strollers, elders walking with the aid of canes, youth, and every life stage in between. Some carried blankets, some carried food, some had humungous cups filled with soda pop, and some had Starbucks cups. Others carried suitcases with their regalia safely tucked inside. Some held the hand of the person they were with, and some were there looking for someone to hold hands with. In the shade of the arena, some were in their regalia and practicing dance steps.

There was no question about it: there was a powerful vibration coming from the arena and it wasn't just the drumbeat. It was like something was alive in there.

Inviting them to come in.

Inviting them to be transformed.

Tilly had been to many Pow Wows over the years, but she'd never witnessed anything like this. This many people. She looked back to the elders. Each of them remained transfixed at the scene unfolding outside the safety of their bus. Tilly couldn't help but wonder what it was like for each of them to look out the window and see nothing but their own people. She wondered how it might feel as an elder to see their people openly celebrating what they'd had to hide for years. What had been illegal for years. And she wondered what it was like for them to see so many people proud of being Native. Tilly could feel the reverence spreading through the bus and noticed Lucy's eyes brimming with tears. She continued to watch the elders. There was no measurement of time for this moment. It was a culmination of the past, the present, and a future of possibility.

In a hushed tone, Poncho's few words described the sentiment on the bus. "Well I'll be…." He removed his cowboy hat and placed it on his knee.

The elders continued to stare out the window. After a few moments, Poncho turned and looked at Tilly. She raised her eyebrows and gave him half a smile.

With pauses between her words, Lucy said, "Look…at all…the Indians." Her tone was somewhere between a whisper and her regular voice.

Sarah's chest constricted and she was about to turn to Annie and say, "I don't know if I can do this." But then, she saw *her*.

The young woman who first visited after the Stitch 'n Bitch meeting where she had shared her dream, the dream that was unfolding right in front of her.

Then when they were in Seligman. She guided Sarah to the Pendleton blanket that Sarah was now using as part of her regalia. And then, a couple nights ago, when they were in Sedona, she had appeared again. Now, the young woman was standing a few feet away from the bus. She motioned with her arm for Sarah to come out and join her. "It's going to be okay, trust me." The smile on her face and the warmth that exuded from her was enough to create a surge of confidence in Sarah. She hoisted herself up and looked down at her sister sitting beside her.

"'Scuse me, Annie, but I got a Grand Entry to get ready for." Sarah still had to register to dance and get ready. There was no time for lollygagging. Or for fear.

Annie's head slowly turned upwards. It was Sarah, but it wasn't. Or at least not the Sarah she was used to. This Sarah stood taller. Her slightly stooped shoulders now straight back, her eyes were aglow and there was something else. Something indescribable. Something that Annie couldn't put her finger on.

Annie stood and stepped back and watched as Sarah walked the short aisle of the bus to where Tilly had opened the door. There, Sarah stopped, turned, and addressed everyone, "This is what we came on this trip for. Or at least what I came for." She turned her gaze out the door and scanned the spectacular scene unfolding before her. Sarah turned to the elders once again and added, "So you can either sit there an' watch or you can come in an' watch me dance. Either way, I'm goin' in now. Tilly, can you please help me get my regalia from the back?" And with that, Sarah exited the bus.

Tilly hopped out and met Sarah at the back of the bus. She unloaded the suitcase and as she hugged Sarah, Tilly whispered in her ear, "I can hardly wait to see you dance."

"I can hardly wait to dance," Sarah responded. She pulled away and Tilly reached down to hand Sarah her suitcase full of regalia. "Thanks, Tilly." The women's eyes held for a moment. "Been waiting all my life for this, so I best be gettin' myself on in there."

Annie reached for her purse and followed her sister's lead down the aisle and out the door. She hustled to catch up to Sarah. Tilly watched them disappear into the sea of people.

Back on the bus, the elders hesitated. Although they all wanted to join in—this is what they'd come for—fear had them stuck to their seats. Fear of not knowing what to do when they got in there. Fear of being judged for not knowing what to do, not knowing each and every protocol. Fear of so many people in one place. Fear of not doing something right. Fear of the unknown. Fear of being arrested, even though that was not logical. They were of a time when ceremonies such as the Pow Wow were illegal, and participation came with a fine and jail time. Fear was swirling around every cell, in every body, of every elder sitting on that bus.

Even though their logical minds were telling them their fears were unwarranted, their lived experiences told them differently.

Eventually, Mabel opened the door. As she stood, she spoke over the top of her seat, "I'm going in to support Sarah. I know what y'all are thinking and feeling. I'm scared, too, but she needs us. I didn't come all this way to sit in the bus when she dances. Grand Entry ain't for two hours. We've got plenty of time to get comfortable in there. So…get over yourselves. Get your stuff," she swung her arm through the air and pointed to the door, "and get a move on." Such directness, some might even consider such harshness, was unusual for Mabel, but it worked. It was what everyone needed.

A reminder that they were all there to support Sarah in her dream of dancing at the Gathering of Nations Pow Wow.

After all, it was Sarah who got the whole trip started.

Poncho stood first, put his cowboy hat on, and beckoned Rose with his fingers to indicate "Come on." She reached up and he helped her out of the seat.

Lucy stood, pulled her shirt down and ran her hands over the front of herself, flattening a few wrinkles. She leaned down a bit so she could see out the window. Her eyes began to fill with tears. Her legs felt wobbly and she sat back down. Seeing so many people who looked like her, who had the same skin color as her, who had short, curly gray hair like her, and many who even dressed like her was like nothing she'd experienced before. Lucy tested her legs again; this time they felt a bit stronger. Taking a deep breath and letting it go with a puff of her round cheeks, she said, "'Kay, let's do this."

47

It's Pow Wow Time

BY THE TIME Tilly had parked the bus and rejoined the elders, Mabel was leading the group toward the entrance. Rose had woven her hand through Poncho's arm. It was then Tilly heard Chuck say to Bea, "Why don't you tuck your hand here into mine. Make sure I don't get lost in there." She watched as Bea reached down and laced her fingers through Chuck's and how he lifted her hand to his lips and placed a kiss on it.

Tilly took a couple steps toward Lucy and held out her hand. Lucy's eyes swam with tears and she placed her trembling hand into Tilly's. Tilly took Lucy's hand and tucked it under her arm tightly and smiled at Lucy, "It's okay."

"I know. I don't know why I'm being such a crybaby." She wiped her eyes with her free hand. Mabel came over and stood with them.

"We can all feel it, Lucy. The Ancestors. They're calling us in there with every beat of the drum. I feel it."

"Me too," whispered Lucy.

"What say we go in there?"

Lucy nodded as a tear meandered down her cheek.

Together, they all turned and walked into the Pow Wow.

It was a blessing they had to be there early for Sarah to register, as it provided them an opportunity to gently transition into the enormity of what was to unfold. When they entered the arena, which would soon be filled with twenty thousand people, they were surprised by how many of the seats were already reserved with blankets and pillows. It took them a few minutes to find an area that had enough vacant seats for all of them and didn't require them to go up and down too many stairs.

Once they had laid out their blankets and settled in for the day, Poncho turned to them, beaming and, as if he was the announcer, bellowed, "*It's Pow Wow time!*" He stood, lowered his voice a few notches, "And what that really means is, it's fry bread time! Who wants a piece? My treat." His humor eased the tension the elders were feeling.

Lucy didn't miss a beat. "Well, if you're treatin'."

"Me too," replied Rose.

As it turned out, everyone was in the mood for fry bread.

"Whaddya say, Miss Tilly? Wanna come help me carry everything?"

Tilly stood. "Love to."

They followed the signs out of the arena to where the food vendors were located. Along the way, a drum group started to sing and Poncho turned to Tilly. "That drumbeat. It hits me right in the ribcage and I can feel it all the way down to my toes."

Tilly nodded, and just loud enough to hear over the singers, she told Poncho, "I feel like I've entered a sacred space."

"I think it is a sacred space, Miss Tilly. Even in this ginormous arena, I feel the presence of spirit."

Just then they exited the arena and were out where all the food vendors were set up. Poncho's mouth fell open. After a second or two of taking in the scene before them, he declared, "Holy Dinah! Look at all the fry bread stands. I'm sure some comedian could do a whole stand-up routine just about the fry bread stands and all us Indians."

Tilly chuckled. This man could move from talking about spirit to comedy in one breath and not make it feel disrespectful. Every day her love for Poncho grew.

"How we gonna decide who to buy from, Miss Tilly?" He rubbed his chin and furrowed his brow.

"Most people who come out will go to the first couple of stands, so why don't we walk down to the end and buy from the last stand?"

Poncho tilted his head and flashed Tilly a smile. "I knew I liked you right from the first time I met you."

Tilly was right, the last stand wasn't busy and in no time she and Poncho were carrying stacks of fry bread back to the elders. As they munched on their fry bread, they watched the final preparations for Grand Entry. All the drum groups were set up around the perimeter of the arena floor and the announcers had a small stage to work from. It wasn't long before the arena was filled with people. Even though they were seeing it firsthand, it was still difficult for the elders to conceive that this many people had come to celebrate, dance, and honor this tradition known as Pow Wow.

Tilly felt the anticipation bubbling in the air. She watched as the male Fancy Dancers took the stairs two by two. The feathers on their bustles bounced up and down, almost as if they were dancing. Beside her, a group of Jingle Dancers gracefully descended the stairs, causing the *chang, chang, swish, chang, chang, swish* sounds to come from the silver cones on their dresses. Tilly noticed a family making their way down for Grand Entry. The gentleman was a Grass Dancer and dressed in green and yellow regalia. In one arm he carried a child, dressed in similar green and yellow regalia. Tilly couldn't tell for sure, but she thought the little one might be about two years old. With his free hand, the gentleman hung onto the hand of a young girl. She had on a hot pink, Fancy Dancer dress with purple and white ribbons hanging from her collarbone area, a beaded white belt and white moccasins that went all the way up to her knees. Her hair was in two perfect braids, tied at the end with pink ribbons. On the other side of the girl was a woman dressed in full buckskin regalia. Her long, black, shiny hair was pulled back into one braid with an eagle feather tucked at the top. The woman was stunning. Tilly watched her with reverence and was in awe of the way she carried herself, chin jutted out, shoulders back, eagle fan held close to her chest. She didn't have to look down to navigate the stairs, her feet simply knew where the next stair was. Tilly would look for her when it was time for the women's categories. If she could walk the stairs like this, imagine how she might dance!

Lucy leaned over to Tilly and said, "I don't really know why I was such a crybaby earlier. I think I get afraid at things like this, you know, about being Indian." Lucy looked around the arena. "I think, Tilly, if you hear mean 'n hurtful things about yourself and your people long enough, you start to believe it." Lucy shrugged her shoulders. "At least I did. So being here, at the World Pow Wow, it brings all that stuff up."

Tilly put her arm around Lucy and leaned her head in until it rested on Lucy's. They sat like that for a few minutes, neither saying a word. It was times like this that Tilly vacillated between profound empathy for what these elders had endured in their lifetime and awe at their extraordinary resilience.

***

In the lower halls and stairwells of the arena, Sarah and the other dancers prepared for Grand Entry. There was something sacred for Annie about supporting her sister like this. She helped Sarah step into the white buckskin dress and then they shimmied it up Sarah's body and over her shoulders where Annie buttoned it at the base of Sarah's neck. Then came the buckskin shawl that Annie placed over Sarah's shoulders. Across the back of the shawl were four bear paws. Chocolate-brown colored beads had been used for the paws and turquoise beads created a circle around each one. Running along the top of the shawl was an inch-wide strand of turquoise beads that came all the way down the front to where the turquoise fringes hung. On the front of Sarah's shawl were four more bear paws, two on each side of her chest. On her feet, she wore white moccasins that had the same bear paw beading on the top. Her regalia was stunning and the blanket she had bought in Seligman, when draped over her left arm, was a perfect match.

Once Sarah was fully dressed, Annie reached into the suitcase and ever so gently pulled out Sarah's eagle fan and handed it to her. Sarah held it in her right hand. She was ready.

When Annie stepped back and looked at her sister, her hands came up to her mouth and reverence pooled in her eyes. "I don't think I've ever seen you look as beautiful as you do right now."

"Oh, Annie." Sarah blushed.

"No! It's true! You are glowing!"

"Oh, you." Sarah teased, but then she looked at her sister. Really looked at her. Sarah's tone softened. "Thanks, Annie. I couldn't've done this without you. The chemotherapy, the sickness, the trip. All of it. I want you to know that I'm forever grateful."

It had been a privilege and an honor for Annie, and she was no longer able to choke back the tears. In an unexpected move, she reached out and held her sister's face. "Seeing you like this is all the thanks I need." The

two women embraced, healing more than years of hurt and misunder-
standings. Healing generations.

Over the loudspeaker came the soon-to-be-familiar voice of the Master
of Ceremonies. Every third or fourth word he seemed to linger on, it was
a cadence common among Pow Wow emcees. "We're going to do one
more song and then it's time for Grand Entry. Dancers this is your final
notice to move on down into the tunnel and get ready. Everyone up there
in the stands, all twenty thousand of you, take your seats. Now, White
Fish Bay take it away. Last song before Grand Entry. Aho, Aho!"

Annie released her sister. "Guess that's my cue. I'm going to go sit with
everyone." She gathered up her purse and Sarah's suitcase. With one final
look at her sister, Annie added, "Go out there, Sarah, and have fun! Enjoy
every single second of this dream come true!"

All Sarah could do was nod. Her stomach was fluttering. Her mouth
was dry, and she had to pee, but that wasn't going to happen. There was
no way she could go to the bathroom with her regalia on. Instead she
took a deep, deep breath and let it out with a sigh. She closed her eyes for
a moment, squeezing the eagle fan just a bit tighter and offered a prayer
of thanksgiving. Imagine, her, Sarah Fraser from a tiny little reserve in
British Columbia, Canada dancing in the Grand Entry of the World Pow
Wow. She couldn't help but chuckle to herself. Plenty of crazy things had
happened in Sarah's life, but nothing as crazy—or magical—as this!

The Master of Ceremonies came over the loudspeaker again, announc-
ing, "Ladies and Gentlemen, boys and girls, please rise and remove all
hats. We're going to start the Pow Wow off with the Gathering of Nations
song and eagle medicine. The eagle here..." The emcee pointed to the eagle perched on his companion's hand. "The eagle is going to go to all four
directions and share his medicine. When this song is over we're gonna
go right into the Flag Song and entrance of the Eagle staff, the Flags, our
Veterans, and our two thousand dancers!"

Tilly helped Lucy to her feet and continued to hold her hand.

When everyone was standing and the noise had died down, the emcee
looked to the gentleman and his hand drum. "Take it away."

The eagle sat perched on his companion's gloved hand and they slowly
made their way around the arena. At the end of each round of song, the
companion would stop and remove the eagle's mask and the eagle would

spread and flap its wings. As this happened, the emcee would announce, "Fill yourself with the blessings." The eagle would flap its wings a few more times and then tip its head for his companion to put the mask on, and they'd move to the next door. This happened at the doors of the arena that represented the four directions.

When they stopped in front of the section where Tilly and the elders were standing, Tilly closed her eyes and opened her arms. It was like the emcee was talking to her, "Fill yourself with the blessings." She could feel the eagle medicine fill her, bless her. She could also feel Lucy's hand in hers and with each flap of those wings, Lucy's hand got warmer and warmer.

When Tilly no longer felt the wind coming off the eagle's wings, with her eyes still closed, she offered only one word. *Kinânskomitin.*

After a few moments, she opened her watery eyes and looked down at Lucy. Lucy was using her free hand to wipe away the tears streaming down her face.

"Can't believe I'm being a big ol' crybaby again, but geez Tilly, I ain't never experienced anythin' like that before. I ain't never felt this proud to be Indian."

Tilly looked down the row at the elders. Her aunties and uncles. Bea had removed her glasses and was using her shirtsleeve to dry her eyes. Chuck stood with his chest out, head back, eyes closed, and his body moved up and down to the beat of the drum. Poncho stood with his cowboy hat held to his heart and his eyes were almost closed because of the huge smile on his face. Rose stood with her purse over the crook of one arm and the other holding Poncho's free hand. Tilly couldn't tell for sure, but she thought she saw the pride welling up in Rose's eyes. Mabel stood with both hands on her heart and her mouth moving. Tilly knew the words she couldn't hear made up a beautiful prayer.

On the other side of Lucy stood Annie. She was looking toward the arena entrance where Sarah would soon emerge. Her camera hung around her neck and she had her phone in her hand. There was no way she was going to miss capturing Sarah dancing. No way!

She'd never loved anyone quite the way she loved each and every one of these Crazy Eights!

The thunderous first beat of the drum was like an explosion, the sound reverberating throughout the arena. Three more beats and then the high-pitched voices of the singers joined in. A chill went down Tilly's spine, and her throat tightened. She felt her shoulders push back and her body become more erect. As she glanced one more time at the elders; they, too, seemed taller.

Something stirred deep within her. Something awakened. A strength that was not only hers, but belonged to those who had gone before her and whose blood ran through her.

The emcee came back on and spread out his words, enunciating loudly, "Oh, *do* it boys! *Do* it! *Do* it!" He made each word linger in the air. "It's Pow Wow time and I'm Pow Wow happy!"

Lucy's face radiated joy as she turned to Tilly. "I'm Pow Wow happy." Tilly giggled and wiped her eyes.

"Aw, now look who's all sappy," yelled Lucy over the drumming and singing.

"I know, I know. What can I say? Grand Entry always makes me cry."

The MC continued. "Ladies and Gentlemen, if you like the singing and dancing, how about a round of applause?" The crowd erupted. Hundreds and hundreds of dancers were making their way onto the arena floor, turning it into a radiant sea of colors moving in time to the drum. The emcee came over the loud speaker again, "Oh what a sight, the pride of the Indian Nations, representing Turtle Island. Over five hundred and sixty tribes in the United States and over two hundred Canadian Indian bands are right here at the Gathering of Nations Pow Wow."

At that moment, Chuck leaned over to Bea. "If only Duncan Campbell Scott could see us now." Bea laughed so hard her head fell back. Chuck was referring to one of the many men in Canadian politics and history who had systematically attempted to eradicate the First Peoples and their culture and language.

"Yeah, looks like his policies really worked to take the Indian out of the Indian, eh?" Bea replied sarcastically, and they both laughed. It felt good, *real good* to know that history did not determine the future. They did.

Chuck took in the spectacle of twenty thousand people of different ages and races who had gathered to celebrate. He leaned and talked loud enough so Bea could hear him over the drumming. "I know that I haven't been a proponent of reconciliation. Thought it was just another government way of making money off of us, and for Canadians to feel better about history."

Bea nodded. More than once on this trip she had heard his tirade against reconciliation. Not the truth part, just the reconciliation.

His eyes swept the scene again, and then, with his hand, he motioned to what was unfolding before them. "When this many people, from all different kinds of backgrounds come together to celebrate and uphold the dignity of our culture and ceremonies, well, this to me is part of what reconciliation is about."

"Yes, my love! It sure is." With every thunderous whisk of the drumsticks on the drum, Bea's knees bounced.

Tilly looked down the line of elders and noticed Bea dancing. She couldn't help but think how much Bea had changed since the beginning of the trip. She seemed younger. Her eyes had a spark, and it was almost as if she glowed.

Just then, Mabel pointed and yelled out to the group, "There she is! There's Sarah!"

Sarah entered the arena floor, and as soon as her feet hit the floor she began to dip and sway to the beat of the drum. She held her eagle fan high, moving it forward and back, almost like she was cleaning the air of anything that might be hurtful.

Annie wasn't prepared for the emotions that welled up in her. For the first time she could remember, maybe for the first time ever, Annie felt proud to be Native.

They all realized how powerful this moment was. Witnessing the remarkable courage and strength of Sarah—after all she had been through over the last few months—to be dancing at the Gathering of Nations Pow Wow was beyond extraordinary.

Grand Entry lasted for almost an hour. Sarah danced the entire time. Each beat of the drum lifted her spirit. She couldn't believe the energy she felt. How vibrant she felt. How beautiful she felt. How alive she felt.

48

All Good Things in Their Rightful Time

TILLY WAS NESTLED on the bleacher between Poncho and Bea when the time finally came for Sarah's category, the Golden Age Women, to dance. The drum group was called and the first four beats of the song were loud. The voices matched them, stirring a genetic memory within Tilly. The memory of someone who came before her and whose blood ran through her. Ancestral memory.

Rose stood. Poncho followed his wife's lead, and then, one by one, all the elders and Tilly rose to show their respect for Sarah and the other dancers.

Tilly watched as Sarah moved clockwise around the arbor, her feet barely coming off the floor, her knees bending with each beat of the drum. She stood tall, her shoulders back, and her head held high. In her right hand, she held her eagle fan while her left arm crossed her chest with the Pendleton blanket draped over it. Her grace and beauty were stunning.

After the song ended and everyone had sat down, Bea turned to Tilly. "I always get choked up watching the elders dance the Women's Traditional." She looked back out to the dance floor, but continued talking. "The tender and graceful way they dance each and every step, in unison with the drum, reminding us how we are to be walking our lives here on Earth. Gently. You know what it makes me think of, Tilly?"

Tilly shook her head from side to side. She knew that Bea was about to share a gift with her. She waited, knowing Bea would continue talking when she was ready.

"Makes me think of the different layers of our teachings." With her eyes forward, watching as the dancers prepared for the next song, Bea began. "Many think humility is about not being full of yourself—about thinking of others—but there's more to humility than that. It's also about having faith that all good things will unfold in their rightful time." Bea went on to share with Tilly that in this busy world, we push, push, push to make things happen. She told her it is our ego that tries to make something happen, usually so that we feel better in some way. "We need to get back to the old ways, of a balance between working hard to make things happen and having faith that if something is in our greatest good, it will unfold." She turned to look at Tilly. "I've come to learn that when I don't get what I want or think I need, I'm being protected. Time always reveals why I didn't get what I wanted. It's one of the ways the Creator and our Ancestors take care of us."

Tilly remained still, letting Bea's teaching settle in. She looked from Bea out to the dance floor and back to Bea. She put her arm around Bea, leaned over, and kissed her cheek. "Kisâhkihitin, Bea."

Bea patted Tilly's knee. "I love you too, Tilly."

Tilly had *so* much to thank Bea for. She had pretty much been a pillar in Tilly's life since the first day they met at the Friendship Centre in Kamloops. Bea had been integral to Tilly's recovery from alcoholism. She'd help guide Tilly's reconnection to her culture, she'd been her witness when Tilly married Mick, and so much more. "Thank you for everything, Bea."

Bea's eyes radiated the love she felt for Tilly. "Just remember, my girl. All good things in their rightful time."

49

Full Up on Love

SARAH SAT ON the edge of the bed and glanced at the clock. "Oh, my gracious."

"What?" asked Annie as she came out of the washroom and navigated the dimly lit hotel room toward her bed.

"It's one in the morning," replied Sarah.

"Noooo."

"It is!"

"Well, I'll be..." Annie's voice trailed off.

"You'll be what?" asked Sarah as she slid her watch over her hand and placed it on the nightstand, then slipped her feet out of her slippers and swung her legs up onto the bed.

Annie looked across at her sister, who was now snuggled beneath the covers. "I don't know what I'll be. What is that saying that the old people have, 'something like being knee-high to a grasshopper.'"

"Annie, those are things white people say. I mean really, no grasshopper hung around long enough for me to get knee-high to it."

"Yeah." Annie giggled. "I guess you're right."

"You know how the ol' people say every race got its own gifts?" asked Sarah.

"Mm," murmured Annie.

"Well, maybe that's one of the white people's gifts. Maybe they can get that close to grasshoppers cuz they're grasshopper whisperers."

The sisters cracked up laughing.

When Sarah had caught her breath, she added, "Yeah, that's a gift to be real proud of, eh? Go introducing yourself and be all, like, 'Hi, I'm Sarah and I'm a grasshopper whisperer.'"

Again, their laughter filled the room.

Sarah sat up in bed. "All this laughin' has me havin' to go pee again." Upon returning and crawling beneath the covers, Sarah commented, "Don't know the last time I was up this late."

Annie reached up and turned the light off. As darkness filled the room, Sarah released a deep sigh. She closed her eyes and her mind wove its way back to Grand Entry. She wanted to replay it again and again. To make sure every single step, every drumbeat, every motion of her eagle fan was etched in her memory forever.

"I can die now," she whispered.

"What? Sarah! Don't talk like that!" Annie snapped. She didn't know how else to respond. Perhaps being empathic or something gentler might have been a better response, but hearing her sister talk about death… well, with everything that had happened this year, it was too much for Annie, and all she could do was scold her big sister.

Sarah rolled on her side to face her sister, whom she could see by the light from the parking lot that streamed through their curtains. "It's true, Annie. I was just thinkin' how today was one o' the best days o' my life. There ain't nothin' else I wanna see. Or do."

"Oh, come on, Sarah, sure there is!" Annie reacted.

"Nope. Nope there isn't. I came on this trip with a big part o' me empty." Even in the shadows of the night, Sarah could see the quizzical look on Annie's face. "I didn't realize it, but tonight, out there dancin', I felt alive. More alive than I have in a real long time. I never in my wildest dreams ever thought I'd dance again, let alone here at the World Pow Wow. It's pretty crazy!" She wasn't sure if she should tell Annie about being able to see the Ancestors dancing with her tonight, or about the young woman who kept visiting her. She wasn't sure Annie would understand. But she'd kept too many secrets from her sister and it had only driven a wedge between them. "I danced tonight with our Ancestors." Sarah paused for a moment. Hearing the words made the experience even more real. "Maybe you couldn't see them, but I could." She filled her lungs and slowly released the air. "They were there, Annie."

Silence.

And then, in a much softer tone than previously, "I believe you, Sarah."

Sarah closed her eyes and as sleep beckoned her, she said through a smile, "You see now why I feel like there's nothin' left to see or do? I done it all, Annie. I danced at the World Pow Wow an' now I'm full up on love."

50

Beading Hall of Fame

IT WAS SATURDAY afternoon and Lucy, Rose, and Tilly were ready for a little Pow Wow shopping. They made their way over to the vendor building and when they entered, their eyes widened as they took in the scene. There were over four hundred stalls. Mostly artisans selling items like stuffed animals made out of Pendleton blankets, beaded items, buckskin clothing, regalia, dreamcatchers, soaps and candles with scents like sage, cedar, and sweetgrass, clothing with sayings, or artwork related to Pow Wow or being Indigenous, toys, books, and of course, jewelry. You name it and you could probably find it somewhere in the vendor building.

"Where do we start?" asked Lucy.

Neither Rose nor Tilly responded; they were still processing the magnitude of what lay before them. Lucy took a step closer to them, partially to get out of the way of the traffic walking in and out, but also because she wasn't sure they'd heard her. She asked again, "Where do we start?"

This time, Tilly and Rose both raised their shoulders, indicating "I don't know."

They had to shuffle out of the way of people again, and it was then that Lucy gave directions. "Let's head this way," she said and pointed to her left. "We'll go clockwise around. That way if we get lost, it should be easy to find each other." Lucy didn't wait for the two women to respond, she headed in that direction, and just as Lucy had predicted, it wasn't long before the elders got separated from Tilly.

Rose and Lucy spent lengthy periods examining the intricacy and detail of the beadwork available for sale. At one table, Lucy picked up a hairclip and admired the way the artist had been able to create such beauty. She groaned out loud as she placed the hairclip back on the table and mumbled, "I ain't never gonna be able to bead anythin' like that again." Lucy looked up to see if Rose was listening to her and said, "'Member that butterfly sequence I did?"

Rose replied, "How could I forget?"

"Mm-hmm. That girl won competitions, first place for years."

"Yeah. It wasn't that girl's dancin' that helped her win. It was your amazing beadwork," said Rose. "And cuz you put a prayer in every bead." Rose knew the depth of Lucy's loss when she could no longer do one of the things she most loved in the world. Beading.

Lucy had been a bit of a legend back in the day, back before the arthritis took home in her hands. Her beading had helped save Lucy when Jenny went missing...and when she never came home.

Rose looked down at her friend's face, it was clouded with sadness. Rose reached out and squeezed Lucy's forearm. "Aw, Lucy. I remember how when you were working on that piece, how you used to hush us. Tell us you were doing sacred work. You'd tell us to behave and speak words that were like medicine."

"Yeah. Well, time changes everything," Lucy solemnly replied.

Rose put the moccasin she'd been admiring back on the table and turned to her best friend. "Ain't that the truth." She gave Lucy a wink. "I still think your work should be in the Beading Hall of Fame."

"Beading Hall of Fame? Is there even such a place?" asked Lucy.

"How should I know? But if there is, it ain't complete without Lucy Louie's beadwork!"

Lucy regarded her friend for a moment. "After all these years of being friends, Rose, I think that's the nicest thing you ever said to me." She reached over and put her hand on Rose's arm. "Thank you."

"Aw, don't go getting all mushy-gushy on me, Lucy. It's the truth, that's all." Rose pulled her arm away and glanced back to the table.

"And there she is—the Rose I know and love," Lucy said. They turned to face each other, smiled, and bumped shoulders playfully.

51

A Visit from Grandma Tilly

TILLY AND THE Crazy Eights spent all Saturday afternoon and evening hanging out at the Pow Wow. Tilly was mesmerized by the drumbeat and loved how the voices of the men carried with them a current of energy that caused her to bounce in unison with the rhythm. She was sitting side by side with Mabel on a plastic bench in the arena, watching the Men's Chicken Dance competition. Both were transfixed by the dancers and lost in their own world until the drumming came to an end. When the clapping finally quieted down, Mabel noticed Tilly sigh deeply.

"What's up, Tilly?"

Damn, how's she always know? Tilly thought to herself. She crossed her arms and lowered her head, remaining quiet. Mabel watched her for a moment, knowing that when she was ready, Tilly would talk. She always did, and this time was no different. After the next song, Tilly started, "I was just thinking how crazy it is that here we are surrounded by twenty thousand people, and I feel so lonely."

Mabel put her arm around Tilly and gave her a squeeze. "Oh, my girl, it's going to get better, but it's up to you to *make* it better."

Tilly felt her chest constrict and she couldn't catch a full breath. The drums had begun again and with each beat she felt her heart might burst. She took a deep breath, but it didn't help. She turned to Mabel. "I need air." Tilly stood and bolted up the stairs and out the closest door, trying to catch her breath. Once outside she leaned forward, putting her hands on her knees, like an athlete recovering. When she felt like she could breathe again, Tilly noticed that she was at the back of the stadium, overlooking the city of Albuquerque. There wasn't a cloud in the sky as the sun released the last of its rays, spreading hues of red, orange, and gold across the city. The air was warm, and yet a shiver ran through her body.

Tilly didn't know what feeling came after "discombobulated," but whatever it was, that's what she was feeling. She closed her eyes, folded her arms across her chest, and tried to warm herself up. That's when her nostrils caught the unmistakeable scent of home-grown tobacco.

The smell.

The smell of Grandma Tilly.

Tilly stood motionless, absorbed in the scent of her grandma. She'd come to Tilly like this before, and Tilly knew that, when she opened her eyes, Grandma would be there. She also knew that no one else could see her.

As Tilly opened her eyes, Grandma Tilly stood beside her. "Quite a view you're looking at, my girl."

"Grandma," Tilly's voice caught in her throat.

"I know, it's been a few days since I visited you, back there in Sedona."

"I knew it. I knew that dragonfly was you."

"Good thing I showed up when I did or who knows what trouble you might'a gotten yourself into." Grandma had never been one to mince words, not even from the spirit world.

Tilly turned away and looked to the ground. She was pretty sure she knew what would've happened with her and Rob that day had Grandma Tilly not intervened. She knew full well that not being happy in her marriage meant she had to do something about it, and that doing something about it didn't mean having an affair.

It was like Grandma could read her mind, "So my girl, what are you going to do?"

Tilly exhaled and shook her head. "I don't know, Grandma."

"Oh, but I think you *do* know. That's why you're out here."

Tilly glanced over at her. "What do you mean?"

"There's no accident you came out the door you did and found yourself right here," Grandma spread her arms out in front of her, "in the glory of Grandfather sun setting. I think you've come out here to use the strength of the sun to fill you up, so you have the courage to make the changes you need."

"You make it sound so easy." Tilly looked away and out at the landscape.

"But it is, don't you see that, my girl? In your heart you know what's right for you. Sometimes you got so much chatter going on in your head that you don't hear your heart."

Tilly could only nod in agreement.

Grandma Tilly continued, "Somewhere you closed up your heart. You can't blame Mick for that. That's your doing. You're the only one who controls if you have an open heart or not. Remember who you are?"

Tilly nodded and under her breath uttered, "Beautiful Light Woman."

"That's right, you're heart is your light. You come from a long lineage of Ancestors who shared their heart. Even when they were hurt and they thought they'd never recover, they opened their heart and loved again. You need to follow the way of your Ancestors. Find the courage to love again. And you need to start with yourself.

"That man back there in Sedona. The one who caused you to feel all twitter patted? He was a gift. He reminded you of who you are, Beautiful Light Woman. He saw that in you. We all see that in you, but the real question is, do *you* see your beauty?"

Tilly closed her eyes. Grandma had always made it clear that no one was responsible for Tilly and her life, except Tilly. Somewhere along the line, she'd either forgotten this teaching or it had simply become easier to blame others...especially Mick. She eased her eyes open, hoping Grandma would still be there. She was, and Tilly took comfort in the lines across Grandma's face, each one a story of a life well lived.

For a long time after Grandma had passed over to the other side, Tilly would lie in bed at night and in her memory she'd retrace the lines of Grandma's face. Now, as Tilly looked at her, each of those lines was exactly as she remembered. Tilly found it funny how she cursed the lines that had begun to appear beside her own eyes and between her eyebrows. She hoped that one day she'd love her lines as much as she had loved Grandma Tilly's.

As the sun continued its descent across the Albuquerque sky, Grandma Tilly gazed across at Tilly. She knew how much her granddaughter missed her. "I'm always with you, Tilly," she said, resting her hand on Tilly's shoulder. "I'm the gentle breeze that tousles your hair, I'm the shiver that goes down your spine, and sometimes I'm even the dragonfly that crosses your path." Grandma winked at Tilly, and Tilly smiled back. She was only beginning to understand the depth of her gratitude that Grandma Tilly had shown up that morning in Sedona.

They stood side by side, watching as the radiant sky changed colors. "I'm everywhere, Tilly. You just need to close your eyes, breathe, and you'll feel me. And when you need help, sit quietly and listen. If you listen, really listen, your heart will give you the answer."

Tilly closed her eyes, wanting to pause this moment in time. She knew that when she opened them, Grandma would be gone.

52

A Knock in the Night

RAP, RAP, RAP. Tilly stirred in her sleep, the sound merging into her dream.

Bang, bang, bang.

This time the knock at the door startled Tilly awake. She glanced at the clock on the hotel nightstand: 3:45 a.m.

Like a phone call in the middle of the night, a knock on the door rarely brings good news.

Tilly swung her legs over the side of the bed and groggily shuffled to the door. Looking through the peephole she saw Annie standing there in her nightie, arms crossed, hair tussled, eyes wide and blinking fast. Tilly was now fully awake. Her hands moved at lightning speed to unlock and open the door. Annie, her breathing shallow, looked desperate. "It's Sarah. Something's wrong."

"I'm coming," Tilly said as she turned to grab her housecoat and then rushed down the hall after Annie. When they entered the dimly lit room, Tilly found Sarah hidden below the covers. Her shivering shook the bed.

Annie leaned in close to Tilly and whispered, "She woke me up about an hour ago. She was burning up then, so I put her in a cool bath, but now she's freezing." Annie crossed her arms and choked out, "I'm afraid I made it worse."

Tilly reached over and put her hand on Annie. "You didn't make it worse. It's the cycle of a fever."

Tilly knelt down beside Sarah and placed her hand on her shoulder. "Sarah, it's Tilly. Let me look at you, love." Sarah slowly pulled the covers down that she had wrapped over her head in an attempt to get warm.

Tilly gently wiped the sweat-drenched hair from Sarah's forehead and placed a kiss where her hand had been. As she removed her lips, Tilly closed her eyes for a moment before looking up at Annie. Their eyes exchanged a knowingness. This was more serious than a fever. Tilly stroked Sarah's cheek and whispered, "We need to take you to the hospital, Sarah."

Sarah shook her head, "No, can't go—" it took immense energy for her to finish "—no insurance."

Out of the corner of her eye, Tilly saw Annie's head fall forward. After a few seconds, Annie squeezed onto the bed beside Sarah. She couldn't stop herself from blurting out, "What? No insurance? We were all supposed to get insurance before this trip!" Beneath the anger in Annie's voice was the fear of what no insurance could potentially mean. *No medical help for her sister.*

Sarah took a sharp breath and said, "With my cancer," a chill shook her body, "I couldn't afford it. So," another gasp, "no hospital."

Annie and Tilly shared a glance, their eyes searching...

Searching for hope.

An idea.

Hope.

A solution.

Hope.

A plan.

They were grasping for anything. Anything that might help them.

"Do you have Tylenol?" Tilly asked.

"No," said Annie.

Tilly began to rise, saying she had some, but, with a shake of her head, Annie interrupted her. "No. No, we aren't going to do this. She needs more than Tylenol. I'll pay. I don't care what it costs. We're taking her to the hospital."

They both expected Sarah to put up a fight, but she didn't.

It was a silent surrender.

In that instant, the three of them knew that Sarah's recovery from cancer had gone sideways.

Tilly hustled back to her room, changed out of her pyjamas, left a note for Mabel, and grabbed the bus keys. Together Annie and Tilly were able to get Sarah into the bus. Annie ran back to the hotel to ask the lobby staff for directions to the hospital.

When they arrived at the hospital, Sarah was having difficulty breathing, so the staff whisked her in. Tilly and Annie stood at the emergency room door, helplessly watching as it closed before them.

From behind a glass window came, "Y'all need to come on over here and get the paperwork sorted out."

Tilly and Annie looked at each other. Tilly put her hand on Annie's arm and guided her to the window and together they began the process of filling out the paperwork for Sarah's admission. When it came time to produce insurance papers, they informed the woman that Sarah had no insurance. "Well, how y'all gonna pay for this?" she questioned.

Annie dug into her purse, pulled out her wallet and placed her credit card on the counter. "Use this."

"You sure?" the woman asked as she looked over her horn-rimmed glasses.

Annie nodded and pushed the card closer to the woman.

"Alrighty then."

After what seemed like hours of waiting in the cold, drafty, and somber emergency room, the doctor came out. Both women stood and Annie reached for Tilly's hand. The doctor explained that they had given Sarah oxygen and she was now breathing a bit easier, but that the X-rays revealed pneumonia in both lungs.

"Pneumonia?" Annie said, shocked. "It's the end of April and it's hot. How'd she get pneumonia?" Annie was trying to make sense of a situation that didn't make sense.

The doctor took a step closer to them and responded, "Sometimes, after chemotherapy, patients are more susceptible to infections because their immune system is weakened. By the look of her chest X-ray, I'd say she's had this for quite a while. Probably walking pneumonia, but now it's more serious." The doctor continued to explain to them the treatment she had begun for Sarah and what they might expect over the next few days. "I have to tell you, though, she's very sick." Being trained as a nurse and having worked in a hospital, Tilly knew exactly where this conversation was going. She put her arm around Annie and guided her to a chair.

Annie could feel her chest rising and falling.

The doctor stood over them. "We've got her hooked up to an IV to try and restore her fluids and on the strongest antibiotics possible." She always hated this part, no matter how many times she had to say it, it never got easier. "But you need to prepare yourselves."

Annie inhaled sharply, her body flinched, and she doubled over. "Noooooo," escaped her lips. Tilly pulled her closer and looked up at the doctor, who seemed like a messenger of darkness hovering over them in their fragile vulnerability.

The doctor looked away for a moment. She needed to get back, but there was never a graceful way to leave after delivering news like this. "Give us a bit to get her comfortable. I'm going to give her something to help. I'll send a nurse for you when you can see her." She turned on her heels and escaped through the emergency room doors.

The two women sat in silence, stunned by the news they'd just received. Each attempting to sort it out in her own way. Again, they had no choice but to wait. And pray.

Annie stared at the bulletin board in the hospital emergency room, unable to think. Actually, that's not true. She couldn't stop thinking. Thinking horrible, horrible thoughts about what this might mean for Sarah.

"Liz." Annie moved her fingers up and down on her kneecaps, whispering, "My Liz. Can you call my Liz?" With tears streaming down her ashen cheeks, Annie repeated, "I need my Liz."

"Okay, Annie. I'll call her." Tilly pulled out her cell phone and asked for the number. Tilly walked outside while the phone rang. She was about to leave a message when at the last moment there was a breathless "Hello?"

"Hello, may I speak to Liz please?"

"This is Liz."

Tilly introduced herself and briefly told Liz that Annie had asked her to call. She told her about Sarah's condition and attempted to answer the questions that Liz had.

Then she called Mabel.

After about fifteen minutes, the nurse came and got Annie so she could be with her sister. Sarah was hooked up to machines and had oxygen tubes in her nose.

Sarah felt Annie come in the room. She tried to open her eyes, but it was too much effort.

Annie sat down beside the bed and took Sarah's hand in hers, careful not to touch the IV that was helping hydrate her sister. "I'm here Sarah, you're not alone. I'm here."

Sarah gave Annie's hand a slight squeeze.

For a couple hours, they sat like that, holding hands, not needing to exchange words as Sarah wove in and out of sleep.

When the doctor came in, she informed Annie that they needed to do a few procedures with Sarah and she was welcome to stay or come back in half an hour. Annie wanted to call Liz. She needed to hear Liz's voice tell her everything was going to be okay. Even if it wasn't.

As Annie walked into the waiting room and headed for outside, she noticed Tilly. And then, she saw them. Each and every one of the elders—her family. They had all come to be there. To be with her and Sarah.

It was Poncho who saw Annie first. He walked over to her and wrapped her in his arms. She laid her head on his shoulder and began to cry.

They all made their way over to where Poncho and Annie were, and one by one they hugged her, wiped her tears away, offered her tissues, and hoped she knew she wasn't alone. Tilly handed Annie her phone. "Liz is waiting for you to call. Whenever you are ready."

"I'm ready." Annie went for a walk and called Liz. Between that call with Liz and the support of everyone, Annie found the strength to face the next few hours and days.

***

A couple of days later, when Sarah had been stabilized enough to travel, she and Annie prepared for the MedEvac flight to Vancouver. Before they left, Poncho gathered everyone in Sarah's hospital room. They stood in a circle around her bed as he spoke. "I think we need to send our sisters off in a good way, surrounded by our prayers. I have a pouch of tobacco here, wrapped in red cloth. I'm gonna pass it around the circle and ask each of you to say special prayers for these two." He paused when he noticed that Annie had begun to weep softly. Lucy wrapped her arm around Annie and pulled her in close.

Poncho continued, "They gonna need our support and prayers as they travel back to Vancouver." He passed the tobacco to Rose who was standing to his left and then he reached to hold Sarah's hand. Rose didn't usually participate in circles or prayers, but this was different. This was for Sarah and Annie. She held the tobacco in both her hands, closed her eyes, and, after a few moments, passed it to her left. Tilly said her prayers, and then the tobacco went around the circle. When the tobacco came to Poncho, he held it to his heart as he said his prayers and then placed the pouch of tobacco on Sarah's chest. It took all the strength she had to lift both hands and rest them on the tobacco. In the faintest of whispers, she said, "Thank you."

"Now just before they take you, we gonna sing you a prayer song." Poncho leaned over and kissed Sarah on her cheek. "Be well, my sister, and know that you are loved." He began with a soft beat of his drum and each of the elders joined him in singing the prayer song.

Not long after, the medical staff came to take Sarah and Annie out to the plane. Chuck put his arm around Bea and his other arm around Mabel. Bea pulled Tilly in close and then Poncho, Rose, and Lucy joined the line, their arms around each other.

The ride back to the hotel was filled with silence. Words could never fill the vacant seats that had been Sarah's and Annie's. In the morning, they would gather and decide on their route home, but for now they each needed time to be with their thoughts and feelings.

The trip, as they knew it, was over.

53

Nature's Medicine

AFTER A RESTLESS night, the group gathered over breakfast to discuss their trip home. As they went around the table, it was pretty much unanimous that they should take the fastest route. Then it came to Rose. She was the last to speak and that's when it all changed.

"I know you all wanna get home to be with Sarah and Annie, and I do, too," she said, nodding her head. "Really I do." She hesitated for a moment and turned to look at her husband. "But, there's still Poncho's bucket list thingamajig, and as you all know, he rarely asks for anythig from anyone." Her eyes slid over each one of them. "So I'm asking you all for a favor. Can we still go to the Redwood Forest so my husband can hug his tree?" Rose startled everyone when she began to laugh. "Geez, never thought I'd be sayin' 'so my husband can hug his tree.'"

"Yeah, especially not you, Rose," giggled Lucy and everybody else around the table joined in.

When the laughter eased, Poncho kept his eyes lowered as he informed them, "I can hug a tree another time. We really should be gettin' home. We've all been through a lot and we've been away..."

Rose didn't let her husband finish. "No, Poncho! The chances of us gettin' to the Redwood Forest ever again are pretty much nil."

"Yeah. I suppose you're right," Poncho admitted.

"I am right," Rose said smugly and then turned to the group. "So, whaddya all think? Can we stop and hug some trees?"

Mabel and Tilly had spent the previous night exploring routes home and knew that heading down off the I-5 to the Redwood Forest was not that much of a detour. Mabel responded, "Yes, Rose. I think stopping in the Redwoods is actually a wonderful idea. I imagine we could all use a bit of Mother Nature's medicine."

Rose's face lit up, her chest puffed out, and her chin jutted forward as she said to Poncho, "See? I had a wonderful idea."

"You always have wonderful ideas, Rose," Poncho replied and then added, "Okay, maybe not always, but…"

"You should just stop while you're ahead," Rose responded.

"See? That's what I mean. You always have wonderful ideas. This is me, stopping." Poncho's grin was as wide as his face, and his eyes danced as he looked at his wife.

Watching these two reminded Tilly that relationships can survive the difficult times. Maybe not always, but here on this trip she had learned of the challenges Rose and Poncho had overcome. And, of course, Bea and Chuck had rekindled their love after thirty years.

It gave her hope. She knew that what was facing her and Mick would not be easy. They would have difficult conversations, a need for deep honesty and forgiveness, and a need to find their way back to the playfulness that had always been a beautiful aspect of their marriage and friendship. Today, she had hope.

It was Mabel's voice that brought Tilly back from her thoughts. "Let's meet at the bus at nine thirty, which will give Tilly and me time to sort out our travel and book hotels."

And that's what they did. The first day was emotionally difficult, as the majority of the driving was from Albuquerque to Kingman, meaning they went through many of the same towns and cities they had traveled through on the way to the Pow Wow. Constant reminders of when the bus was full and everyone was healthy.

The first night they spent in Kingman, at a Hampton Inn. The hotel was short on rooms, so Lucy was sharing with Poncho and Rose. When they walked in, Lucy immediately noticed a yellow sticky note on the headboard. She walked over and read it, then cracked up laughing.

"What are you laughin' at over there, Lucy?" asked Rose, who had just come out of the bathroom from washing her hands and face.

"They must've known you was comin' Rose, cuz they left a special sign here. Just for you."

Rose squeezed her eyes. "What are you talkin' about?"

Lucy read the sign out loud, "Duvet covers and sheets are clean for your arrival." She started to laugh again and Poncho began laughing as well.

Rose couldn't help herself, she succumbed to the laughter bubbling in her chest.

***

The trip from Albuquerque to Crescent City, California took them three days, with highlights along the way. The elders especially loved the windy and scenic drive from Redding down to Arcata. At one point, they stopped along the river to stretch their legs. The day was warm and sunny, and before Tilly knew what was happening, the elders were rolling up their pant legs, removing their socks and shoes, and wading into the river.

Chuck was the first one in and after a few steps, he leaned his head back so the sun landed on his face. He opened his arms and said, "Thank you." Tilly remembered him telling her near the beginning of the trip that sometimes the most powerful prayer is only two words. "Thank you."

While the elders were enjoying dipping their toes in the river, Tilly walked a short way along the bank until she came to another clearing. She removed her backpack and pulled out the pouch of tobacco Bette had given her. It was almost empty, and Tilly realized how good it felt to have been offering prayers of gratitude and guidance. This time was no different. As she crouched down, tobacco tight in her hand, she began to pray. Serenity eased into her body and settled in. She could feel it. Her shoulders relaxed, her breath deepened, and her jaw slackened.

When she finished her prayers and opened her hand, the wind gently tossed the tobacco across the rocks and into the river. Tilly watched as the tobacco floated away. Eventually it would make its way to the Pacific Ocean. She loved the notion that the prayers she had just sent off would join the ocean that was just a few steps from her home back in Vancouver. And, for the first time since they'd left almost three weeks ago, Tilly was excited to get home.

They made only one more stop that day, Crescent Beach lookout. This time they all piled out and stood in awe of the grandeur that lay before them. The open ocean, the varying shades of blue and the layers of white-caps that seemed to roll forever. The white sand spread out before them and reminded some of them of photographs they'd seen of Hawaii. After a few minutes of taking in the beauty, they started to take pictures of the scenery and of each other posing.

Bea hadn't moved to get in the photographs. Instead, she stood absorbing the roar of the waves and feeling the breeze on her face. She imagined the waves bringing in and filling her with positive energy and vitality and as they rolled out they took with them hurt and mistrust. She had taken a huge leap in loving Chuck, and although it felt right and like a piece of her that she didn't even know had been missing was back in its rightful place, it was still extremely out of character for her to be so impulsive. Just as she was thinking this, Chuck came and stood behind her. He wrapped his arms around her waist and asked, "Have you ever seen so much beauty as we have on this trip?"

She leaned back into him, feeling the warmth of his body and shook her head. "No."

"Me neither, but the most beautiful sight on this trip…" He was quiet for a moment. "No. The most beautiful sight of my life was when you asked me to go to the Grand Canyon with you."

Bea playfully slapped his hand that was wrapped around her waist. "Yeah, and then we didn't."

He smiled and whispered in her ear, "That's true, but we still have to get to the Grand Canyon one of these days. Maybe we can make it a family trip, with our girls and the grandchildren." This time, instead of slapping his hand, she placed hers over his.

The next morning, they were all up early, excited to experience the Redwood Forest. They stopped at a place called The Trees of Mystery. It was located at the center of the Redwood National Park and, as Tilly and the elders discovered while there, the land they walked on and where the trees had grown and lived for centuries was known by Native Americans as "a place of spirits." When Poncho read this out loud, he stopped and looked around. "I can feel them. The spirits." At that exact moment, a brush of wind blew through, and the branches on the trees danced, almost as if the spirits were acknowledging them.

Lucy and Rose weren't quite up for a hike through the woods and decided instead to take the shuttle to the gondola ride. Along the way they saw trees of all shapes and sizes, some bigger than they could've ever dreamt. As they sat waiting for the rest of the group to walk up the trail and join them, Lucy asked Rose, "How do you think Sarah's doing?"

Rose shook her head from side to side. "I don't know, Lucy, but I don't have a good feelin' 'bout it."

Usually Lucy would be angry with Rose for being negative, but this time, this time Rose had spoken what Lucy felt in her heart. They sat quietly, both lost in their own thoughts until the rest of their group emerged from the trail. "Well, there you guys are, we were beginnin' to wonder if you got lost," remarked Rose.

Poncho took a couple of moments to catch his breath. "Nope, just enjoyin' the glory of it all."

"Did you hug your tree?" Lucy asked.

"You betcha. Many of them," he proudly replied.

Mabel smiled at Poncho and added, "That's for sure! We had to stop every few feet so he could hug another one."

"That'd be my husband," Rose said as she too smiled at Poncho, who stood grinning and soaking up the love.

Later, after they'd made their way back down and had browsed the gift shop, they boarded the bus. Poncho stood at the front and cleared his throat. "I just wanna take a moment to thank everyone for agreein' to stop here. It was real good medicine for my spirit." He looked directly at his wife and said, "I'd especially like to thank Rose, for makin' my dream come true."

"Aw, isn't that sweet," teased Lucy.

What Rose wanted to do was give Lucy a dirty look and say something mean to her husband. But she wouldn't this time. Rose was starting to like how it felt to be kind. She turned to Lucy. "Yes, he is sweet." She looked up at her husband who was still standing at the front of the bus grinning at her. Their eyes met. "You are welcome, Poncho. It made me happy to see you so happy." She patted the empty seat beside her. "Now come sit down. You're embarrassing me."

"I know." He giggled. "Why do you think I did it?" He made his way to his seat where his wife welcomed him with a roll of her eyes and a kiss. Poncho's giggling became contagious and before they knew it, everyone on the bus was laughing.

54

Arriving Home

AS THEY DROVE through Vancouver and got closer to the Friendship Centre and to what would be the completion of the trip with Tilly, a variety of emotions wove their way through the bus. The elders would spend the night in Vancouver and they all would visit Sarah and Annie tomorrow before heading home.

Tilly offered up a silent prayer. *Grandfathers and grandmothers help me to have an open heart with Mick, to be honest with him and able to be vulnerable and go to the places we need to go, to have the conversations we need to have, to say what I need to say, and the ability to hear what he needs to say to me.*

With the last part of her prayer, Tilly remembered one of Grandma Tilly's teachings: *We've been given two ears and one mouth for a reason.*

When they came to a red light, Bea leaned over and asked Tilly, "How are you feeling about seeing your family?"

"I can hardly wait! I've missed Piper and Grayson like crazy!"

Bea continued probing. "And Mick?"

Tilly could feel her grip tighten on the steering wheel. She had mixed feelings about seeing her husband.

Bea was her usual persistent self. "Tilly, how are you feeling about seeing Mick?"

Tilly rested her elbow on the open window frame and then leaned her head into her hand. The light turned green and she pushed down the gas pedal. "Nervous." That one word hung in the air.

They drove in silence. It was at the next red light that Bea resumed the conversation. "You must guard your tongue. I'm not saying hold your tongue because sometimes there are things we must say, but remember your words can either be medicine or poison. Choose your words and how you say them very carefully. Let them be medicine."

"I will, Bea. I will."

Finally, they reached the Friendship Centre. Pulling into the parking lot, Bea reached over and placed her hand on Tilly's arm. "Are you ready?"

Tilly nodded.

Bea tucked a strand of Tilly's hair behind her ear and rested her hand on her friend's cheek. Tilly closed her eyes and leaned her face into Bea's hand, seeking the comfort.

"Thanks, Bea." She opened her eyes and looked into the beautiful, loving face of this elder who had supported her, guided her, and nurtured her for many years. "Thanks for everything."

"You're welcome, my girl. I love you." Bea removed her hand from Tilly's face. "It'll all be okay." She moved back in her seat and watched as Tilly's twins burst out of their car and ran toward their mother.

"I believe that," Bea said, but Tilly didn't hear because she'd already opened her door and was running toward the two lights of her life, Piper and Grayson.

Tilly held her children for a long time, making up for all the hugs she'd missed. It was Grayson who pulled away first, looking back at Mick. "Come on, Dad. Get in here." He pulled him in so hard that Mick bounced right into Tilly. As uncomfortable and awkward as this was, they both knew their children were watching, so they each put an arm around the other and leaned in. Mick kissed her on the cheek. "Welcome back, Tilly."

Tilly removed her arms from around her children and cradled Mick's face in her hands and kissed him. A lengthy journey had just unfolded before them and she had no idea where it would take them, but she did know she was willing to fight for their marriage.

55

The Long Walk Back

THE NEXT MORNING Tilly woke to the soft sound of her husband snoring beside her and rain falling on the roof. To say it felt good to be home was an understatement. Something had changed in Tilly, or perhaps she'd simply found her way back to herself. Now, it was time for her and her husband to find their way back into their marriage. Last night, after she'd gotten home from a visit to Sarah and Annie, she and Mick had begun talking, acknowledging that there were many conversations they needed to have. It was Mick who suggested they walk the Stanley Park seawall for the next four days. "As we walk, we talk. We can get it all out and leave it there for the tide to take away."

"I like that idea," replied Tilly.

They got the twins off to school without incident and climbed into Mick's truck for the drive to the seawall and their first day of walking. The rain was torrential and the temptation for her and Mick to go somewhere warm and dry was almost too much. Any excuse to avoid the conversations seemed justifiable to Tilly; somewhere in the night she'd lost her nerve to share with Mick what she'd been feeling and thinking and to listen to him.

He looked at her and shook his head. "No. No, we aren't leaving because of a little rain. We're going to do this, Tilly." He zipped his raincoat up, lifted the hood over his head, and opened his door. He turned to Tilly, who slowly reached for the door handle.

For a while they walked in silence, their heads down as the rain assaulted them. At one point the wind gusted so hard it blew Tilly's hat off. Mick went chasing after it and when he came back Tilly said, "Mick, this is ridiculous." Feeling defeated in many ways, she said, "Let's just go back."

"No." He put his hand on her elbow and pushed her forward. "Come on, walk. We both agreed to this." She quickly moved her arm away, turned, and walked swiftly in front of him. He matched her pace and they walked in silence, hands tucked into their pockets and heads down.

After almost an hour of walking in silence, Tilly stopped to use the washroom. When she came out she saw Mick standing with his back to her. She looked away abruptly, her body ached. The exhaustion of the last week flooded her and all she wanted to do was go home and have a long, hot soak in the tub.

Slowly she made her way over to him, unable to look at him. "I'm done for today, Mick. We're not even talking." She wished it could be easier, and not just the torrential rain and wind part of this scenario, but all of it.

Mick's mouth barely moved as he faintly said, "But we're together and that has to count for something."

She wasn't sure it did count. It was just like it had been for months. Empty. Void of any meaningful conversation. Tilly rocked gently from foot to foot. The motion reminded her of how she used to rock Grayson when he was colicky.

Grayson. Piper. Their children.

She had never understood why couples stayed together "for the children," but now she did. Tilly thought about how many times in her life she had judged others for their actions. These last few weeks she'd come to realize that everyone simply does the best they can.

"I have an idea." She still couldn't look Mick in the eye. "Why don't we each get ten minutes to talk? We can say anything in that ten minutes, but we have to talk. No silence. And the other person can't respond, unless they're asked a question." Out of the corner of her eye, she could see he was looking at her. "You know," she lifted her shoulders and cocked her head to the side, "maybe if we just start talking, eventually we'll get to the real stuff we need to talk about." Tilly inhaled deeply and her words came tumbling out, "Because I don't know about you, Mick, but I suddenly feel nervous...and afraid...and I need some help to get started."

He nodded. "Me too, Till. Me too."

So that's what they did. It forced them to listen to each other and to reflect before responding. They talked more the first two days than they had in the last couple of years. Trying to find their way back, back to who they were before it all got to be too much.

At different times, they both had to swallow their pride and dig deep within to find the words that could help them build the bridge across the chasm.

On the third day, they had to walk the seawall twice. There were excruciating times, like at Siwash Rock where Mick had asked her if she still loved him, and how he'd let out a deep sigh of relief after she said yes. Or at the pool by English Bay where she'd learned that he too, had been lonely in their marriage.

When they got back to the truck, Mick went to open her door for her, but stopped. He stood real close and said, "We've both made mistakes, I know that now. This isn't all your fault, I'm also responsible for the state of our marriage." His voice broke on the last words and tears streamed down his cheeks. Tilly reached out and pulled him in tight to her body. He wrapped his arms around her and burrowed his face in her neck. Holding each other up, they released their shared pain.

The last day of their walk the sun was bright, the tide was high and the water glistened. They teased each other playfully and the conversation flowed with ease. They no longer had to keep track of the time. They were talking about what they needed from each other when Mick suddenly stopped. "Tilly, turn around." She did and was about to keep talking, but the look on her husband's face caused her to pause.

"You know what I really miss?" he asked.

She hardly moved her head from side to side, her chest tightening.

His eyes darted back and forth between hers and then slowly swept down her body. Mick stepped toward her. He lifted his hands and cradled her face. Tilly trembled, and he pulled her in for a long kiss. Tilly's arms instinctively wrapped around him, pulling him even closer. After a few minutes, their lips separated, but their bodies remained as one. Both were breathless, their eyes remained closed, holding the moment in time. Mick whispered, "I miss kissing my wife."

Their eyes connected.

The chasm had just been crossed.

Tilly tilted her head. "Maybe you should kiss her some more then." She raised her eyebrows teasingly. "You know, make up for lost time."

That's just what Mick did.

56

So Much Has Changed

THEIR FIRST STITCH 'n bitch meeting back in the basement of the community hall was awkward. Each of them had placed their projects on the table, but no one began to work. Instead they looked around at each other, uncertain of how to proceed now that so much had changed—within each of them and within their group.

Surprisingly, it was Rose who spoke up and stated what everyone was feeling. "I don't want to meet here anymore." She looked around the gray walls of the basement. Even though art had been put up, and the community had tried to make it feel welcoming, it reminded her of Residential School.

Rose bowed her head, and her shoulders began to shake. Lucy moved her chair closer and put her arm around Rose, while the other women stared, dumbfounded. They'd never seen Rose like this before.

After a few moments, Rose took in a sharp breath and then squeaked out, "Sorry."

Mabel shook her head from side to side. "There's no need to be sorry. Tears are medicine, remember?"

Rose began to share, "It's just that ever since our trip, I feel like I've been cracked wide open and comin' in here tonight," she paused while a few more tears fell, "there's just too many memories. The smell, the door handles, the floor…everythin' reminds me of the hurt and I don't wanna be reminded of the hurt." Rose inhaled deeply. "That's what I realized on our trip. I've been livin' in the hurt and I don't wanna live there anymore."

They sat in silence. Eventually Mabel spoke up, "Just because this is where we've always met, doesn't mean it's where we *have* to meet."

The women had never considered this before.

Their trip had affected each of them differently, but they all felt the need to speak up for themselves. They each felt more inspired to decide what *they* wanted for the rest of their lives, however long or short that might be.

***

The next week they began meeting at Rose's house. She and Poncho had a huge, round kitchen table. It had been a gift to Poncho from his favorite Chinese restaurant in town. Whenever he was running errands, which was often, he'd stop in and have the smorgasbord. A few years ago, when the restaurant was closing, they gave Poncho *his* table. It was perfect for when the kids and grandkids came over because they could easily squeeze everyone around it. The table even had a Lazy Susan in the middle. Not only was it perfect for family meals, but now it was also perfect for Stitch 'n Bitch. Besides, Rose had decided she wanted to find more ways to fill their house and her life with love, so having the ladies over once a week was just the thing to help with that.

Lucy teased, "Now that we're sittin' in a circle an' I can see you all, I think I like the ol' square table better."

Sarah

Sarah spent a week at Vancouver General Hospital. Her family traveled down to be with her and between her family, Annie, and Tilly, Sarah was never alone. Even if her family had not been there, Sarah wouldn't have been alone. The young woman stood beside Sarah's bed the entire time she was in the hospital. Sarah wasn't sure if anyone could see her, it didn't really matter because having her there gave her immense comfort. Every day at lunch, Tilly would bring a big pot of hot soup and baked bannock and the whole family would gather in Sarah's room and eat together. Without question, this was the highlight of Sarah's days and better than any medicine the doctors gave her.

She knew something had changed in her body. Or rather, something had come back. The cancer. The doctor confirmed this, informing Sarah the cancer had spread to her lungs. Sarah knew this meant her time was limited, and she had best spend what was left of it in meaningful ways. For Sarah, that was with her family.

She was grateful to go home, and be back on the land that she was connected to. Her family set a hospital bed up in the living room where Sarah could see the river and watch the birds. When Annie left, her daughter set up a laptop beside the bed and made it so all Sarah had to do was push a couple buttons and she could skype with Annie in Toronto.

The Stitch 'n Bitch ladies took turns dropping in to visit and bring food. Even though Sarah had virtually no appetite, she appreciated that the ladies fed her family. Mabel had videoed Sarah dancing at the Pow Wow and that was Sarah's favorite thing to do when any of them came to visit. It brought back such beautiful memories.

In the quiet of the day or the early morning hours, the young woman would visit. Sarah knew the young woman had been sent from the other side to help her prepare for the transition from Earth to the Spirit World.

Annie

Annie stayed with Sarah for only a few days after she came home. While she was more than welcome to stay longer, her help was no longer needed. Sarah's oldest daughter had finished university and would care for her mom…and Annie was ready to go home.

She found it odd that when she got home to her Liz and their life in Toronto, she craved the quiet and gentler pace of living on the reserve. Of living with Sarah and her family. Annie longed for the smell of fry bread. Although she attempted a few times to make it, it always turned out like hockey pucks and tasted like the pages of books that had been dropped in the tub. As well, Annie longed for time with the Stitch 'n Bitch ladies. Sometimes, she'd stay up late so she could FaceTime with them at their meetings. And, of course, she missed Chuck and Poncho. She hungered for family, for community, and for her culture. It wasn't the kind of hunger that causes your stomach to growl, but rather the kind that causes a longing in your soul.

Annie wasn't sure how to attend to the hunger. She didn't feel comfortable going to any of the elders' lunches or gatherings at the Friendship Centre. Maybe one day, but not yet.

Instead, she returned to the library, this time as a community member and began devouring books written by Indigenous authors. On the trip, Lucy had given Annie her first book by an Indigenous author, *Monkey Beach*, and she was hooked.

She also started smudging and offering prayers every morning.

After a couple months of reading and adjusting to retired life at home, Annie summoned up the courage to go to an elders' luncheon at the Native Canadian Centre in downtown Toronto. When she opened the door and entered, Annie was greeted by the now familiar scent of sweetgrass.

Lucy

Lucy found herself bored once they got home. She had never been one to sit around and do nothing, but the trip had reminded her how much she loved being with people. She was reading the community newsletter and saw that the school was looking for an elder to come in a couple days a week. They were calling it Elder in Residence.

Lucy showed it to Rose and told her she was thinking about going over to the school to talk to the principal and check things out.

"Yes!"

Lucy's head snapped back. Yes? Was this her Rose? Usually she was a NO and sometimes, if you got lucky, she'd eventually get to a yes.

Rose continued, "Do it Lucy! Those kids an' the teachers, matter o' fact, the whole school, would be lucky to have you."

Lucy's eyes welled with tears. Not so much from the kind words Rose had shared, but more from witnessing how her friend was changing. To the Rose that Lucy always knew was in there. It made Lucy realize just how much the trip had impacted each of them, in their own way.

The next day, Lucy went up to the school and before she knew it she was introduced to and sitting in a class with grades 3, 4, and 5. The teacher was telling the students that tomorrow they'd be going down to the river as part of their science unit.

Lucy put up her hand.

"Yes, Lucy?" the teacher asked.

"Umm. Do you think I could come with you?"

The teacher gave a sideways glance to the principal who gave a nod of her head.

"Sure Lucy, we'd love that."

"Great!" Lucy turned to the students. "There's this real special spot I want to show you. My daddy used to take me there when I was a tiny girl. In the springtime, just like now, he'd show me how to find the spots along the river where the water wasn't flowing as fast. I'd have to sit real still and watch for flying ants. Sometimes, I'd sit there and sit there and sit there. No ants. Then some days, they'd be everywhere. The flyin' ants are like little messenger. They tell us the trout are running."

"But trout don't run, they swim," said one of the students.

Lucy giggled at herself, which made it okay for the students to giggle as well. "Sometimes I say the silliest things."

The next day, down by the river and with the children, Lucy felt alive. Like, really alive. Just as she had on their trip.

It was also the first day of many that Lucy was the school's Elder in Residence.

Bea and Chuck

While they were away, neither Bea nor Chuck spent much time considering what life would be like when they got home. Or just how much of an adjustment it would be for each of them. And their children, who, for most of their lives had only known their parents as being separated and not really all that fond of each other.

Chuck moved in with Bea and one of the blessings was that he traveled for work. This gave each of them some time alone—time that, over the years of being single, they'd become accustomed to and needed.

Bea continued her work as a counselor at the Friendship Centre, but the way she worked with clients deepened. The trip had taught her, again, the importance of forgiveness. And that, yes, we can learn to love again.

One Sunday morning as they were returning home from a walk, Chuck turned to Bea. "You know all those years that we were blanket married."

"Blanket married?" she asked as she opened the front door.

"Yeah, you know. We got to do everything married couples do under the blanket," he said mischievously.

Bea gave him a sideways glance as she headed up the stairs toward the kitchen. Chuck followed and continued talking, "But we never got properly married, and I was thinking, well, I was thinking, that maybe—maybe that was our problem."

She shook her head. "No, Chuck. Our problem was that we both liked the sauce too much."

"Yeah, I guess you're right, but, see, there's my point."

"What point?"

"We don't drink anymore, so…I don't know, I was thinking that maybe…" He looked out the window for a moment, summoning his courage and taking a deep breath.

He pulled the ring box from his chest pocket and using the kitchen counter to steady himself, he got down on one knee. Chuck opened the box, revealing the engagement ring with the two eagles coming together and the diamond set between their beaks. The ones he had bought when they were in Las Vegas.

An audible gasp escaped from Bea. She looked at the ring, then to Chuck and back to the ring. She had not seen this coming.

"Bea MacArthur, mother of our children, grandmother of our grandchildren, the love of my life and the only woman who can bring me to my knees, will you marry me?"

Again, Bea looked from the ring to Chuck. "For real?" she asked. "For real this time?"

"Yes, Bea, for real."

Bea studied him for a few moments. "I don't know, Chuck. What if we're making a mistake?" She crossed her arms. "A big mistake?"

Chuck reached up, uncrossed Bea's arms, and took her hands in his, holding them to his chest. "We're not making a mistake, Bea. I love you and you love me."

The tension left Bea's shoulders. Chuck continued. "We aren't in our twenties anymore. We can make this work. I know we can. I believe in us." It was this last sentence that caused the usually stoic Bea to release her tears.

He asked again, "So, what do you think? Want to get married? To me?"

She reached down and cradled his face in her hands. Looking deep into his eyes, she smiled and said, "Yes, Chuck, I'll marry you."

"Oh, thank goodness, because I was beginning to think—"

But before he could finish she cut him off. "Shut up and kiss your bride to be." Very few people ever saw this playful side of Bea, a part of her personality that Chuck always seemed to bring out.

With his face still cradled in her hands, Bea leaned down and met Chuck's lips with hers. After a few moments, Chuck pulled away. "You know, I could do a much better job at that if you'd help me up to my feet."

"Oh, I think you're doing a mighty fine job." Bea pulled on one arm and with the other, he pushed up on the counter until he was standing.

57

Six Months Later...Making Peace

AS SOON AS she got the call that Sarah was back in the hospital, Annie caught the first flight west. A few days after she arrived, Sarah slipped into a coma. Annie and Sarah's daughters did what they could to make the hospital room a loving space, including covering Sarah with the quilt that the Stitch 'n Bitch women had made for her. In the center, they had put a photo of Sarah dancing at the Gathering of Nations Pow Wow.

On day four day of the coma, Annie was resting her head on the bed and had Sarah's hand in hers. At first, when she heard "Annie," she thought she was dreaming. Realizing it wasn't a dream, she sat straight up.

Sarah's eyes were half open. She turned her head toward her sister and asked, "'Member the tulips?"

"The tulips?"

"Your..." She took a few short, raspy breaths before continuing, "... bucket list stop."

Annie nodded. Of course, the tulips. She leaned in closer to Sarah.

"'Member. How you told me...'bout forgiveness...'bout how. You forgave. Father Murphy 'n the nuns?"

"Mm-hmm."

"Well. I forgave 'em too. For everythin' they did to me. And to you. I made. My peace. With 'em." Sarah closed her eyes.

Tears streamed down Annie's cheeks.

58

Family

LUCY WAS THE first to receive the call that Sarah was awake. She immediately called Rose and between them they let the Stitch 'n Bitch group know. Mabel also called Tilly, and just as Annie had done, Tilly caught the first available flight. Within a few hours, Tilly and the Crazy Eights were gathered in Sarah's room.

At the top of the bed, on either side of Sarah, stood Poncho and Annie. Tilly and the others formed a circle around the bed, just as they had back in California.

A lifetime ago.

Everyone knew that Sarah's hours on Earth were numbered.

Poncho smiled down at Sarah and removed his cowboy hat. "Some say you're simply transitioning to the other side of the creek, where you can still see us and we can still feel you."

The left side of Sarah's face lifted in an attempted smile. Over the last couple of days, she had found a sense of peace in knowing she was saying her good-byes. And although she was no longer afraid to make this transition, she knew that wasn't the case for her family.

Sarah knew that family isn't always about blood relations. Family is also those whom you love and who love you.

Every person around her bed had woven their way into her heart.

They were family.

Sleep was drawing her in once again. In the distance Sarah heard the faint beating of a drum. She turned her head toward the sound.

***

Annie invited Tilly and the elders to sit with her and Sarah. Once settled, they remained quiet, alone with their thoughts and feelings.

Time is a funny thing. Ten minutes can feel like ten hours and one hour can feel like a blink of an eye. There is no telling how long they sat adrift in their own thoughts.

It was Tilly whose soft voice brought them all back to the present. "I've wanted to do this for a long time, but we haven't all been together since our trip." She reached into her pocket and removed a tobacco tie that she had taken to always carrying with her. As she rubbed it between her fingers, she began to share. "I want to say kinânksomitin. Thank you to each of you." She looked at each elder in turn. "Thank you for the kindness you gave me on our trip." The emotions rising in her chest and forming in her eyes surprised her. "Well, the only other time I've felt so cared about was with my Grandma Tilly. You all took such good care of me when I was supposed to be taking care of you." She couldn't help but smile and laugh softly at the memory. "I really was lost on that trip." A few of the elders nodded. "But I've made lots of changes and want you to know that Mick and I found our way back, and not just back, but to a better place. It was hard, real hard, but it's been almost six months now, and there's a big change in our marriage and our friendship." Tilly paused. "So, I just wanted to thank you. Each one of you." She took her time connecting with them as she looked around the circle. She would forever be grateful for the role each played in her life.

Tilly had not intended to share more, not just yet, and not with Sarah so close to crossing over. But suddenly, this seemed like the right time. "There's one more thing." Tilly was totally unaware of how her face lit up. "We're going to have a baby."

"Ahhh," escaped from a few of them in the circle. Chuck and Bea exchanged knowing smiles.

Poncho pushed his chair back, stood, and walked over to her. "Oh, Miss Tilly, that is the best news I've heard in a long time." He pulled her in for a hug. In his ear, Tilly whispered, "A gift from the Creator, Poncho."

"Yes, Miss Tilly. A gift for sure."

Rose leaned over and whispered to Lucy, "That explains things."

"Explains what things?" Lucy looked confused.

"You know." Rose drew a line around her waist with her hands. "The little pudge around her tummy."

Lucy playfully slapped her friend's hand. "Rose."

Rose lifted her shoulders. "What? I'm just sayin'."

Sarah groggily asked, "What?"

Annie moved closer to Sarah. "We thought you were asleep."

Sarah's eyes smiled, but it was too much effort to lift the sides of her mouth. Her eyes closed again.

"It's Tilly. She's got some news," Annie whispered. She motioned for Tilly to come near.

Tilly took Sarah's hand in hers and whispered, "I'm going to have a baby, Sarah."

This time, Sarah's smile was effortless.

***

The drumbeat was growing louder. Sarah could see the young woman now. She was dancing as she drew nearer. Every movement of her shawl beckoned Sarah to join her in the Spirit World.

After a few moments the young woman reached out to her and smiled. "Take my hand, Sarah. I've come to dance you home."

Gratitude

THIS BOOK HAS been one of the most enjoyable and entertaining projects I have worked on yet. I could see these characters as if I was watching them from behind a lens. Some days they made me laugh and some days they made me cry, but all in all, I have fallen in love with each and every one of them. I feel like they are Ancestors with whom I've had the privilege to story tell.

I am grateful to the Lkwugen and WSÁNEĆ people for the gift of living on your unceded territories as I wrote this book. This land, the water and the stars we live below, are beautiful medicine for writing and raising a family. Kinânskomitin.

For my family. My wife Rhonda, who takes incredible care of me all the time, not just when I'm writing. Thank you for all your help with this story! You have been instrumental in helping me with this book. I loved all the conversations we had about the characters and their antics! For my children, Sadie and Jaxson, you are the most precious gifts I've ever been blessed with and your love is fuel for my writing.

We all need people in our lives who support us, encourage us and believe in us...even when we don't believe in ourselves. My family are some of these people, as is the group of women known as my Soul Circle. Since 2013, our circle has met every two weeks. These women are touchstones for me and my time in their presence is always healing, motivating, and inspiring. Thank you Anne Marie Hgoya, Brooke Semple, Carmen Spagnola, Carolyne Taylor, and Robin Arnold.

My dear friend, Kelly Terbasket for being the greatest travel partner!!! I could not think of anyone more creative, fun, and easygoing to have come on the research trip with me. I will always remember our laughter, our adventures, and cherish the memories. Thank you for being mi socia for almost thirty years.

I am thankful to everyone who agreed to be early readers and provide feedback; Rhonda Peterson, Shirley Smith, Jocelyn Caldwell, Carolyne Taylor, Kelly Terbasket, Della Preston, Shannon Lundquist, and Margo D'Archangelo.

Much gratitude for the grant I received from First People's Culture Council in 2015. This grant provided me with the financial means to do the research trip and travel the same route as Tilly and the Crazy Eights. This trip provided me with the foundation, photographs, experience, and inspiration to tell this story.

On July 12th, I put a couple of tweets up as part of #CanLitPit 2017. Second Story Press was one of the presses who liked the tweets and were interested in seeing the manuscript. I am grateful to Margie Wolfe for her interest in the story and to Second Story Press for publishing *Tilly and the Crazy Eights*. It is an honor to work with you!

Grateful to the editors who have helped with this over the journey of the book: Barbara Pulling, Ronda Kronyk, Kathryn Cole, and Richard Van Camp. Each of you came in at different times during my writing process and contributed in profound ways!

About

MONIQUE GRAY SMITH is Cree, Lakota and Scottish and a proud mom of teenage twins. She is an accomplished consultant, writer and international speaker. Her first novel, Tilly: A Story of Hope and Resilience, won the 2014 Burt Award for First Nations, Metis and Inuit Literature. She is also the author of several books for children, including You Hold Me Up, My Heart Fills With Happiness, and Speaking our Truth: A Journey of Reconciliation. Monique and her family are blessed to live on the traditional territory of the WSÁNEĆ people near Victoria, British Columbia.